Dream Time

Dream Time

Sarah Starr

authorHOUSE®

AuthorHouse™ UK Ltd.
1663 Liberty Drive
Bloomington, IN 47403 USA
www.authorhouse.co.uk
Phone: 0800.197.4150

© 2013 by Sarah Starr. All rights reserved.

No part of this book may be reproduced, stored in a retrieval system, or transmitted by any means without the written permission of the author.

This book is a work of fiction and, except in the case of historical fact, any resemblance to actual persons, living or dead, is purely coincidental. Any portrayal of customs and spirituality in the text does not necessarily reflect the belief systems of any Indigenous peoples.

Published by AuthorHouse   10/02/2013

ISBN: 978-1-4817-6890-0 (sc)
ISBN: 978-1-4817-6891-7 (e)

Any people depicted in stock imagery provided by Thinkstock are models, and such images are being used for illustrative purposes only.
Certain stock imagery © Thinkstock.

Because of the dynamic nature of the Internet, any web addresses or links contained in this book may have changed since publication and may no longer be valid. The views expressed in this work are solely those of the author and do not necessarily reflect the views of the publisher, and the publisher hereby disclaims any responsibility for them.

Acknowledgements

My heartfelt gratitude goes out to Frances, Valerie, Pauline, Jo, and all those who have cheered me on through the writing.

Special thanks also go to my spiritual mentor, Arona, who proof read the manuscript and gave me her loving encouragement throughout the whole project.

Finally my deep appreciation to my husband John, whose love, patience and technical help has known no bounds.

Dedication

For Rachel, who existed for only a short time and who now sleeps with the Angels.

And for my mother Joan, who loved children and was also rather fond of ghosts.

Said the Voice of the Continent:
These newcomers will destroy the cycle of life; the dry spells will become droughts, sand will eat up the good lands, fire and floods will wipe him out.
If they do not know the secret of life, the secret of the trees, how can they survive?

Said the Herald of the Future:
They will bring knowledge and engines from overseas, new animals and new plants.

Said the Voice of the Continent:
I shall turn their inventions against them . . . I am old, and they are frail and new. I have conquered one race, I shall conquer another.

Said the Herald of the Future:
Nevertheless, they shall survive. And they will come to you at last in love, and will honour and serve you. They will take your strength and secret power and raise it to another plane.
You will be hearth and home to a new race.

From 'A Mask of Australia' by M.B. Eldershaw.

Introduction

Dawn broke, and his world was illuminated. An intake of breath broke the morning hush as he spread his mouth into a wide yawn. He lay beneath a gum tree, beside the embers of the previous night's fire. He had walked through long hot days and dreamed through many nights of silence before finally arriving under her boughs. He had marked his way alone through these heat parched lands, following the timeworn tracks of his ancestors.

Killara was the son of a Wise Man.

He was aware of his latent power and longed to be able to use it. But first he had to complete the challenge set by his elders: a journey traversing the whole of his World. Today it brought him to the coastal fringe, and as the sun rose he smiled with all the confidence of royalty. He had almost reached the sacred site of the Great White Snake. As a child he had learned how she rested at the edge of this beautiful bay. Now Killara clicked his tongue against his teeth in happy appreciation.

But first today he would be tracking small lizards like goanna. On his own he caught smaller game so as not to waste anything. This also left him with a lighter load to carry. Killara felt happily boyish as he climbed to a rocky viewpoint to get a good look at the bay below. He quivered with excitement as the morning sun provided its assured warmth, falling lightly now over his slim frame. It was still early. He looked down into the sea and reflected upon his task. That evening he would find her site and give thanks to the Great White Snake, and enjoy a celebration feast under the stars.

His dark eyes took in the expanse of azure softness, effervescent as it lapped against the golden sands of the bay. A huge sky displayed several flag-like clouds as if in jubilation for this part of his quest. Sunlight danced gently on the surface of the water, lighting up the ocean with so many jewels. Although kinder than the arid interior, his heart still missed the ochre reds of his own country. He recalled the woman he was to be joined with when he returned. She was young, but already accomplished in gathering, cooking and basket weaving. He was sure she would provide him with strong, brave sons.

Killara looked out again at the indigo horizon. After a while he spotted something strange. He narrowed his eyes, straining against the brightness of the sun. Sure enough, a white flash was floating through the waves. It seemed to be heading towards him. Now it changed into several slivers of cloud, but a large solid form was below it, moving through the water like a whale. His people knew how to float on water with crafts cut from tree trunks, but this was much larger than that and able to move faster. He saw a similar craft following the first, and then another after that.

They were coming into the bay.

Gunfire roared, rudely assaulting his ears. All at once his earlier joy evaporated, and instinctively he fell onto his haunches. Something this alien must spell trouble. Nervously he decided to watch a little longer and flattened himself down on the scrub grass. He stayed there, watching for some hours. He heard noisy calls echoing across the bay, and thought they did not belong here. From his watch point he saw how they poked at the earth with strange implements, laughed at the trees and hacked at the vegetation. If they did not understand his world how could they live here, how would they know how to survive?

Killara sighed, and for a moment wished he was back in his own country. As the Wise Man's son he had respect and trust. That was the real key to his future within the tribe. But what he did not know, and would never have any real use for, was the date that particular day: *26th January 1788.*

Chapter 1

Darwin, September 1973.

The gate had been unlocked the day I met Daphne Green. She waved regally from the veranda railings as I climbed the driveway past tall mango trees and even taller palms. 'Sorry I'm late,' I said, 'the car broke down.'

'You didn't walk all the way from town?' she replied, 'And in this heat?'

'Oh no, I got a lift from the rental agency.'

Miss Green fussily poured glasses of iced lemonade. I sat on a rather hard chair and looked around me. The house on Monkey Puzzle Street seemed immediately odd, as if masking some sort of secret. I felt uneasy, and shifted in my seat. Miss Green's hat was tied on to her head with a chiffon scarf, the brim obscuring her eyes as she continued, 'You must be Rachel; how wonderful you're English. But you must have realised how much hotter it is here than in Brisbane? It's enough to make you go completely troppo.'

'Troppo?' I asked, gulping lemonade.

'Yes, mad my dear, *quite mad.* It's more the humidity than the heat that does it. Last year there were two murders and five people wounded, all with shotguns. That's why I always get away for the wet season.' She put down her glass and grinned in a bizarre fashion, showing her well preserved teeth. I stifled a tense giggle, and the lemonade fizzed painfully up my nose.

'Well now, I've just got time to show you the house and the garden before my car arrives,' she blustered, 'and of course you must tell me all about yourself.'

I followed her through darkened rooms while bright pictures of native art shone out at me from the walls. 'I like your pictures.' I ventured to say.

'Thanks very much,' she said, as if she might have painted them herself. 'They're only prints you know, the originals are in the Art Museum in Melbourne.' She hesitated by a large sideboard. 'If you like Aboriginal art you might like to visit the museum in town. But what do you think of my antique furniture?' And she rubbed the wood finish. 'The heat has completely ruined it.' She proceeded until we reached a closed door. 'This is my bedroom, but I keep it locked while I'm away, you see.' She demonstrated unnecessarily by trying the handle. 'I understand you will be studying here?' She added, ushering me away from the door.

'That's right; I'm writing my history thesis. It's on Australia's first settlers.'

'Oh; how interesting. But will you be staying here alone?'

'For now yes, but my cousin is joining me in about a month. She's coming up from my uncle's place in Brisbane, like me.'

'Well now, that's all right then. I expect you will be busy until she arrives, but be sure to look out for one another, if you get my meaning.' She gave me a half wink. I smiled in reply but had no idea what she was trying to say.

She led me through the kitchen and out into the sunny garden. With obvious pride she presented her fish pond. 'Now then,' she said as we approached the edge, 'you must be sure to feed these little darlings daily. It must be every day without fail you know, because they get very hungry.' I gazed into the sparkling water. White lilies were flowering on the surface and three colourful fish were snaking through the stems. They came to the surface of the pond expecting food, and Miss Green was unable to resist the urge to give them extra rations. She showed me where she kept their food, and chattered away to them while the flakes drifted softly onto the water. Small beads of perspiration gathered on my face, while larger ones dripped down my back. The sun singed into my head and I realised I'd left my hat on the veranda.

Miss Green was laughing softly, but I had stopped listening to her and was thinking about the paintings in the house. Perhaps she was laughing at me, a real fish out of water. All at once home seemed a lifetime away and suddenly I missed all the noise and bustle of London. She sped off across the garden, flowing chiffon and leaving me to trail after her. Near to the corner fence she stopped abruptly, nearly knocking my sunglasses off with the brim of her hat. 'Now this is really the most important part of the place,' she announced solemnly, 'and I do ask you to treat it with respect. As a special request I ask that you don't step beyond this brick line.'

What had once been the foundations of a small shed or outhouse lay before me. Miss Green had fallen silent, and her cheeks looked rather ashen. 'This is hallowed ground, you know. You can probably make out the remains of a little house. It was here that my friend Mulga used to sometimes stay.' She paused and then added, 'He was an Aboriginal artist.'

I swallowed audibly before saying, 'Where is he now?'

'He's dead, my dear.' Her voice lowered to a dull tone. 'He had a sudden heart attack one morning. Nothing could be done for him. He has returned to the Dreaming, now.' Her words trailed off weakly, and she looked desperately at the brick ruins, as if she were looking into a grave. I reached over and touched her shoulder, and she rummaged around her pockets for a handkerchief.

'I'm very sorry; you must have been fond of him.' I said. She turned her head away from me to blow her nose.

'We were friends you see, unusual as it sounds.' She gave her nose a good blow. 'He stayed here and did lots of art work, and every now and then he went on a walkabout. But he always came back, until one day.' She looked up and I caught a glimpse of a brave smile challenging her saddened eyes. 'It's probably difficult for you to understand, but he was such a good friend! In fact one of only two *real* friends I have in this life. This can be an awkward place to live, if-' and she looked at me carefully before saying, '-you were not actually born here. I come from Adelaide, although I'm pretty sure my ancestors came here from England in the 18th century. One day I intend to trace my family tree, and I may even visit the old country.' I started to reply, but the words were lost to a shrieking galah. It took flight from above our heads, and landed noisily on the house. I imagined it was watching us, and rapidly felt a chill crawl up my dampened spine.

A more composed landlady led me down wide steps where the garden was deeply overgrown. Brown leaves littered the ground and rippled as the insect world beneath sensed our steps. Around the corner and underneath the stilts of the house she pointed out a dingy room, and said, 'This is the storm shelter.'

I peered inside, through the wire mesh door. 'It looks like a store room.'

'It's a shelter in case of cyclones, you know.' She added vaguely, 'goodness, it is full of junk isn't it? I must get down to clearing it out one day. There's a camp bed somewhere, it might be an idea to find it in case of an emergency.' I tried to conceal this shock but my face must have betrayed concern. She gave my hand a gentle pat. 'Oh dear girl, please don't worry. It's extremely unlikely the weather will get that bad. But, if a storm should hit here it's better to know where to come if necessary. After all, this *is* the wet season, you know.'

Perhaps that was supposed to give me comfort. I took a last look into the dingy shelter. 'What's that thing?' I pointed to a small wire cage amongst the jumble.

'Oh, that's the possum trap dear. I nearly forgot to mention it! I've got several of the little blighters in the roof space. They're nocturnal you know, and can drive you mad at night. If they get too troublesome just bait the trap with bread and honey or apple slices, but not mango, they won't go for that. Then pop the trap into the loft for a couple of days.'

'But what do I do if I catch one?' Unexpectedly I felt insufficient, and woefully unprepared.

'Well, then you take the trap to the East Point reserve and release it. It won't hurt you,' she said, 'but be careful. If it has babies it's more likely to be aggressive.' She bent down and rummaged around in a box just inside the shelter. 'Here you are,' and she handed me some leather gloves, 'use these with the trap, just in case. Now I must be going, I really don't want to miss my flight. I do hope you will be alright, my dear.'

The early light streamed in through the window and silently caressed the bed sheets. Stillness engulfed the house, following what had been a noisy and disruptive night. No rainstorms had awoken me but Miss Green had been right about the possums. Abruptly wrenched from my heated slumbers at 1am by what can only be described as possum obscenities, I was unable to get back to sleep for over three hours. Heavy possum feet and bickering possum protestations had echoed from the roof space and had brought forth a few swear words of my own.

Intending to visit the storm shelter I hoped the possum trap was in working order. Another night like that was less than desirable. I passed Miss Green's bedroom and being naturally inquisitive tried the door handle. I knew it was locked, but something seemed to draw me to try it. *Curiosity killed the cat*, my mother used to tell me. I touched it and immediately felt a surging sensation up my arm. This was not like a static shock; it was somehow different. My hand was numb, and my fingers were tingling. I took my hand away and then put it back. No surging that time. Perhaps I was tired after my night with the hateful possums. Uncle Sid was sure to be angry if he found out the house only had one usable bed. I decided not to tell him. When Kim arrived I would just have to rough it on the sofa.

It was still early, only 9am, but the heat was already building as I searched the kitchen for something to eat. Miss Green had left some bread and milk in the fridge, and I found some tea in a tin. Yawning, I made tea and toast, and ventured towards the veranda. But a crash and the splinter of breaking glass made me jump, and I nearly dropped my breakfast. Turning, I saw the kitchen clock dashed to the middle of the floor. I walked back to the kitchen. Its glass face had shattered, and lying next to it was the nail on which it had hung. A feeling of guilt washed over me, and I knew I must replace it.

I picked up the nail and considered what had happened. It seemed impossible that the nail could have flown out of the wall and into the middle of the floor. The clock hung above a window which was a good five feet away. Pulling up a chair with the toast between my teeth, I climbed on to the draining board and examined the exit point of the nail. I pushed it back into the hole, trying to make sense of this defiance of gravity. Surely if the nail had dropped out on its own, then the clock would have fallen straight down, into the sink? I let the toast drop out of my mouth and it landed plop, onto the drainer. Nervously I let the nail fall from its point of exit at the wall. Sure enough, it landed in the sink with a metallic clink and didn't even bounce. Uneasily I looked out into the garden, towards the little house. Someone or *something* was watching me, I was sure of it.

Uncle's car had broken down as I arrived in Darwin, or I could have driven to town. He followed me part of the way up from Brisbane in Aunt May's car, leaving me to drive the rest of the journey alone. It was straightforward he insisted, just keep driving and you will end up in Darwin. At least that was fairly easy, but now added to my list of chores was: *find a car mechanic.*

I followed a map I'd found in the lounge. As I explored my new world I mused over what Miss Green had told me. She mentioned the gardener would be visiting the house to mow the lawn. I hoped it would be soon. I hadn't yet noticed any other life apart from the invisible but not inaudible possums and the barking dog next door. Anyway Miss Green had written lots of details down and put all the information on the sideboard in the lounge. She had said the gardener really just cuts the grass and tidies up, but I thought it could do with a lot more than that.

At the bottom of the hill the road divided in two and the frangipani trees either side stood like sentinels guarding their territory. I took the right fork to follow the most direct route to town. The trees, with deep green leaves and waxy white flowers appeared unreal, almost dreamlike. Roadside gardens displayed shrubs of Geralton wax smothered in tiny pink flowers and appearing so perfect they could have been made of silk. Soon the houses were gone and I travelled through a parched wasteland. I had to walk along a scrub lined path but was forced to stop and take off my sunglasses. Wiping the sweat from my forehead I struggled to wave the biting flies away. I cursed under my breath. My hat repositioned I struggled up an incline while damp air hung like a burden on my back. It was becoming difficult to breathe and my braided hair pressed like a hot iron into my neck.

There seemed little point in complaining, but I cursed again. I let out a wet snort as I came to the summit of the hill. Wet through, my clothes tackily clung to my body. London seemed further away than ever, and I yearned for cooler climes. With all its faults, now I could only think of how I wanted to be there. From this far away even my father did not seem so bad. I missed my little sister, and thought I would weaken and cry. Uselessly I tried again to wave away the unceasing flies. How was I going to stand the months ahead, and how would I be able to work in this unbearable heat?

Eventually I reached the town, my mouth dry as leather. Rising before me shiny stone and glass contrasted violently with the ochre earth. These buildings towered over that which had endured since the first dawn. Near to the shopping mall I happened upon a group of Aborigines, slouched in a drunken haze on the ground. They saw me looking and pointed towards me with crooked fingers, shook their beer bottles and hissed words that I supposed to be an ancient dialect. I thought I heard one of them hiss, *mutant*. They lay among the litter and broken glass and had lifeless stares. Thin, shabbily dressed kids stood around with unflinching faces. Their hair was matted and their feet were bare. They appeared shipwrecked, stranded in a world that made no sense. I was unable to help them, and hurried away.

I headed through the modern automatic doors into the air conditioned vacuum of the mall. A Peter Sarstedt song rang out from the speakers: *'I'll buy you one more frozen orange juice on this fantastic day!'* My hair stuck to my face and the cold air began to chill my skin. I could appreciate if you lived here long enough you might end up crazy, but I had been here for less than two days and felt like exploding. I was starting to feel queasy, and badly needed to quench my thirst. The deafening possums at the house had been replaced with ear splitting music in the mall. And even here, was something really watching my every move? I pulled myself together and headed to the general store in search of a clock. Having come all this way, I was determined to find one.

When I exited the mall the Aborigines had vanished. I wondered where they had gone. Perhaps they were lying in wait ready to ambush me as I crossed the scrub, back to the relative comfort of modern habitation. Or they might jump out at me later from the gardens, camouflaged by thick vegetation and flowering shrubs. Apprehension followed me all the way on the hot trudge back to the house. But even with my bag of shopping the trip back felt shorter than the journey going. In what seemed to be only minutes I found myself back at the large metal gate on Monkey Puzzle Street.

Sarah Starr

The house beckoned to me as I unlocked the padlock; tempting me inside, urging me to come back home. As I hastened up the drive, something inside me surrendered to its call with every step I made.

Chapter 2

A week had passed following Daphne Green's escape from the wet, and still I hadn't got the possum trap into the loft. There had been no rain for at least five days, but the heat and humidity remained fierce. The battered old radio in the lounge issued worrying *yellow* warning alerts because of storm activity out at sea. With no television I had little excuse to procrastinate over my thesis. However, rather than beginning work I seemed determined to provide my own diversions. I had been out walking and exploring most days, and in the evenings listened to the radio on the veranda.

My first visit to the shore revealed a deserted beach, apart from some craggy rocks and flapping notices about Box jellyfish. Crocodiles, it said were also to be avoided around the creeks and lakes. There was real danger here. From a rocky ledge I watched the waves as they rolled in and stretched out again. The water hissed gently at me as it clutched the tiny pebbles on the shore, and I felt a long lost smile stretch onto my face. There had to be a certain comfort in knowing this ocean had been around for millennia.

History had captured my imagination since childhood, and I longed to teach it to others. And since learning about the explorers who had discovered this continent I had held a secret ambition to come to this land.

Away from the house I felt more relaxed than I had done in years. At Monkey Puzzle Street I felt continually anxious, and still thought I was being watched. Perhaps it was nothing more than fancy. Since childhood I had disliked being shut in, confined as I would have to be in the storm shelter. But by the shore the sea foamed in and out like a frilly petticoat, laughing and singing the way it had done for thousands of years. I couldn't be sure, but it seemed to be trying to say something.

Faded memories of home searched my mind for a place to live. Into my thoughts came Belle and the school playground where we skipped and played hopscotch and shared the secrets of small children. After school we sometimes visited each other's houses for tea. Belle's parents were Scottish and her father had a set of real bagpipes that we were sometimes allowed to blow. I huffed and puffed but never got a note out of them. My mother was not at all keen on Belle, and made lots of spiteful remarks about the Scots. Banging the pans on the stove, when Belle came to tea she always lost her temper. We were sent up to my room if we got the giggles and had to stay there until we were sorry. After that, I didn't think she would ever want to be my friend again. She would be gone forever, before I had the chance to tell her my deepest secrets.

I sat on that same rock for hours, just looking out at the steady horizon. Time passed gently while the gulls swooped over and over into the waves. When a steady breeze came up I knew it was time to leave, to start the hot walk back to the house. Once there I sat at the heavy dining table and looked for a long time at the blank paper in the typewriter.

I met Biff Johnson when he brought a newspaper round one afternoon. His dog Ringo came with him, and immediately started to explore the garden.

'Don't mind him,' Biff said, he's always had a thing about this garden.' A sun wrinkled postman, he told me he much preferred living with his dog since his divorce some 20 years previously.

'How long are you staying?' he asked.

'My rent's paid until April,' I told him, 'and my cousin is due to join me soon.'

'One of these days Daphne Green will stay put in Adelaide, and then the house will sit empty and rot.' he said.

'Can I get you some tea?' I wanted to be polite, but hoped for his refusal.

'I only drink beer love.' But he didn't laugh and I couldn't tell if he was joking.

'I don't suppose you know any car mechanics?' I said carefully.

'As a matter of fact you're speaking to the right man there.' He went home and brought back the number of a mechanic friend of his, insisting he was a good bloke. While he was gone I flicked through the paper. An article told about an Aboriginal man who had recently escaped from a crocodile attack. He saved himself by poking the croc in the eyes very hard, with both thumbs. The animal had let go of him but had left the poor lad with puncture marks right down the side of his torso. A gruesome picture of his wounds was next to the article.

Biff urged me to contact the mechanic before the police got a chance to impound the car. 'And there's storm activity off the coast,' he said 'but I expect a smart kid like you has got your shelter ready.'

The cyclone shelter was a mess. Over by the far wall I could just make out a folding camp-bed, the rest of the space being taken up with junk and gardening paraphernalia. The possums, *little blighters* as Miss Green called them, had left me with no alternative. Stretching over a rusted bicycle I grabbed the possum trap. Only the size of a cat basket, it felt surprisingly heavy. Moisture dripped from my face and I had to rest, like someone middle aged. The airless atmosphere was stifling, and my throat was dry. A spider clung to one of the bars of the possum cage. A closer inspection confirmed my dread. It was a poisonous variety, a Redback spider.

I directed a shot of anger towards Uncle Sid, living comfortably in Brisbane. Aunt May was probably just about to light the barbeque for lunch. Kim was most likely on her way home from surfing, her blonde hair swinging in the sunshine. She didn't have to worry about jellyfish that could kill with one sting, or the gnashing jaws of crocodiles.

I knew I had to get the storm shelter ready. Biffs' paper had a useful article in it, explaining how to get a box together with some tins of food and water bottles. But I was unable to move, as if stuck to the upturned crate. Inside this cage my only company was the chirping song of cicadas. It was impossible to see beyond the garden walls, and I began to feel shut in. The insect volume increased, urging a deeper, primal panic. Familiar feelings of weakness crawled over me, providing their own grimy comfort. If Belle had been with me I was sure she would reassure me the way she had done in the past. I closed my eyes and tried to conjure up her face. But I saw the door to the old cellar: the entrance to my prison.

Dream Time

An icy chill ran through my heated veins. Quickly I opened my eyes. A glance out through the shelter door confirmed I was not shut in, that I was indeed safe. However, it was becoming clear that unwanted memories could turn this place into a prison of a different kind.

Tears tried to fight their way free, but my eyes just stung with sweat. I had no choice but to stay here, there was simply nowhere else to go. Grabbing the possum trap I slammed shut the shelter door. I realized my throat was parched. The front door was nearby but I decided to use the back door near the pond. The climb up the steps was rewarded by the shade of tall palm trees. I placed the trap by the back door, remembering then to feed the fish. Their food tin was on the kitchen sill and as I reached for it the sun hid momentarily behind a dark cloud. The flakes fell in silence on to the water while a dull thud came from behind, like a falling mango. It was so loud it caught my breath. Then I was alerted to a different noise, one like a soft cry coming from the undergrowth.

Beyond the pond the trees parted to reveal the dingy remains of the old Aborigines' house. I approached warily, curious to find out what was making the noise somewhere amongst the rubble. Kneeling on the coarse grass I scanned the piles of rough bricks. Stinging ants climbed into my sandals and up my bare shins, oblivious to where they were going. Flicking them onto the grass, I shifted position onto my haunches. The heat was compelling me to go into the shade of the house, and my mouth was like parchment, but I continued to look. Perspiration drenched my clothes, sticking the fabric to my skin.

I began to feel nervous. I had been asked not to intrude here by Miss Green, after all. Why had she said it? And what was that noise? Was it my overactive imagination, the same

• 15 •

one that kept telling me *he* had knocked the clock off the wall?

A dry smile twitched at my lips, and I admonished myself for such foolishness. The isolation and the confounded heat were getting to me, and it was time to pull myself together. I decided to go inside for a cool drink. Just then a momentary breeze drifted past my face, gently lifting my hair. It felt different, like a feather stroking my skin. Then it grew swiftly into an aggressive wind, stinging my body and blowing dust into my eyes. Larger clouds moved across the sky obscuring the sun and shadowing the foundations of the little house. Truly frightened, I turned to run. But my body cowered as a sudden crack of thunder exploded overhead. I jumped to dodge a falling palm frond. Gasping for breath I felt my heart pump like an engine while I stood in frozen panic.

Several mangos hit the ground like missiles as my eyes darted around the scene. A crack of lightning split the heavens in two like a silver blade, releasing soft fat raindrops along with my helpless tears. Soon water was everywhere, noisily crushing the leaves and dust into the earth. I grabbed a nearby tree for support as a ripping groan of thunder sent shock waves through my body. The responding streak of lightning illuminated the shrine in which I stood, and before me I saw the dark eyes of an aged painted face, the hair long and matted.

A scream rang out but unaware it belonged to me I ran from it. I tried to get to the back door but the rain was so heavy now it was blinding. My foot caught on something and I struggled to free it but then I tripped forward and fell headlong onto the rubble.

It seemed like weeks later when I finally awoke.

A painful head accompanied my throbbing body. Opening my eyes, slowly the lounge came into focus. Through the screen door I could see the long veranda that flanked it. I thought I saw a figure leaning against the balcony rail. I rubbed my eyes, and then realized it was a man smoking a cigarette. He was looking out into the still falling rain, and seemed to be enjoying the precious release it provided. I tried to move, but the pain in my hip released an involuntary moan. The man stubbed out his cigarette on the veranda rail and entered the lounge. His heavy work boots clacked loudly on the wooden floor, and the noise reverberated through my brain.

'Wondered when you were going to wake up,' he said cheerfully as he headed for the kitchen. 'You need some ice on that head.'

'What happened?' I watched him as he returned with a glass of water and the ice, wrapped in a tea-towel decorated with birds of Australia.

'I wanted to ask you that.'

I put the ice pack to my forehead, where I felt a large lump. 'You found me?' I said unnecessarily.

'Yep, you were knocked out cold; hit your head on a large brick.' I winced as the ice stung the lump. Embarrassed, I realized he must have carried me inside. I took a closer look, hoping he didn't notice. He appeared strangely familiar, but I didn't see how I could know him. How odd, that he should be coming to the house at that very moment, and odder still how he had managed to get in through the gate.

'Well, I'm really glad you found me, and thank you for bringing me indoors. How long do you think I was out there?' I took a mouthful of water from the glass.

'Not sure, maybe a few minutes, maybe longer,' he said casually. He hoisted a foot onto his opposite knee and scratched his shin. 'Damn mossies.' He cursed. 'Oh, by the way, I'm Luke, the gardener.' I shook his large, outstretched hand, and made an effort to sit upright.

'Pleased to meet you Luke; I'm Rachel. Did Miss Green mention me?' It was painful to smile. 'I'm supposed to be finishing my History Degree.' I added.

'She said something about a clever Pom renting the place.' I thought this was rather insensitive and winced, but he sailed on, 'She usually rents the place out during the wet. Mind if I roll one up?' He reached for a tobacco pouch in the pocket of his scruffy shorts, and carried on anyway, before I had time to object. 'I came by today to see if the lawns needed mowing. Anyways, just before I got here down it came thank God, so I thought, may as well shelter under Greenie's trees until it finishes. And that's when I found you laying there, out cold; sparko.' He gave a lopped sided grin as he finished rolling up the cigarette. 'Guess I'll have to come back at the weekend to do the lawns. Anyway I've got a key for the gate, so you don't need to stay in for me.'

I shifted round delicately, ignoring his last remarks and hoping Miss Green had not called me a Pom. 'I've never seen rain like this. Is it always this heavy?'

'Well, sometimes it starts and then stops again, and that's bad. Other times it rains for hours, even days without stopping, like now. If it gets really bad you need to get ready with your cyclone stuff. Keep listening to the radio. But try not to worry too much about it; we've managed to escape for years without a hit.'

'Well, I'm glad about that.' I had to drop my gaze, as his eyes were boring into me.

'D'you remember what happened before you fell?'

I tried to recall, and shivered as I remembered the face. 'It might sound a bit silly,' I said beginning to feel uncomfortable.

'Try me.' He looked straight at me, again with those steel eyes.

'Well, I was in the cyclone shelter getting the possum trap. Oh yes, then I remembered I had to feed the fish, but while I was doing that I heard something in the garden and went to investigate. I got spooked and must have fainted, but it felt like I was tripped.' I could remember my foot getting caught up. 'And I saw something.'

He lit his cigarette. 'Like what?' He was giving me that look again.

'This is going to sound ridiculous.' I glanced away, wishing I hadn't mentioned it.

'Was it near that old ruin?' he said, apparently concerned.

'Well yes, as a matter of fact-'

'This is really weird.' He got up abruptly and started to walk up and down rather noisily, puffing away on the cigarette.

'Have you seen something too?' I asked, hoping for reassurance. 'What I saw, well I could have sworn it was the same person Miss Green told me about, you probably know about him, the Aborigine who used to live here.' He stopped pacing and sat back down heavily.

'He never really lived here, just stayed with her now and then and did some painting. She told me this when I first started doing the garden, but I already knew about it on account of my dad being the gardener before me.' He took a slow drag and exhaled the smoke through pursed lips. 'Well you've met Greenie; you know how she can rabbit on.'

'So, have you seen something as well?'

'I never said I saw anything.' His eyes narrowed as he took yet another drag on the cigarette, pointing it in the direction of the garden. 'But what happened to me out there to this day remains a mystery.'

Chapter 3

A glance at the clock told me it was early, only 5am. I stretched out in the bed, luxuriant in the knowledge that the temperature would remain relatively cool for the next few hours. As a bonus the usual concert of insects was taking its daily break, but my head was pounding. Just an hour later I heard the volley of tennis balls from the club two roads away, and the occasional groan as a shot was lost. Ringo barked sporadically from next door but otherwise all was peaceful as the day began its dawning. I padded out to the kitchen, my body still sore. I searched for motivation, but it was hard to find any. From the veranda I watched the palms and mangos stretching their green canopies up into the morning sky.

The typewriter sat expectantly on the dining table, the paper stirring gently in the breeze as if to entice me to work. A few stray geckos scrambled silently across the mesh screening the windows in search of flies. Inside the lounge a lone gecko with no tail scanned the walls for insects. I followed his trail and christened him Stumpy. I thought how Belle would have liked him. In her block of flats pets were not allowed, but she had a shelf full of plastic trolls in her bedroom. They had vivid hair and funny expressions. Before we went off to different secondary schools she gave me a troll with orange hair called Jock. She had named him after her grandfather who lived on the Isle of Skye.

I stretched carefully into my morning yoga routine and found my thoughts pulling back to meeting Luke, and my odd experience with the little house in the garden. I thought this was probably all we would ever share. He was very different to anyone I knew, but at the same time something about him had seemed familiar. Our conversation ran over and over through my mind and my yoga suffered for it. He said he thought the little house was haunted, and I should steer well away from it. It seemed he accepted my ordeal as a solid confirmation of *his* encounter. In the five years he had worked for Miss Green he'd never met any problems until one particular day. Then he had heard some sort of music coming from the area of the little house.

The sound had been quite soft to begin with and he had moved nearer to the spot to see if anyone was hiding there. It was not unusual for Aborigines to come to the back door asking for money, he told me. If this ever happened, if I left the gate open accidently for instance, I was never to give them money as he conferred, *they'll only spend it on booze*. But on that day he searched the garden and found no one. He could still hear the strange music that got louder and louder, and then so loud he had been forced to put his hands over his ears and run to the safety of the lounge. The music had contained chanting which he insisted had made him ill, so much so he was unable to eat or sleep for two days while a strange fever ran through his body. Miss Green arrived home late that afternoon to find him unconscious on the sofa, and had looked after him until he was well enough to go back home. My head throbbed, but at least I had escaped that trial.

Luke had put the possum trap into the loft before he left, and after lunch I used some rickety stepladders to check it. While my eyes adjusted to the gloom I could feel the extra heat up there pressing down on the tin roof. I saw the trap was still empty, apart perhaps from the spider that sought refuge in it. I reached up to close the hatch lid but through the gloom noticed a large object. It was propped up in the middle of the roof space. Squinting through thin shafts of light, it didn't seem worth the bother of investigating. I had my work to get on with and laundry to hang on the line. But something urged me to just take a closer look. This was irritating because my hip gnawed with pain and my head felt fuzzy. I swung my body round and sat on the edge of the hatch opening. Climbing into the loft I swung jerkily from one roof joist to another. As I came closer to it I saw a large box propped against a supporting beam, rectangular in shape and set on its narrow end. Coffin like, I shocked myself in thinking and stopped dead in my tracks. Teetering on a joist I turned to go back. But curiosity gripped tightly now. Sweating, I moved closer to it, the heat in the loft at melting point.

Taking a deep breath I clambered in front of it and could see inside. With trembling hands I reached out and felt wood. It was something oval shaped. When my eyes adjusted I saw quite clearly the shape of a fish. Rather, it was a dolphin on an oval shaped shield. Perhaps it was made from bark with the dolphin painted in the Aboriginal style in hundreds of orange and yellow dots and squiggles. It was facing north, out towards the ocean, partially protected by the box that housed it. But why was it here? Had Miss Green forgotten it, or was it here for a reason? Perhaps it was some sort of lucky charm to protect against cyclones. That seemed reasonable to me. I breathed easy and my queasiness began to evaporate. I stood up as straight as the roof would allow, chuffed with this unexpected find. Before the feeling had a chance to diminish I lowered onto the stepladder and with considerable dexterity closed the hatch with a gentle clunk.

The same afternoon I started work in earnest. Soon my tapping at the typewriter was interrupted by a knock at the back door. I thought it might be Luke, and hastened through the kitchen. But to my surprise, there stood two Aboriginal men. They were propping each other up unsteadily and were dressed shabbily just like those I had seen near the town. One of them was clutching an empty gin bottle.

'Can I help you?' I asked politely, holding the door firmly with one hand, and wondering how on earth they'd got in through the gate.

They looked through me with blank expressions. The one without the bottle said, 'Taxi missus,' and held out his hand, while the other held tightly onto his empty vessel. I remembered what Luke had told me, pulled out the pockets of my shorts and said, 'No money.' very firmly.

'Taxi missus,' they said again in drawling voices.

'No money.' I said, as calmly as I could, and gently closed the screen door. Through the dark mesh I could see them skulking off reluctantly round the side of the house. I walked out to the veranda where I watched them leave through the open gate. Perhaps Luke had forgotten to close it? I could hardly believe it had been open all this time.

A cooler breeze stirred past me as I leant over the veranda rail. The sky was threatening rain again. Chirping cicadas sang a slow lullaby, and it wasn't long before I relaxed in one of the chairs. The heat was less intense but still perspiration ran from me and each breath was an effort. Uncomfortable on the hard chair, even so I dozed off into slumber. When I woke again I felt as though I was being watched, and remembered the gate needed closing.

Groggily I forced myself to first see to the fish. They rose to the surface of the water and opened their mouths hungrily. I had never met such greedy fish. They swam round and round, the mesmerizing action inducing a leaden stupor. And there it was again, the strongest feeling that someone was watching me. But all I detected were the trees with their gently swaying branches. As I closed the gate and bolted the padlock the chirping cicadas fell unusually silent. There was no activity in the street, and the growing humidity promised a quiet evening for the Tennis Club. I made my way back to the lounge, and settled on the heavy chair at the end of the dining table. Finally I continued my account, with only my lethargy and Stumpy for company.

There is no dusk in Darwin, day moving into night in one smooth orchestration and in a matter of a few minutes. A cloudless sky reveals different constellations to those in the northern hemisphere, and the stars are scattered like twinkling diamonds upon indigo velvet. The moon was in hiding that evening and I switched the lights on earlier than usual as gloom descended. By now my head was really throbbing, and my hip was just as painful. A purple bruise had developed on my forehead although the swelling had subsided. I felt sure to find matching bruises as time went on to accompany my grazed ribs.

In spite of this I was pleased with my days' work and I tidied my papers with satisfaction. I fried meat and onions for supper, but by then felt so exhausted I didn't think I would have the energy to eat it. The smell attracted dozens of blowflies that bounced at the window mesh in a vain attempt to reach the food. They continued to fruitlessly torpedo the screen for some time after I had finished cooking. I sat down to eat and tried not to think about the cockroaches that were most certainly lurking beneath the table. The sleepiness deepened as I ate, and afterwards it took all my energy to clear the dishes and wash up. The time was only 8pm but I collapsed onto the bed fully clothed and slept as though tranquillized.

Sleep, like a drug, or bad illness, can leave you feeling strangely more alive, while dreams can take you to places you have never been before. But nightmares deliver you to the deepest of horrors, and are remembered for all of your life.

Morning found me well enough to investigate the trap in the loft. A large possum had been successfully caught and spat angrily at me. Feeling brave, I lowered the prey and put the cage in the kitchen. The animal glared at me from behind the bars until I covered the trap with a blanket. I felt better, but could not shake off my bad dream since waking. Luke arrived in his utility truck soon after getting my call. Grateful for his help, I was also more than happy to have his company. My eyes were heavy from my long sleep and the disturbing dream I now carried.

Luke peeped under the blanket and whistled through his teeth. 'Hey, she's a real beauty isn't she?' He grinned at the possum like she was a pet. Then he said, 'Can you join me for the ride to Point End? It's a nice run out.'

'Oh, yes please, I need to get out of here for a while. But can you look at something in the loft first?'

'Okay, but it should be empty; I cleared it out for Greenie the week before you arrived.'

'Really? How strange, I found a large shield in a box up there yesterday.'

He climbed the ladder quite swiftly for his large frame and disappeared into the dark space aloft. I followed and stood on the top rung, and could see him walking as I had, from joist to joist through the gloom.

'It's in a big box in the middle of the loft.' I called out.

'There's no box up here.'

'What? It must be there.' I struggled up through the hatch and joined him at the very spot I had seen the shield. Seeing the upright beam that had supported the box I realized with a sinking heart it had vanished.

'But I did see it yesterday,' I said, 'I came up here and saw it. There was a dolphin painted on it.' He looked down at me doubtfully.

'How's your head feeling?'

'So you think I imagined it? What reason would I have? This house—it's driving me mad and it's giving me nightmares!' I wrung my hands together wishing I hadn't shouted. I knew I must look like a nervous wreck.

'What *sort* of nightmares are you having?' he said, in what seemed to be a semi-serious tone.

'Weird stuff I don't understand.' I said, immediately feeling like a fool. But I had to tell someone, and it might as well be him. He could mock me if he wanted. 'All I can tell you is that after seeing the shield I felt a bit brighter, and then two Aborigines turned up asking for money, so I sent them away. Then last night I was just so exhausted I went to bed early and had a nightmare.' I paused as a terrible thought occurred to me. 'Do you think I'm going troppo? Or, maybe I really have got concussion?' Luke steadied himself against the rafters and gave me an uneasy look.

'It's a distinct possibility.' he said. You did take a bit of a whack on the head when you fell.' We made our way shakily across the loft. 'Have you vomited?' he asked in his usual forthright manner.

• 27 •

'No I haven't. But I did feel sick when I was up here yesterday, it was so hot. Really, I don't feel at all bad today.'

'Okay, let's get out of here and get you into some fresh air. A change of scene might help you to recall your bad dream.'

Chapter 4

Out through Darwin we drove past dwindling habitation and were soon on an open dirt track. Low scrub lined the road, and the odor of scorched earth rose up on the hot air. The road stretched ahead like a red carpet and we drove right along the middle, Luke ready to move over if anything came from the opposite direction. But the way remained clear, apart from a large sunbathing lizard and a huge eagle that landed its prey by the coarse scrub. Luke looked over at me and remarked, 'Bit different to London driving, I'll bet.'

'It's amazing! We only get the odd fox in Croydon.' I said. The cage, safe with its cargo was firmly tied down in the open back of the truck. *Murray's Gardening Services* was emblazoned on the cab doors. Luke explained Murray was his father's name, but due to ill health he didn't work so often now.

The brick-red land stretched as far as my eyes could see, up ahead and on either side of us. A few blackboy, gum and acacia trees dotted the open landscape, adding greens and browns to the palette of reds and blues. I had to admit it felt good to get out of the house and away from the town and today even Luke didn't seem so bad. I relaxed into my seat and my shoulders softened a little. The open windows provided some air movement but no respite from the intense heat. The sun blazed relentlessly through the windscreen, singeing already tanned skin and forcing my body to perspire. It was annoying that my skirt was so short and I placed a headscarf over my exposed knees. Luke was concentrating on the road, wincing at every bounce and taking an occasional puff from the roll-up balanced between his lips. The truck was thrown around on the rough track, much worse than I had experienced on my drive up from Brisbane.

'Rains have washed away some of the road,' Luke said, his voice raised, 'might be in for a rough ride.'

I thought of Uncle Sid and how he had left me to drive here alone. I felt sure he had forgotten all about me. Years ago my mother had cried the day her brother sailed away to Australia, and next to my father I had waved from the dockside as the ship became a smudge on the horizon. Mother said Sid would come back home before we could say *knife*. But Uncle had had no regrets about being a Ten Pound Pom, and had opened a bistro with Aunt May as soon as they were settled. The Christmas knees-up with my parents was the only thing they missed, while Kim forgot about me at once. One morning in the bistro, Uncle pressed the advertisement into my hand. Aunt May gave me a cup of tea and they both said how much better it would be for me to study in Darwin, and what a very good environment it would be to write my thesis.

Luke's voice broke into my thoughts. 'Tell me about your dream and the blokes who turned up yesterday.' I described the visitors and how I must have forgotten to lock the gate, blaming the blow to my head. 'Those guys won't harm you,' he said, 'but you did the right thing, or they could be on your doorstep every day.' We whizzed along the road and clouds of red dust flew up behind us. I hoped he wouldn't ask me about the dream again. 'What about your nightmare?' Again he raised his voice above the engine.

'It was about a woman, an Aborigine.' I said, sighing. 'She spoke to me. And I became part of her story; in fact it was as if I had taken her place.'

'Can you remember what she said to you?'

'That's just it. Her words have burned into my mind, and I can't stop thinking about her.' Luke nodded and waited for me to begin.

'Well, here goes.' I cleared my throat and raised my voice. 'I saw a little settlement that appeared to be composed of two large sheds, a small house and a small barracks. There was also a tiny chapel and a very small hut at one end of a redbrick courtyard.

People were in the courtyard, sitting on the hard ground and having to answer to their names. I knew these were not their true names; and they were unable to understand this strange language that was spoken to them. I was sitting in the middle of the yard and my husband was down at the front. He was trying to explain that he needed to be near to me, that I was his wife and that it was his duty as a husband to be next to me. He was pushed roughly back into line and prodded with one of the guards' long weapons. Not a spear, but a biting vicious thing made of a hard shiny substance. I had heard, rather than seen one of them used, and had covered my ears as its roar bellowed out across the silent scrubland. It had been aimed high into the sky, and used to warn two of the captives who had managed to run away into the bush. I had been told that another time the biting thing was aimed at a kangaroo and something flew out of it and killed that roo. It hit it in the head and killed it very quick. But when they used it to scare those two runners we never saw what came out of it, even though we searched on the ground for hours. Some said the sky spirits had caught and gobbled up the thing that would have killed the runaways. A pale boss man tried to find those men but they were too clever for that. He came back from the bush after two days and did a lot of shouting at us all. He is here now and is walking round us. He stops next to me and prods me with a long stick. I don't like him and I don't look at him and his scar face. He walks up to one of the other boss men and points at me.

That frightens me.

I try to get near to my husband but they keep us in separate huts, one for women and children and the other for the men. I am very sad; I do not understand who these people are and why they want to make us live like this. A woman tells me one of the runaways is my brother. He is going back home, a long way away but he knows how to get there. He has gone back to our people. We live on the coast where the dolphins swim, but now I live inland with my husband. Somehow I know we will escape, and find a way to be together.'

I paused and said, 'That was when I woke up.' The truck slowed as Luke steered it over to the roadside. We came to a complete halt before he turned in his seat to look at me.

'After we drop off our passenger, how do you feel about joining me for a beer?'

I had momentarily forgotten about the possum under the oilcloth. Feeling foolish again, I wished I hadn't disclosed the dream in such detail.

Dream Time

'You mean go back to Darwin?' I didn't feel ready for the trip to end. 'Okay, if you want.' I looked away from his gaze and out at the squat blackboy trees with their jet trunks and crazy hair. He reached into his pocket for his tobacco and rolled a slim cigarette.

'There's a place inland near the Daly River.' He smiled with the lighted cigarette in his mouth. 'We might even see a croc on the way, if we're lucky. Thing is, after what you've just told me and with what you saw in the loft, there's something I think you should know.' I started to reply but he raised a thick finger, saying, 'Not now, I'll tell you when we get there.' He started up the truck and we sped off once again towards the reserve.

As we drew into Point End the vast sky loomed above us, devoid of all clouds. Even this near to the coast the air was still and damp. Luke placed the cage on the spiny grass and invited me to open the trap door. The fat possum bounced weightlessly into the heady atmosphere, letting out small shrieks of jubilation. How my sister Jade would have loved seeing her. Luke said she looked pregnant, and would soon need to find a nest for her babies. I worried she might starve as it seemed to be such a barren landscape, but Luke assured me otherwise.

'It must have been unbearable for her, shut up in the cage like that.' I said. 'Being shut in is the thing that really frightens me.' Out here in the open I became exhilarated by the open landscape with its vast canopy of never ending blue.

The pub was further inland, and soon we were driving past dense bush and splashing through shallow creeks. Luke warned, 'Watch out for crocodiles! Mind you, we'll be lucky to spot one. Even with the recent rain it's drier than it should be for this time of year. By now the creeks should be overflowing, and that allows the crocs to move to other hunting grounds.'

'I'm still going to look out for them.' I replied.

'Good on you!' he said, and gave me a twinkling smile.

As we moved further inland the sky turned dull, weakening in a cloudy haze. The road, long since lined by trees, became pitted and narrow. We saw no wildlife, and even the birds fell silent. They were probably right up in the tree canopies. Luke thought we were due for a thundering downpour. By the time we arrived at the pub it was gone midday and my entire body ached. The wooden building appeared makeshift and grubby, a disappointment after driving for so long. But I needed to stop, even if it was just to stretch my jelly-like legs. Luke grabbed my elbow and helped me from the cab. 'Come on Rach, let me buy you a beer.' he said.

Hospitable the Daly Tavern was not. Nor was it much cooler inside than it was out, although an old ceiling fan was trying valiantly to make some form of air movement. It circled endlessly as if pirouetting to the music coming from the worn and rusted jukebox. The bar ran the length of the interior, while the walls were dotted with pictures of men holding up dead fish. A dartboard took pride of place at the end of the room, and by the bar a *'Saucy Sheila'* calendar hung, no doubt for the regulars' amusement. A few beat up old tables, stools and chairs dotted the floor. Two locals were playing a game of darts, but they stopped to check us out as we entered. An old timer in a dusty hat and dungarees sat at the end of the bar. As we approached he stopped drinking and wiped his mouth with a gnarled hand. The landlord stood grimly behind the bar with his sleeves rolled up, a seemingly malevolent glint in his roving eye as he looked me up and down. Feeling immediately uncomfortable I wanted

Dream Time

to leave, but desperately needed stronger refreshment than the insipid water we had shared on our journey.

Luke held out his hand and the Landlord's eyes brightened, a huge smile spreading across his lined face. 'Luke, you old dog,' he said in a gravel voice, 'where have you been? We thought you'd been made into croc tucker!'

Luke smiled sheepishly. 'Sorry it's been so long, Vince. Been busy, mate.'

He eyed me up again. 'I can see why mate!' He exploded into laughter.

'Oh no, this is a friend, Rachel, this is Vince.'

'Pleased to meet you,' I said, nodding my head towards him. Luke pointed to the old timer who was smirking into his beer.

'That's Scratcher, and over there's brothers Dave and Marty.' I waved weakly and said 'Hi,' while Luke ordered some drinks. I would rather have sat outside in privacy, and after all, the temperature difference was negligible. But Luke said we would be eaten alive by flies and mosquitoes, so we sat at a table in the corner of the room. I was relieved to see everyone went back to behaving normally, Vince and Scratcher striking up a strong debate about Barramundi fishing, while Dave and Marty resumed their rather vocal game of darts.

The beer tasted good and I tried to sip it, but my deep thirst urged me to take large gulps of the cool golden liquid. The jukebox was playing *I want to be loved by you,* sung by Marilyn Monroe, creating an unlikely feminine feel to the room. Vince was telling Scratcher about a really big fish he had caught up river. It had put up such a struggle he was dragged from his boat and nearly became a croc's supper himself. Luke put down his glass and wiped his mouth with the back of his hand. Dave came over and slapped Luke playfully on the shoulder, causing him to spill beer onto his shirt.

'Dave, you drongo!' he said, 'I'll be stinking like a brewery all the way home!' Dave feigned a look of shock.

'That wouldn't normally bother you mate.' He looked at my knees while he went on, 'I just wanted to ask when we're going fishing again?' Luke stood up and gave his friend a light punch in the ribs.

'Soon mate, I'll call you with a date. Excuse me Rach.' And he headed to the gents to rinse off the beer. I knew I wanted to go straight back to Darwin as soon as I finished my drink. Dave sat down next to me and told me what a good friend Luke was.

'Do you know anything about fishing?' he said. I had to admit my ignorance about the subject, disappointing him momentarily. Then his eyes widened, and he started to point out the pictures on the walls, telling me who had caught what, and how much each catch weighed. After a while I realized it wasn't so bad being there after all. All this time Marty had been throwing darts alone, and now he was impatient for a proper game. He shouted at Dave to join him. Luke returned and hung his wet shirt on the back of the chair.

'I've got to sit here half naked, now.' He looked down and frowned at his singlet.

'Dave has been teaching me fishing facts,' I said, and his frown turned to a smile.

'That must have been a quick lesson,' he said, avoiding his friends' eyes.

He took the empty glasses back for refills. From my position I saw his back as he leaned over the bar. It reminded me of the first time I saw him on the veranda. But now I could see a large scar running over an exposed shoulder, like

Dream Time

the tight grip of a burning tarantula. The skin had silvered where the scar lay, and was furrowed where healing had failed to bring normality back to the upper limb. He brought the drinks over, and noticed the shock on my face. Our eyes seemed to fuse together for the briefest of moments. His glance moved to his left side.

'That's my old war wound.' he said. Marty looked up from his game and laughed. 'You really know how to charm a girl, don't you Luke!'

I ignored the dart players. 'Was it a fishing accident?' I asked. He inhaled the last pitiful bit of smoke from the end of his cigarette.

'Not fishing, no Rach. I got this in Nam.' The words came out quickly with the smoke. A shiver ran through me and I put down my glass.

'You don't mean Vietnam?' He looked into his beer and for the first time I sensed his vulnerability. I saw his eyes flicker towards the dart game.

'I'll tell you about it another time. I served over there with Dave.' He may have sensed my awkwardness then because he bent his head to find my lowered gaze.

'It's fine now, almost as good as the other one.' He flexed both arms theatrically, but the left shoulder seemed to fight uncomfortably against the tightened scars.

'It must have been a dreadful time.' I had no idea how such an ordeal might have affected him. At university I had attended anti-Vietnam rallies, and was aware of the conflict as reported by the media. But here were two first hand survivors of the war I had marched against. Luke's scars served to bring the horror of it all much closer. I took a breath and rather feebly told him about my home made banner and rallying efforts in London.

'I was one of the lucky ones,' he said, almost whispering, 'I came back.'

The juke box was silent, the opening fizz of cans and bottles providing an occasional release. Luke sipped his drink and turned away to light a fresh cigarette. His rough cheek betrayed a lone, struggling tear. He coughed and wiped it away in one swift movement. Unexpectedly I wanted to comfort him, and found his hand in mine under the grimy table.

'It's good to know you marched against it like that.' he said, 'Out there we had each other, but I felt completely cut off from the rest of the world. We felt dumped, forgotten.' He squeezed my hand and a shock connection shot through my veins, like the feeling of the locked door at Monkey Puzzle Street. He finished his beer but small beads of liquid clung to the stubble around his mouth. 'Nam is a story for another day. I really want to tell you about my dad.'

'Okay.' I was puzzled to know how this would explain anything.

'My father can name his entire family line, going back as far as 1788 when the first fleet landed.' Fascinated with history I wondered if I could use any of this information for my thesis.

'I'm not proud of my ancestors,' he continued, and confessed one of his forefathers had been guilty of a gruesome crime.

'You mean like a skeleton in the cupboard?' I said, perhaps a trifle too eagerly.

'Yeah, but this is a real skeleton. I'm going back seven generations down my father's line to when he committed the murder.' I nodded, hoping he would continue. 'I'm descended from a naval officer who was aboard one of those ships.'

Dream Time

I couldn't help interrupting. 'So your dad traced your family tree back to that date?'

'He didn't have to trace any of it. From the time that officer lived, every first-born son was given what they called the family *Trophy*, and that included the family tree.' He paused, and puffed thoughtfully on the cigarette. 'The officer had a son called Tobias. He committed the murder, and until Dad's day it was considered something to be proud of. Tobias passed the trophy on to his son, so the story goes. He made him believe it was something good, like a sort of cleansing act.

'Who did he murder?' I suddenly felt sick.

'Dad told me it was an Aborigine.'

'Oh no, are you sure?' Luke nodded, and a tortured look entered his eyes as he lowered his voice.

'Apart from Dad, I come from a line of malicious men.'

'Isn't that a bit strong? After all, it happened a long time ago. I know from my studies that hundreds of natives were killed by white settlers.'

'But that doesn't make it *right* does it?'

I had to agree with him. 'Well, so what can you do about it now?' Then it hit me. 'Are you telling me this has got something to do with the nightmare? And the shield in the loft?' His eyes met mine with a new intensity.

'I think so.' he said. 'Let me tell you more about Dad. He was told about the trophy when he was fifteen, was very upset over it and stormed out of the house. He felt a great wrong had been done, and it hit him hard because he had memories of an Aborigine mate at school.' He paused to roll a new smoke. 'Also, during the Second World War he served alongside Aboriginal soldiers; he's told me how brave they were. He's always been against killing of any kind, luckily during the war he never had to shoot anyone as far as I can tell. He's 61 now and still does a few hours gardening but he has to go easy on account of his blood pressure.'

'My uncle Sid has high blood pressure.' I said unnecessarily.

Luke continued, 'The thing is, Dad has always felt bad because of the Trophy. When I got that fever round at Greenies place, he really began to worry. But since this wet started he thinks we've been put under some sort of curse. I'm beginning to agree with him now, but he's on these really strong tablets for the blood pressure, right?'

'Right . . . .' I said, wondering where this would lead.

'So a few weeks ago just before Greenie left town, he called out in the middle of the night.' He stopped and shakily lit a fresh cigarette. 'It's about 2am, for God's sake. I got up to see what he wanted. There he was sitting bolt upright in bed, looking straight ahead and terrified out of his wits. He grabbed my arm and pleaded with me to get rid of the warrior at the end of the bed. I told him he was dreaming. Then he said *He's there at the end of the bed, behind that shield.*'

My stomach did a summersault. 'Oh no, that can't be possible.' And I pushed my drink away.

'At the time I put it all down to the tablets, like I thought what you saw might have been concussion, but after hearing your dream I remembered that night with Dad. And the native who was murdered, all those years ago? I happen to know it was someone from a tribe who lived right off this coast.'

I got up shakily, made for the lavatory, and once there was violently ill.

Chapter 5

The radio was playing Fleetwood Mac. I turned up the volume to drown out the noise of the wind. The words sent a tingle down my spine, and brought the nightmare back into my consciousness.

> *Now when the day goes to sleep and the full moon looks,*
> *The night is so black that the darkness cooks,*
> *You come sneaking around trying to drive me mad,*
> *Busting in on my dreams—making me see things I don't want to see.*

That evening I had only the rain and the radio for company, but my head felt much clearer now I had been sick. Outside vast sheets of water fell out of the sky, cascading from the veranda roof in long silver chains. I sat in my favourite place out there sipping warm tea. Luke had dropped me off earlier at the gate, insisted I should take it easy for a few days and promised to be in touch soon. That alone was gratifying. He was determined to find out more about the artist Mulga, saying he would visit the town library and ring Miss Green for possible information. I agreed to keep a note of any further phenomena. He suggested we meet up for a meal the following week to compare notes. I was already looking forward to seeing him again. I was shaken by his story, and confused as to why I felt so involved in it. My emotions were heightened, but I had no intention of losing my grip as others had, one drop at a time, like the persistence of the rain.

I drank my tea and stretched my sore muscles. A few stray geckos were braving the roof struts in search of food. They appeared to be even clumsier than usual, unable to catch even the slowest of flies. I watched their awkward movements while I tried to relax but found myself worrying about the future. Luke may have shared his family secrets but I was not nearly ready to tell him mine. The rain fell and fell, and eventually I closed my eyes.

Memories of home threatened to whip me like punishments. It was already October and back home autumn should have arrived. Heralded by the russet tones of the leaves, this season possessed soft evenings, large moons and weak shadows that lengthened with the hours. My parents would be busy preparing for the long winter sleep, clipping back shrubs and clearing out moss from gutters.

In my youth we had harvested fruit and vegetables from Grandfather's allotment for jams and chutney. In their steamy kitchen I often helped Grandma with her baking. At Christmas she made sure we all had a wish while we mixed the thick pudding together. Even my mother was ripped away from her wine and cigarettes, joining in and risking chipping her painted talons. Those times it felt like we were a real family. Grandma died before Jade was born, and then things changed for the worse. When my sister was old

Dream Time

enough we played at pretend cooking and I stirred in wishes that Grandma would come back from heaven. Mother said they had never seen eye to eye, but I missed her sorely. I couldn't understand my mother's apparent indifference.

On the sideboard in the dim light sat the letter to my parents, awaiting its postage home. The distance between us had given me courage to write words I had never dared say, and this knowledge had eased a part of my heart. But I thought it unlikely they would understand, or were even missing me. I thought of Grandma and Belle now, as I listened to the radio. I had not seen Belle for years, not since junior school. And the little troll she gave me was now thousands of miles away, on a dusty windowsill in a house that should have felt like home.

I opened my eyes, strode over to the letter and ripped it to shreds.

Alone in the dark before Jade was born I thought I had seen Uncle. It was Boxing Day, when he and Aunt May usually visited with Kim. But that day I was locked in the cellar. Cold terror forced me to run up the stairs where I stayed with my hands over my eyes. Waiting; chilled and frightened until I was let out of that icy hole. My father released me that evening when everyone had gone home. He said if I became strong I would not have to go back there again. I counted twenty three steps down to the flagstone floor, and sat on the twenty-first step to kid myself I was safe. Grandma believed it was a lucky number, but how much truth was in that I could never be sure. If Belle ever misbehaved she was sent to her room with no tea. But there she did have her trolls for company. If only I had been stronger, and not weak like I felt right now. Even Kim's company would have improved my solitude.

I picked up the pieces of torn letter and put them in the bin.

I returned to the veranda and caught the scrambling geckos fighting for insects. The rain flowed onto the ground making little rivers and provided a gurgling melody. Tonight it replaced the usual chirping of cicadas and croaking of frogs, drowning out the radio as it became louder and heavier. My sighs went unheard as I looked out into the inky night. The mango trunks stretched up in front of me like giant guardians, their branches and swollen fruits silhouetted with raw electric light. A silent possum tripped gingerly down a fine branch to reach a ripe fruit. I hoped it would not find a way into the roof, but at least I could use the trap if need be. I became sleepy and turned up the volume for the *Evening Falls Show* and unintentionally dropped off to sleep. When I awoke some time later the wind had strengthened and felt cold round my legs. It whistled through the mango leaves, propelling fruits to the drenched ground with soggy splashes. Startled, it took a few seconds to realise where I was, and I soon made my way to bed.

The telephone was ringing angrily. In the morning calm its shrill tones echoed eerily through the house. I lifted the receiver, and at once heard my uncle's roar. 'G'day Rachel, how's it going up there?'

'Oh, alright thanks Uncle. How are you?' I was still bleary.

'We're all good here, except for Kimmy. That's why I'm phoning really. She took a tumble off her surfboard and broke her leg, so she won't be up to travelling for a while.' My heart sank as I took in the news.

'I'm really sorry Uncle; I hope she gets better soon.'

'Your aunt thinks you might be lonely up there on your own.'

'I'm okay, don't worry about it.' I said, hoping not to betray the strain in my voice.

'Is everything all right up there? How's the wet going?'

'Well it's very oppressive, and there's not much rain compared to the usual amount, I'm told. And this house, well it's a bit weird.' I was hoping he would ask me why.

He laughed and said, 'Well, you are at the top-end love, it's bound to feel hotter, it's not like anything you're used to.'

'I suppose so . . . ,' and my heart sank further.

'Well, if you need anything, just ring. Your aunt sends her love and hopes you're able to get all your writing done. Bye love!' he boomed.

'Bye Uncle.'

The line went dead, and he was gone before I had the chance to tell him about his broken down car. I pulled my night-robe round me as a shiver ran up my spine. So this was it, alone as I always had been, as it seemed I was destined to be. Had Kim really intended to join me, I wondered? Even if she had broken her leg, surely she could have spoken to me on the phone. I tried hard not to think about them. The nightmare popped into my head and annoyed, I tried to push it away. I did a few yoga stretches but I could still see it as clearly as if I had lived it myself. I sat at the kitchen table but I was really sitting on the hard ground surrounded by my fellow captives. I glanced around the room, expecting to see their anguished faces. The dream had not just seemed real; I was sure now it had *been* real.

The heat stoked up as the morning progressed, along with my further frustration at Uncle's call. Maddening thoughts ignited a growing anger that grew the more I tried to shut it away. Barging onto the veranda I slammed the screen door behind me and set Ringo barking. The distant hum of voices drifted over from the Tennis Club, their mocking laughter joining with Ringo's drum-beat barking. I gripped the veranda rail with all my strength, suddenly wanting to scream out loud. Things were getting on top of me, I could feel my weakness.

My eyes stung with frustration, but then something moved at the corner of my vision and I turned abruptly. I jumped away from the rail, and screeched with enough force to silence Ringo. A huge twig with legs was coming towards me along the railing. As long as my forearm, it's thin wings were neatly folded along its misshapen body. Like a tightrope artist it placed one skinny leg delicately in front of another, a concentrated determination in its bulbous eyes. I backed off towards the screen door, keeping my eyes firmly fixed to this monster. But to trick me the wind blew up from nowhere, throwing my hair across my face and obscuring my vision. When I looked again the insect had vanished and I retreated into the lounge, closing the door firmly behind me.

Somewhat relived to be indoors, even so my hands were trembling. Moments later I was surrounded by airborne missiles. I could see they were cockroaches. They must have come in on the wind in the few seconds when the door was open. Were they really able to fly, or was this another part of Luke's wretched curse? And fly they did, everywhere and anywhere and always just out of my reach. I tried catching them when their fat bodies flopped on the floor, but it was no use.

I found an empty jam jar and tried trapping them one by one, but they escaped as soon as I got anywhere near. Just the sight of their spindly legs made me sick to the stomach. They buzzed around me, slapping into me and catching in my hair while I cried out hysterically for help. My fury shifted to wild panic as I struggled to find a solution to this vile infestation. Finally I removed one of my sandals and chased after each one in succession, smashing them into the furniture, onto the walls and against the hardwood floor. Cockroach entrails smeared the place as finally all were dispatched. Left sobbing and exhausted, I sank to my knees amid the putrid scene I had created.

Hours later I finished cleaning up. Still shaking from the effects of unleashed adrenaline my mind was resolved. I would have to return home to England. I could not suffer another day in this house. Even the thought of retreating to my relatives in Brisbane filled me with dread. I was too feeble to withstand this place, and every fibre of my body screamed defeat. But my mind was made up. My meeting with Luke was in a few days, but I could call him before then. I needed to find a flight home as soon as possible.

After a while I felt apprehensive about admitting failure to him, of all people. I couldn't expect him to begin to understand, being as we were from two different worlds. But I had started to trust him, even though I hated to admit it. I didn't know why that was so.

Standing under the shower I let the water wash over my body. Someone was there, watching me as I bathed. She saw the water rinse away the insect grime and perhaps knew how it was able to soothe my frayed nerves. I didn't care anymore. I told myself even if she had won the battle, it was stronger of me to leave than to stay.

Chapter 6

The appropriately named *Darwin Hotel* was modern, with a glass roofed lobby and large potted palms. The marble floors and soft furnishings gave a feeling of opulence, and I was relieved I had taken some trouble over my appearance.

'Stone the crows Rach, you look like a film star!' Luke blurted out the words when he picked me up in the truck. I was just as surprised to find him looking smarter than I thought possible. He had shaved closely, and his hair was combed back. He wore a bright blue shirt that matched his eyes, jeans and soft shoes. We laughed at each other's new look and he told me 'I've got lots to tell you.'

In the hotel bar we perched like two elegant birds, sipping our cool drinks. Somewhat elated, after the first cocktail I had to balance carefully on the precarious stool. 'Before anything else,' Luke said, 'I want to thank you for being a mate,' and he clinked my glass with his own, continuing, 'it's strange, but I feel so much better for telling you about the family Trophy. I really appreciate you not judging what happened.' His openness stopped me in my tracks, and I found myself smiling encouragement. I raised my glass.

'Here's to friends.' And our glasses clinked again. 'Actually,' I said, 'I wish I had called you the other day, but anyway I've come to a decision.' I recounted my fright with the praying mantis, and my woeful battle with the cockroaches. I looked at him sheepishly. He seemed almost hurt because I hadn't phoned him, and asked when my cousin was joining me. After relaying my uncle's call, he urged it was even more important I should ring him if anything worried me. A waiter showed us to our table and we ordered from the menu. While we waited for the food Luke got out a small notebook from his pocket. Excitement twinkled in his eyes as he read from it.

'Okay, here's what I've got. I'm still trying to get hold of Greenie, so I found this at the library. There's a Queen of all the dolphins, her name is Ganadja and she's revered as sacred. Some native people can communicate with her and with other dolphins.' He paused and took a drink. 'To them, the reefs round Australia are a purifier for the oceans. The seas are thought to be like the blood in a human body, because to them the Earth is one huge living entity'. He looked up from his notes. 'I'm wondering if it's Ganadja on the shield, does that make any sense at all?' I put my elbows on the table and leaned forward.

'I've read a bit about the Aborigines, and how important the land is to them. But a Queen of the dolphins? It would be really something if that was what I saw.' The waiter brought griddled seafood and salad, and we ate thoughtfully until I broke the silence. 'If they believe the whole Earth is a living, breathing, intelligent organism, no wonder so much respect is given back to the land from them. It must be like

• 49 •

having a loved relation. And when you think about it, man wouldn't have a home without the Earth.'

'That's about it,' Luke replied, 'no planet means *no us.*' He finished eating and placed his fork prong side down on the plate.

The waiter brought coffee. 'What if the shield belonged to the artist?' I said, the thought just occurring to me. 'Would that make sense? After all, we know he stayed in the garden.'

'Maybe the warrior was a younger version of the artist.'

'You're joking surely?' I stirred my coffee. 'I don't know why, but I'm not really convinced any of it is to do with Mulga.'

'Go on,' he urged, as he rolled his first cigarette of the evening. 'Why?'

'I can't really explain why, but my instinct is telling me all this stuff is to do with the woman in the dream. Maybe it's because her presence is so strong, and because I can sense her watching me in the house, like she's trying to get rid of me.' Luke placed his coffee cup onto its saucer.

'Suppose she's connected with the family murder? But then why would she blame you, rather than me?'

'That's a good question, but I've had too much wine to work it out.' His eyes washed over me, and I knew I couldn't tell him about my decision just yet. I finished my coffee. Perhaps the shield had been pure illusion, devoid of any real substance and dissolving overnight like a cobweb. But I had touched it and it had seemed so real. How Murray had seen a similar apparition, and why his warrior resembled my own vision in the garden remained a further mystery.

Luke changed the subject. 'Tell me about Kim, is she your age?'

'She's a year younger, so we should get along.' I said.

'Don't you like her?'

'Oh yes, but she always seemed a bit spoiled to me. When we were younger she visited us in London but had huge tantrums if she didn't get her own way. I've got a younger sister who never behaved like that.' He raised his eyebrows in a manner I took to be admonishment. 'We didn't really get on in Brisbane.' I wished I hadn't told him that.

'What about your aunt and uncle? Do they have tantrums as well?'

'No, Aunt May is okay, and Uncle is just fat.' I slumped back in my seat. He roared laughing, and I joined in with relief.

'What about your family?' I said. He told me his mother had arrived as an orphan child in the 1930's, and had died when he was 8 years old. When he was old enough he joined his father in the business, and as an only child even now he longed for siblings. He was very fond of his neighbour, a single lady called Bea. She had become a second mum to him over the years, being a close friend of his father.

'I had a happy childhood.' He looked relaxed as he finished his cigarette. 'Now you know I'm half Pom and half Aussie, so no jokes please.'

It was getting late when we arrived at the house, laughter spilling out of the truck prompting a disgruntled woof from Ringo. The night sky revealed what must have been trillions of stars, like so many diamonds scattered across black velvet. The full moon hung low in the sky but was iridescent, like a huge pearl. Luke took my hand gently in his and led me to the back door. We looked up at the night sky. Truly spectacular, the more we looked, the clearer it became.

'Be even better if the moon wasn't so full.' he said. Looking west, he pointed out a triangle of stars called

Indus: the Native American. Further westward *Delphius* the Dolphin appeared diamond shaped with a long tail. Looking upward I could just make out the larger constellations Andromeda and Pegasus. I was fascinated. Tonight Luke wasn't the awkward ox I had at first supposed him to be.

We made some fresh coffee and sat together on the veranda. The fruit bats flitted among the mangos, noiselessly feeding on the juicy fruits. Luke seemed reflective and for a while was silent.

Eventually he said, 'Where do you think we end up?' I saw he was rubbing his scarred shoulder.

'When we die, do you mean?'

'Yeah. I sometimes wonder if Mum's in heaven.' I placed what I hoped was a reassuring hand on his, and wasn't sure how to respond.

'I'd like to think my grandmother is up there,' and all at once her face was fresh in my mind. 'Perhaps they're having a cup of tea together.' He continued to sip his coffee thoughtfully.

'She liked a cup of tea like my mum then? Mum believed in life after death, even about reincarnation.' He paused before saying, 'What about you, Rach? Do you believe in it?' I choked on the hot coffee.

'I don't know really Luke; I haven't given it much thought.'

'I was the same until Dad told me about this friend of his called Jeff. They were on active duty together in Japan, in the Second World War. This happened while Jeff was under enemy fire one day, advancing through dense jungle. Suddenly from nowhere a battalion of soldiers was making straight for him. He could see they were dressed in ancient battle clothing.'

'What did it mean?' I said, leaning forward in my chair.

'Well, he couldn't believe his eyes, but the soldiers ran towards him with swords and with their shields raised against heavy breastplates. He couldn't hear any sounds; he said that was the strangest thing of all. Then he realised he was the only one there from his squad. Terrified, he watched as they got closer and closer, certain he would be killed right there and then.'

'Oh; how dreadful!'

'But when they reached him they disappeared into thin air, and were gone as quickly as they had come. Jeff caught sight of his mates again, and they drove back the real enemy, who had been firing all the time. It's a miracle none of them hit Jeff. Afterwards he told Dad he had witnessed a past life memory. He said they can happen at times of deep fear.'

'What d'you mean by past life memory? Are you saying he could remember the earlier battle?'

'Yes, but I think it's more like slipping back in time for those few seconds. I guess it's like visiting another dimension, time travelling even. It completely changed his life. After the war he joined the Spiritualist Church.'

'That's creepy, Luke. It's an incredible story, but I'm not sure if I believe it.'

'Even after the weirdest month of your life?' I laughed. Before I knew it he reached forward and kissed my face.

'You know,' he said, 'you remind me of Mum.' He moved closer, and when our lips met a song of joy engulfed my body. It seemed we embraced for only a moment before he had to leave. I walked him to the gate and he said, 'Thanks again for being a mate, Rach. I feel as if I can tell you anything.' His voice cracked slightly as he spoke. Then he climbed into the truck and gave a long wave goodbye as he sped away up the empty street.

I tried to sleep that night, but my body tossed and turned on the hot mattress for what seemed like hours. Was it possible the Spiritualist Church could send the ghosts away from here? On the other hand it might simply make matters worse. I for one didn't wish to end up talking to dead people, like Jeff.

Eventually I came to a fresh resolution as the memory of Luke's kiss replaced any plans of my return to England.

The day dawned bright and clear, with a rolling expanse of blue sky and not a cloud on the horizon. In the back garden I greeted the fish cheerily, pirouetting on my toes as I dished out their food. Still on my toes I tripped through the house and practised my yoga with added zest. I wrote a new letter, telling my parents about Kim's leg and adding that I was well and had made a new friend.

I didn't mention anything about Luke but I hoped he was my new boyfriend. Until now I had not had a proper boyfriend. I somehow missed the 60's sexual rebellion, and while my fellow students lived for the moment my head had been buried in studies. My father drummed into me that I must work for my keep, having no right to expect him to keep me. So I studied hard but to some I appeared boring, prudish even. Life at home had always been tense, but it became far worse during the cold war that hung over the world at that time. My parents had lived through the blitz. They had witnessed at first hand its indiscriminate destruction. Perhaps it was seeing families torn apart that made them how they were. Young children were evacuated to the country only to return not to their homes, but to streets of rubble. It must have seemed hopeless. But day after day they witnessed how British stoicism endured while families

Dream Time

coped with private loss and despair. For their generation, war was something they had no wish to re-visit.

At the same time they saw the 60's relaxed ethos as annoying. They believed the threat of war remained real, and if it started nothing, especially long hair, could prevent it. Our neighbourhood was duly issued with instruction manuals telling us to shelter beneath the stairs or under a sturdy table, stock up on tinned food and water, and listen to the radio for the three minute warning. But these guidelines provided little reassurance to my parents. They knew in their hearts that a nuclear bomb would exterminate the whole of London, and probably a much wider area. All through this *my* only fear was the prospect of being shut away under the stairs.

Luke's kiss had been a love bomb. It had ticked away all night long, destroying any thoughts of leaving. It had landed in my heart and now my emotions were in ruins. All morning I was filled with joy, unable to concentrate at all. Eventually that afternoon I was able to work on my thesis. The typewriter keys clattered away busily, only stopping while I fetched a drink or chatted briefly to Stumpy. The same evening just before the sun went into hiding the heavy gate clattered open. Uncle's station wagon climbed the drive noisily, with Luke sitting at the wheel. He had a very pleased expression on his face. He'd taken the keys some days before and all this time had been getting it fixed. I dashed out to the drive as he came to a halt.

'Thank you so much Luke!'

'Glad to be of service.' he replied with a smile, 'You can take me out for a spin sometime if you like.' He fumbled in his pocket for his cigarette papers, suddenly appearing clumsy. 'D'you feel like a drive right now?' He dropped his tobacco, and had to start a fresh cigarette.

• 55 •

'That sounds nice. Where shall we go?'

He cleared his throat. 'Well, it's just that Dad says he wants to meet the girl I keep rabbiting on about.' My gaze met his ocean eyes, and my heart skipped a beat.

'That's great!' I said, almost squealing the words. 'I just have to get my door keys.' Inside the house I tingled at the prospect of meeting Murray and desperately hoped he would find a reason to like me.

Chapter 7

Luke's house stood on the outskirts of town, surrounded by what had to be the best garden in Darwin. A lemon gum grew to one side, while wattles and banksias filled the borders. The drive was flanked by a hedge of pink Geralton wax, but the house was predominantly white. I wondered if Auntie Bea had bought the tinkling wind chimes by the front door. To my surprise more feminine touches were found inside, including a lace cloth on the dining table. Various ornaments were arranged carefully on shelves, and I guessed they held special memories. The face of a young woman looking out of a frame caught my attention. I saw she had thick auburn hair, and Luke's eyes. He followed my gaze and picked up the picture. 'That's Mum when she was twenty.' he said.

'She's beautiful Luke.' He went to find his father while I waited anxiously on the sofa. On a bookcase opposite there were pictures of Luke as a baby, and ones of Murray as a tall, strong looking man. Now he exploded into the room in a coughing spasm.

'Welcome Rachel.' he said, wheezing the words and holding out his hand. 'Welcome to Darwin, and to our home.' I rose immediately and shook his hand. I could see the once tall man was shorter, but still possessed the same amiable face. He regarded me with somewhat narrowed eyes. 'I've heard all about you from Lukas, and I can see you're a good girl.' He waited to catch his breath. 'There's two types of people in this world; hard ones and soft ones. I can see you're a softie, just like my Ruth.'

'Thank you.' I sat on the sofa and tried not to fidget. Luke passed an inhaler to his breathless parent. 'Thanks Son. I don't ever have to ask him, he always knows when I need it. He's a real Godsend to me.' And he slapped Luke weakly on the knee.

'I can see that, Mr . . .'

'Call me Murray, please.' he said, almost booming the words as his lungs began to recover. 'Not as fit as I used to be,' he said with a bowed head, 'I've got high blood pressure and this flamin' asthma, but my Luke takes care of the gardening business now. I do a bit for the Parks Department now and then. Did you know I helped design the Botanical Gardens?' He looked up at me now with pride in his eyes.

'Oh, I must tell you how beautiful they are, I sometimes take a walk through them in the afternoon.'

'Yep, one of my finer moments, I guess. It's probably my only claim to fame.' He smiled at his son, and rested his voice for a while.

'Mum used to take me to the gardens every week when I was small.' Luke said. 'I must know every inch of them.'

Murray sat back in his chair. 'Now, Lukas tells me you're studying, all alone in that house. And I know you've had a bit of a fright. You must come over to us if ever you feel lonely.' He paused and had a bit of a cough. 'Aren't your parents worried about you being here all alone?' I made some excuses about my family and hoped the lightness of my account had not come over too falsely. I told him about my father and his hardware stores that had been in the family for generations. I didn't mention my father had hoped to hand his business down to a son.

'Sounds like you've got a good home back in London.' he said. 'And how do you rate Darwin compared to home?'

'It's very hot.' I said, and realised at once I had stated the obvious. He threw back his head and laughed hoarsely.

'You're not wrong there!' He spluttered and started to cough again. I didn't like to admit that in this short time I had already hungered for the soft greens of England, and that they continued to beckon from the far corners of my memory. Luke had left the room, and now returned with tea and biscuits.

'Hope you're not giving Rach the inquisition, Dad.' he said, winking at his father while he poured the tea. I noticed there was a knitted cosy on the pot, even in all this heat. He passed me a cup of the scalding liquid.

'Just being polite son. It's a good thing you like tea Rachel, because we go through gallons of the stuff. My Ruth was a great lover of tea; well she came from England anyway.' I noticed how he tilted his head to one side as he drank. 'Sad to say we lost her when Luke was just a boy. He doesn't like to talk about it, but we miss her every day.'

'I'm very sorry.' I glanced over at Luke, busy handing out the biscuits. 'Which part of England did she come from?'

'From a little village called Ludlow, in Shropshire. Do you know it? She came over here as an orphan. Poor child, she was only 5 years old. She went to a family in northern Queensland. I met her at a dance just before the war and a few months later we tied the knot.'

'Did you ever visit England?' I said.

'No, never wanted to, after what they did to her.' He blew weakly on his tea. 'Ruth never went back either, but she never forgot Shropshire. He raised his cup as if in salute to her. He looked over at Luke, then back at me, as if remembering something. 'This fright you had. It sounds quite like what I saw.'

'So it seems.' I glanced at Luke, recalling the loft incident. 'Do you think it could be the same thing?'

'Well, I don't know about that. But in all my years I can honestly say I've never been as terrified as when I saw that warrior bloke. Then there was that thing happened to Lucas.' He nodded his head in Luke's direction. 'We never did work out what *that* was all about.'

'I think it could be to do with the house.' I said.

'No!' Murray cut in, 'It's a curse on us, on our family, and it's well deserved when you think about it. I'm only sorry you've been caught up in it Rachel. Very sorry, in fact.' His eyes dropped, and he looked sadly into his teacup. A shiver ran through me and I wriggled uncomfortably on the sofa. Murray began coughing and had another puff on his inhaler.

'So let me just check. These incidents have only just started?'

'Yes, a few weeks ago.' Murray said. 'Ever since that time at Daphne's with Lucas.'

'Since the time I arrived in Australia.' I stated through trembling lips.

Murray raised his hand in a silent goodbye from the window while Luke walked me to the car. We agreed to meet again the following evening. I drove the car out of the drive and onto the hard asphalt road. I had enjoyed meeting Murray and learning about how Ruth loved English tea

Dream Time

and Waikato scones. It was obvious that Murray had loved her deeply. The drive home was smooth, but my mind was uneasy. I didn't want to be responsible for triggering the curse they were both so sure about. Murray had told me how he thought women were the stronger sex, that it was not war but women that made men out of boys. But I felt weaker than ever, now.

Luke said Australia was a land of contrasts, character and diversity. In the cold light of day it didn't seem possible it was also a home to ghosts. I thought about this while I hung out the washing the following day. It was early, the temperature was still cool and I found myself humming involuntarily. Biffs' balding head appeared over the fence and he called out, 'You like the Beatles then?' Embarrassed to be caught off guard, I felt my face colour up. I had not seen Biff for days, and Ringo seemed to be left on his own for much of the time. 'I'm not keen on the Fab-Four,' he said, 'but the dog was named after the drummer. Not my idea; the ex-wife's.' He held up a hand as if to stop my response. 'I prefer Count Basie and Glen Miller. Now that's what I call dance music.'

I took a deep breath and chanced it. 'Do you happen to know anything about Mulga, the Aboriginal man who painted here?' Almost instantly he backed away from the fence, distaste spreading across his features.

'Nasty business that.' he said, 'Daphne had no right encouraging bongs onto her property.'

'Bongs?' I said.

'You know,' he screwed up his leathery eyes impatiently. 'Abbo's, bongs; black fella's. You want to steer clear of *their* kind, young lady.'

'Why?'

'Because they're not like us, are they?' He gave me a look of deep exasperation. Can you imagine discussing the cricket

• 61 •

score with one of *them*? No, we should keep to ourselves and they should keep to themselves and that's the best way for everyone. You must have seen them all over the place, drunk as skunks with their half-caste offspring trailing behind them?' The heat in my face turned to anger.

'But surely it's western people who have produced those children?' I added, 'As far back as the first settlements the white men raped the native women, you know.' Biff gave a look of shock.

'Now I know you're studying and a clever girl, but don't believe all you read in books. I'll bet most of it is made up anyway. And as for bong lovers like her,' he pointed at Miss Green's house, 'they only cause trouble and more problems. Some of them black fella's get out of hand and need locking up; I'll bet you didn't know that!' His voice reached fever pitch. 'Only that doesn't work either because when you lock them up they die off, just like that. Now you tell me that's' normal.' He threw back his head triumphantly.

Appalled, I tried to challenge him. 'You mean they commit suicide.'

'Nah, there's not a mark on them. Not suicide, young lady. They just expire, like a fly expires in a jar with no air holes. It's something to do with their spirit. You can't contain them you see. That's why you should steer well clear.' Biff was calmer now but was making no sense at all. I opened my mouth to ask another question, but he walked away with a bouncing Ringo at his heels. I could just hear him saying, 'They're not like us, just not like us at all.'

That afternoon I had to keep busy. Still bristling from Biff's remarks, I prepared the car bill for Uncle, and looked through the *Darwin Post* for a possible part-time job. The extra money would be very handy, and I needed to get away from the house and the creepy feeling of being watched. I bashed away at the typewriter until my sweaty fingers slipped off the keys and became trapped painfully between them. I knew I should really stop for a while, but Biff had infuriated me, and I needed to vent my anger somehow.

The weather had turned particularly humid, and Stumpy was suckered to the lounge wall beside me, occasionally licking his eyes with a long tongue. It was still unusually dry for the time of year, *Trevor the Weather* said on the radio. We could expect more wet and windy weather; temperatures remaining at around 30C, and humidity remaining high for the next few days. Trevor said a teenager had gone crocodile hunting and had come home minus an arm. He was in Darwin Infirmary and had been given three pints of blood. The disc jockey played *Down Town* by Petula Clarke to cheer him up, and then played *Congratulations* by Cliff Richard for Eve and Don Harris for their 25th Wedding Anniversary. The afternoon morphed into evening, and faceless record requests softened to a background hum.

By 6pm the sky had clouded and the wind blew up around the garden, whistling through the spiny grass. As if on cue, the weather began to obey the radio's predictions. I laid the dining table with place mats and cutlery, and had beer cooling in the fridge. Thankfully I could not find any cockroaches underneath the table. A vase of yellow wattle and purple acacia provided a welcome splash of colour from the sideboard. I stood back to admire the room, but was not at all sure my cooking would please Luke. I opened a beer to calm my nerves. I was looking forward to seeing him and spending another evening together. But apart from my faltering heart something undefined hung between us. Something I was presently unable to comprehend.

'That's how a lot of people feel, more than you'd think, in fact.' Luke said. I had relayed my earlier conversation with Biff. We opened beer cans and sipped the cool liquid. 'I guess some people are frightened of what they don't understand.' He continued as I nodded agreement, my mouth full of beer. 'Oh, and Dad says hi, he really liked you.' I swallowed and smiled with relief.

'I liked him too.' I said, 'A lot.'

'I worry when he can't get his breath, but he's still quite a strong guy really.' I lowered my gaze.

'It's great you get along so well. I hope he lives to a really old age.'

Luke put down his beer. 'I hope so too.' he said. I wanted to show off my little mate Stumpy, so we went looking for him, and just caught sight of him disappearing under the locked door.

'Why do you think this door is locked?' Luke said, still holding his beer can.

'I think it's full of Miss Green's valuables.'

'We could always break in.' A mischievous glint entered his eyes. The beer was beginning to take effect, and I sniggered at the thought.

'No, we mustn't.' Luke feigned seriousness, and stood to attention.

'Someone's got to rescue Stumpy.' he said, and marched outside to the truck. He came back in with a screwdriver from his toolbox. He commented it looked like a big storm was coming and said to look out in case he had to kip down in the storm shelter. He unsuccessfully wiggled a piece of wire around in the lock. I snorted back a laugh, but beer bubbles rose up my nose and made me sneeze. After the clumsy lock breaking he tried spying through the keyhole, but I'd already tried this on previous occasions with no luck. Suddenly he pulled his head away.

'Ouch!'

'What happened, Luke?' He looked slightly mesmerised and rubbed his face. 'That felt like an electric shock, it made me jump.'

'I got the same jolt when I first arrived. I touched the handle. What could it mean?' I felt my eyes probing for an answer.

'It means this house is seriously weird,' he said, 'I think you're right about that. Are you sure you want to live here?' My eyes broke away then, and I didn't have the courage to tell him I felt safe so long as he was near.

'I don't know, and that's the truth. Only I get the feeling we'll only find out what's going on if I stay here. This house has got to be connected somehow with your family trophy hasn't it?' Suppressing a hiccough I added, 'It's just so weird.'

Luke went outside to light up a smoke while I fried steak for supper. As usual the cooking sent more flies into a frenzy bombing towards the smell and torpedoing the window mesh. We ate our meal, but Luke seemed deep in his own thoughts.

'Great tucker.' he said eventually, as he polished off the last bit on his plate. Forgetting about Miss Green's room I cleared away the dishes. I could see the site, but not the remains of the little house from the kitchen window, and called out.

'Hey, did you ever meet him?' He joined me in the kitchen.

'Who, Biff?'

'No not Biff, Mulga the artist.' I nodded in the direction of the garden.

'Not really, no. I saw him from a distance a couple of times, but never met him face to face. Come to think of it, I never heard about him doing any pictures of dolphins either.' He dried the dishes while we both looked out into the garden, half expecting to be spooked by something out there in the gloom.

'Are you sure you don't mind being here?' he asked again. He placed a heavy arm round my shoulders, and we walked out to the veranda.

'I'll let you know if I can't stand it.'

'I'll hold you to that.'

It was muggy out there under the tin roof and night had closed in like a thick cloak. Powerless to the elements we flopped onto a low bench. Huge storm clouds were gathering and bats flashed from tree to tree in search of mangos. The wind came up and my muscles tightened as we waited for the precious rain. The house remained quiet and still, refusing to divulge its secrets. And the night continued to press down as the minutes evaporated. It seemed for the moment at any rate, there was nothing more to say. Drawn towards him I became weaker than ever, and incapable of resistance. Like a spell my senses were further intoxicated by the desire in his eyes. Gently he pulled the ribbon from my hair, sending it tumbling over my shoulders. Sliding his hands around my waist he seduced me into the deepest of kisses. Cigarette smoke was on his breath but I found myself rising towards him, reeling in ecstasy while every nerve strained for satisfaction.

Slowly we drew together as if magnetised. Sparks of excitement flew from our intimacy, lighting up the dim veranda. The most ancient of rituals was begun. We drank from the cup of joy and immersed ourselves in each other's essence. Our bodies then yielded to the oldest dance of love. At the final crescendo the wind flurried into a gale and Mother Nature released her deluge.

The warm rain lashed down onto our fizzing bodies and across the veranda, dashing harder and faster still against the walls of the enigmatic house.

Chapter 8

It was dark when I woke. I was in bed and Luke was sleeping beside me. I turned on the light, panting with fear from the dream, the nightmare that had woken me. I had seen the Aboriginal woman again. My eyes blurred as I tried to focus in the raw electric light. My arms were as black as charcoal against the bright, white sheets.

I reached out to Luke and shook him clumsily with a dark hand. 'Oh my God! *Oh my God!*' My whole body felt numb. Surely I was still asleep?

He groaned sleepily and sat up. 'What's up Rach?'

'My arms Luke, look at my skin!' I held them up for him. 'Look at them!' I was sobbing now, my body rocking back and forth on the bed. Luke's gaze was blank. 'What's the matter with them?' he said, 'They look okay to me.' I shot out of the bed and over to the mirror. Swallowing acid bile, my legs were buckling beneath me. But my reflection confirmed it; in the glass I saw my own arms and my own skin. Luke appeared behind me, a worried expression spreading across his face.

Dream Time

'Come back to bed and tell me all about it.' he said. I crawled back to the comfort of his embrace. He held me close and smoothed my sizzling forehead.

'Not another nightmare?'

I recalled the nauseating episode. 'Yes, like the last one when I was really in the dream. I was the same woman again, feeling all that she felt. Am I becoming possessed?' Luke held me tightly.

'Oh, Rach.' he said, almost whispering the words.

'I'm really scared.' He stroked my damp hair away from my face. My heart was like a lead weight, and it was some time later before I got up for breakfast. I couldn't talk about the dream for fear of weeping.

Luke suggested I get it down on paper before the days' events had a chance to blot it out. Still in my night robe I clattered away on the typewriter while he made toast and fried eggs in the kitchen. The words landed angrily on the paper like so many blows. The rain had not ceased overnight, and sharp winds rattled the house. They made me jump intermittently. Luke brought in breakfast, saying he thought there was sure to be tree damage after the storm. I flinched involuntarily when he spoke.

'Oh, I'm sorry; I'm really on edge.' I confessed. He sat down beside me and squeezed my shoulder with his spade hand.

'Whatever is going on here,' he said, 'we will sort it out. When Mum was alive she knew this lady who could communicate with spirits. I think they called her a clairvoyant. She moved out to Katherine, but it wouldn't be difficult to find her. She may be able to help us get to the bottom of it and make it go away.' I looked up into his honest face and my fat salty tears fell onto the keyboard.

'I'm sorry.'

'Hey, we're mates right?' His eyes melded with mine and a feeling of safety returned.

'Yes, good mates!' I managed a smile. After breakfast I gave him my account of the dream.

> I am standing on the baked earth, looking at my dead husband, waving away the flies from his broken chest. Beside him lies my dead brother. Both of them have been killed with the biting rod, blood still wet and warm on their cold clammy skins. My brother's mouth is open and his body is covered in dust. The dust sticks to their blood. I am crying out to the Great Spirit, but I cannot hear my own voice. The sun is getting ready to hide for the night and the evening air chills my bones. I can feel the child within me moving and my heart aches with sorrow.
>
> 'Get away from there Maisie!' The Boss man with the scar is coming over. I'm on my knees beside the bodies, my howling sparking off cries from the parrots in the trees. Boss man pokes me with his walking stick, and I fall to one side.
>
> 'Stop that caterwauling! Get up and go back to your hut, and let this be a lesson to anyone else thinking about escaping!' I do not understand these words, and I am dragged away by a guard with pale skin, hair and eyes.
>
> 'Come on dirt-bag,' he growls. I try to look back at my husband and my brother. They are lifted on to a cart and I want to know where they are going. I struggle and writhe because I want them

Dream Time

to have a proper funeral; I want them to return to their spirit home.

'Got a right wriggler here,' says pale man, slapping me hard across the face. He throws me inside the women's hut and I land on my right side. The child inside me stirs again, and the other women in the hut surround me protectively. I ask them to offer up a song to Namarrgine, a magician who steals the souls of babies. I ask him to spare my son. They move and sway together, singing and groaning and touching my shoulders in grief and hopelessness.

I rock my painful body on the hard wood floor of the hut. My child must live and I must escape from here and return to my people. The song says we will send Namarrgine to eat the pale white men, and he will allow my son to live. We will hold a ceremony to honour our dead. I will go on to bear a strong son, and when he is old enough he will learn the story of his father and his uncle. A low moaning is heard on the wind but it is coming from the men's hut. The pale men cannot stop us from singing. We sing to the Ancestral Spirits who have protected us from the beginning of time. Within us we carry their strength and resilience. I hold my husband's child inside me but now he is fighting to be born and pain rips through my body.

The guards are walking around the huts with sticks; clack, clack, clack, along the walls, trying to hide our song with their white noise. The women raise their voices, and we hear from the men's hut a sacred verse adding power to our cause. We can hear their voices above the clacking of the sticks and I can feel the women's tears falling onto my body. Like rain the tears flow from my eyes, from the women's eyes, and from the eyes of the children, as we pray for the life of my baby.

Luke put the paper down on the table. 'Jeeze.' he said, 'No wonder it upset you so much. She has a name, *Maisie*. And she's pregnant.' I nodded. 'This is when you woke up?'

'And then I saw my arms were hers, and well, the feelings of pain and despair were overwhelming.'

'Her heart must have been broken.' He glanced at the paper on the table. 'I wonder if she lost the child.'

'I hope not,' I said, 'but now I've written it down it occurs to me the Trophy murder might have been her husband.' He rolled his first smoke of the day and leaned back, looking at the ceiling for a moment.

'Hey, now that makes sense. You know if you can remember it I think you should write down the first dream; in fact all the strange things that have been happening.'

'Good idea, a record we can look at and refer to.'

'That's it.' His eyes narrowed as he sucked in the smoke.

'But I don't want any more dreams Luke.' My eyes began to sting. 'I don't want to be driven crazy!'

'Hey its' okay, I know you're not nuts.' He took hold of my hands. 'But there is something I've just thought about.'

'What is it?' My heart started to pound, as if joining with the rhythm of the rain.

'In the dream Maisie is understandably angry because of the murders. But with you living here and us meeting,' he squeezed my hands. 'What I'm trying to say is, if it was my

Dream Time

forefather who murdered them, maybe you're being punished because of meeting me, and getting close to me.'

'Are you saying we should stop seeing each other?' The dreams were awful, but to be abandoned because of them would be unbearable. 'It may be that she thinks I can understand her. Maisie is being held against her will, perhaps she knows why I also hate being shut in.'

'How could she know, you haven't even explained that to me.'

I fell into his arms and held him. 'I can't tell you yet, but one day I will.' Outside the rain lashed against the house and dribbled noisily from the roof, little bits of spray passing through the fly mesh like the smoke from his cigarette. The radio was on, playing Simon and Garfunkel's *The Sounds of Silence*.

> . . . *Because a vision softly creeping,*
> *Left its seeds while I was sleeping,*
> *And the vision that was planted in my brain,*
> *Still remains, within the sound of silence.*

He laid his head heavily on my shoulder and I stroked back his thick wavy hair. There would be no work today.

The rain fell for two whole weeks, and the skies continued grey and oppressive. Sometimes accompanied by wind and thunder, otherwise the water ran everywhere. It flowed from gutters, oozed from drains and collected in great sheets on the roads. It flooded the fishpond, forcing me to empty bucketfuls while my feet sunk into rust coloured mud. The little house foundations drowned in peace while the storm shelter ran with silted water. Further outback, Trevor the Weather informed us creeks were filling and flowing into rivulets joining previously dry riverbeds. In the centre of Darwin the kerb dwelling Aborigines were absent, while only a few *Driza-Bone* frocked bodies dashed from shop to shop. The temperature remained high and steam rose from the roads in the briefest of moments when the sun strained through the drizzle. At these times the tennis players returned as if they had been standing at the club entrance for such a moment. Insects and birds emerged from unseen hiding places and took the opportunity to feed and preen.

Damp evenings brought the loud chirping of tropical frogs, replacing the familiar song of the cicadas, and announcing the start of their spawning season. The monsoon was finally here, cleansing and nourishing the Earth, washing away built up tensions and diluting my fear with love. Tautened muscles began to relax, and my head and lungs finally cleared. Some days though, it was as if time had ceased to exist. Then I could find myself wandering aimlessly through the house, as the slow wheel of night followed day, as surely as summer follows spring. Like a succulent flower the memory of Luke's first kiss accompanied me everywhere, closely followed by his soft caress and the feel of naked rain on flesh. On paper, the dreams were no longer as terrifying, reduced now to this flat dimension. A new feeling of hope was growing within me, while all around was slowly submerged.

I drove into town and visited the library but more often, the cathedral. Sometimes Luke joined me at the library, where we sat at a long table pouring over books and papers. I looked up anything I could find on Aboriginal history, sacred places and customs. Luke scoured old newspapers in an attempt to discover some facts about Maisie and her family. The first editions he saw of the *Darwin Post* and the *Northern Territory Leader* were published in 1856 and

Dream Time

1870 respectively. Predating these, the Bush Telegraph must have been operating, sending messages around the state by mounted courier. In any case, the papers mainly printed news of white men's achievements, worldwide events and messages from Queen Victoria. Isolated footnotes reported killings and arrests of Aborigines, but no names were given and nothing was mentioned about their role as custodians of sacred sites. One area in particular hit the headlines in 1851, when a white man found gold near Ballarat, Victoria. The resulting gold rush turned the area into a noisy smelly quagmire, driving surviving tribesmen further and deeper into the bush.

Inside the dimly lit cathedral a waft of incense made my nose itch. Silently I prayed for the ghost of Maisie to please go back to wherever it was that ghosts live. It was cool in the church, and somehow time dissolved away as I sat there for what felt like only minutes, but was in fact hours. Softly coloured hues from high windows fell on shafts of light. Like streamers through the air they moved wordlessly while the muffled sound of feet on flagstones assailed my ears. Pitying eyes were on me from the marble statues, the dead knowing only of their own world now while they smirked, perhaps amused by ours.

Luke had suggested it; a priests' blessing for the house. He had seen it done in the movies, when a troublesome ghost needed to be sent packing. I almost plucked up the courage to enquire about it when a priest hastened through the aisles as if late for a wedding. The candles danced and spat as his bustle disturbed them. I was surprised to see he was not wearing robes but the apparel of shorts, shirt, sandals and long socks. Only the dog collar of his faith betrayed his servitude to the Almighty. He looked elderly, and perhaps carried more stomach than was healthy. Although balding,

I could see the faint hint of ginger hair below his freckled scalp.

It was only then I remembered that Belle had been freckled over her face. She had told me once, when we were supposed to be doing gym, that it was her Guardian Angel who had given them to her. She said they stopped her skin from turning red in the sun, and were even under her hair. We all had a Guardian Angel, she said, so that when there was no one else to look after you, they could take over and make sure you were safe. I was not at all sure if any of this was true, at that time or now. If I had one where had they been in hiding at my darkest times? I shifted position on the hard pew. I asked the marble saints to protect me from ghosts, and to forgive Luke's ancestor for his wrong doing. I tried to find the priest to ask for the blessing but he had vanished through a door behind the altar. I was left cold and alone in the middle of the silent nave, surrounded by laughing, flickering candles and the blind, staring saints.

Luke dropped by one rainy evening. After eating we turned up the radio and danced together in the lounge. We slid all over the smooth Jarrah floor attempting to twist and jive. Luke was funny and clumsy all at once, and made me fall about with laughter. He spun me around and out onto the veranda, tipping me backwards over the rail and pretended to wash my hair in the rain. Only when we were exhausted we flopped down and played cards, Luke smoking contentedly and sipping cool beer. The tropical frogs continued to serenade us from beyond the garden, while large snails and slugs came visiting, slithering onto the veranda and congregating on the back doorstep.

Weekends we visited Murray and I helped Auntie Bea get the meals. We showed them how we danced together and they laughed so much Murray had to have extra doses of his inhaler. He told me again how I reminded him of Ruth as tears glistened in his tired eyes. This was a life I had no idea existed, and I prayed it would last forever.

My prayers were also needed elsewhere. I swallowed hard and rechecked the time by the reception clock. I held the letter of a week past in my now sweating hand. It said: *I am pleased to invite you to attend an interview for the position of Housekeeping Maid, on Tuesday 24th November at 2 pm. Please make your arrival known to the lobby receptionist. Yours sincerely, Elizabeth Clarke, Head Housekeeper.*

Trembling, I waited patiently in the palm-fringed lobby of The Drover Hotel. The shock of receiving the letter was still trying to register. In the Darwin Post the advertisement had said: *Evening Maid required for Housekeeping dept, may also be required for some waitress duties in the restaurant. Please apply in writing to The Drover Hotel, Esplanade, Darwin.*

My stomach churned as a reminder of my missed lunch. Silly thoughts of dancing with Luke threatened an uncontained, nervous giggle. Then from years ago a misty memory filled me with warmth, even in the blast of the air conditioning. I was standing alone and unwanted in the playground. Belle appeared and invited me to hold one end of the skipping rope. We were both 5, but I was in awe of her because she could skip with a double rope. Until now I had not made any friends, and was unable to join in any games. But Belle took my hand and showed me how to skip like the other girls.

'Rachel Hardy?' The voice pulled me sharply back to the lobby. 'I'm Mrs Clarke, the Head Housekeeper.' Her crisp words were accompanied by a sort of optical stammer.

'Good afternoon.' I held out my hand and she took it in a strong, painful handshake. 'Come this way please.' I followed her tall frame obediently through a door in reception and along a back corridor. Her head, topped with iron-grey hair, did not look round until we reached a small office. She indicated a chair while I tried not to notice her fluttering eyes.

'I'm really looking for someone who can be flexible,' she said, pausing when I said 'Yes,' although I was not really sure what she meant.

'Good,' she said, 'because we are near to the Christmas season and I will have to share the successful candidate with the Restaurant. Whoever gets offered the post will be required to fill in for evening housekeeping duties, waitressing and possibly kitchen preparation. Would you be prepared to do this?'

'Yes, of course.' I swallowed audibly.

Smiling, her eyes flickered again. 'You will of course be given training and instructions in all aspects of the work required. Furthermore, as we are in the wet season this is a temporary position, so you will probably only be needed for a few months. Is that acceptable to you?'

My palms felt damp. 'Yes, that's fine. Thank you.'

'Now let me see,' she sifted through her papers, 'Ah yes, I have your phone number here. I'll call you with a start date in the next few days.'

Outside the hotel entrance the rain was still teeming but I didn't feel wet. I would be on trial for one week Mrs Clarke told me, ushering me back through the lobby. Christmas was coming, and it seemed more than a few businesses were keen to partake of festive lunches. The restaurant already had bookings from banks and shops in the area, and they expected to be busy. The previous year they had been fully booked for evening dinner from early December. The Drover Hotel had its good reputation to consider, and I would need to be professional and courteous at all times.

I tightened my coat belt and made a run for the car. Distant palm trees waved at me like inside out umbrellas, and the ocean horizon was smudged with clouds. Shop fronts loomed grey and ugly in the damp, dimming light, and water ran from my soggy hat, splashing to the ground and up my legs. With wet feet I stamped through the sidewalk puddles in celebration. On trial or not, and no matter how temporary, I had a job that would take me out of the house, and away from the ghost of Maisie.

Chapter 9

"Botany Bay is on the Kurnell Peninsula, south of Sydney Harbour. It was here that Governor Phillip and the early settlers suffered many hardships, not least of all being malnourishment and starvation. The crops that grew so abundantly in the kind British soil failed and withered here in the seemingly lifeless earth. England had ceased to exist for Phillip and he began to feel abandoned and betrayed. The convicts possessed few skills, were argumentative and aggressive prompting frequent floggings. These were delivered in public to try and foster a better level of general behaviour. Men outnumbered women by four to one, leading to the inevitable fights and disruption. Small farms were made around Parramatta, but because the men had no experience of cultivating crops severe food shortages occurred . . . ."

I checked my watch and was relieved to see my break was not yet over. Although the chairs in the staff room were uncomfortable I needed to continue my research into the history of Australia. I had some books on loan from the library that appeared promising, but like so many seemed to

Dream Time

be mostly about the first settlers. I could find next to nothing about the natives of the continent. The staff room was drab and I was alone. On the walls were pinned Staff Rotas and faded notices about Health and Safety. Union news was also displayed along with items for sale. Among them a tinsel Christmas tree for five dollars, with the message, *Call Angie on 22489 if interested.*

The turndown shift had turned out to be easy work, mainly because the hotel rooms were quiet at this time of year. This was my second evening shift, Mrs Clarke trusting me tonight to pick up the room status from reception and perform my duties unsupervised. The Housekeeping department was on the lower ground floor and in total darkness when I arrived at 7pm. Nervously, I collected a trolley from its subterranean storeroom. I hated being below ground level and escaped as soon as possible. I took the lift to each floor and using my pass key entered the rooms that appeared on the sheet as occupied. The routine went: tidy bathroom, empty bin, place clean towels in bathroom if needed and turndown the bed. The morning breakfast menu and a wrapped chocolate placed on the pillow were the final touch. Mrs Clarke said putting the menu there guests' couldn't fail to see it and so order from it. But if I stayed in the job long enough I would find out what very strange things some people did. Her eyelashes had fluttered for a long time when she told me that. I wriggled in my candy-striped uniform and was sure I had been issued with a size too small. I went back to my book.

"In 1790 England sent the Second Fleet to Botany Bay. This consisted of food, supplies and more women. It became known as the Death Fleet, because so many lives were lost due to overcrowding and poor diet." I skipped on a few pages. "Australia's only inhabitants prior to 1788 were

Stone Age people, thought to be the common Ancestor for all mankind. It is generally accepted by Anthropologists that these people originated from Northern India, having trekked along the Torres Straits before the landmasses divided. Along with the Aborigines, came the Dingo. They adapted to the land together and became wandering in nature, or nomadic. Unaware of how much he had to learn, the white man erupted into this last isolated continent in 1788. With his possessions, it seemed he was at an advantage, but he was soon to find the best way to survive was to adapt and keep moving. Some years later Governor Phillip received orders from England to treat the natives with kindness. But thinking he was helping matters he captured young men and held them virtual prisoner. He taught them how to wash themselves, to comb their hair and how to eat with a knife and fork. Those who did not die of western diseases such as smallpox, whooping cough and tuberculosis escaped back into the bush, never to be seen again."

I finished my shift and parked the trolley in its basement spot. In the gloom I was almost certain I heard my uncles' voice, and even called out, 'Uncle Sid?' Spooked, I bolted from the dark pit and ran to the car park, only pausing to lock up on my way out. I pushed the car key into the ignition. A face pressed up against the window and I jumped almost out of my seat.

'Oh!'

The disembodied head had a chubby hand that knocked on the glass. I lowered the window.

'Are you Rachel?' it asked. 'I'm Mr Blatto, the restaurant manager. I'm so sorry I frightened you, I saw you running and wanted to make sure you're okay.'

'Yes thanks, I'm okay. I just need to get home.' I managed a tight smile.

Dream Time

'Goodnight then, and be careful, Miss Rachel.'

Now that Kim wasn't coming to stay, I doubted I would hear from her again. We were going through another wet patch, and Trevor the Weather announced we were up to amber status on the cyclone alert system. I visited the town in the rain and bought Christmas cards. I would need to send one home; then there was Murray, Luke and Bea and also my relations in Brisbane. It couldn't have felt any less like Christmas. The power of the wet was draining me, sucking me dry. But Luke insisted the last few months had been nothing compared to what we could expect in January. With that in mind I was sure to end up with webbed feet.

More and more, Maisie was inside me. I could hear her soft voice carried on the damp wind, echoing through my ears. When I felt hungry my thoughts turned towards grubs and berries, and roasting insects over a small fire. If I was thirsty I saw myself digging into the ochre earth with a small stick to retrieve a buried frog. Sweet liquid came from the frog when it was squeezed to quench the dry thirst. And she was running, always running away, as far as she could from the scar faced man. Like viruses, these visions wove their way into my system and replicated themselves with little resistance from my defences. I wanted to find the priest with the freckled head, if I could pluck up the courage to tell him about it.

One day, as if God had turned off a huge sprinkler, the rain stopped. Within minutes the skies became light and blue, the clouds dispersing and lifting like a curtain for the grand entrance of the sun. Birds stretched their wings and sang out merrily, while the insect world commenced their usual, though not recently rehearsed overture. Above this welcome concert, I heard Biff shouting from his garden.

'Hey, I've got a parcel for you!' He came up to the fence and joked, 'Looks like it might be an early present from Santa!' I examined the package for a return address.

'It's from my parents. Thanks Biff.'

'Just as easy to bring it home with me,' he said adding, 'your mail box is too small for it and I didn't want to risk leaving it outside on the path.'

'That's good of you Biff; would you like to come over for some tea?'

'Nah, you're all right. Just wanted you to get it safely, and if I don't see you before the holiday, to wish you a good Christmas.'

'Oh thank you, and happy Christmas to you and Ringo.' I watched as he walked away through the overgrown grass, the dog bouncing at his heels.

'Oh, I'll be seeing you next week anyway,' I called after him as I remembered. 'I'm waitressing at your Postie's lunch.'

I put the parcel on the dining table and opened it excitedly. This was unexpected and the sort of thing that only happens when people really care about you. Inside was a letter, a slightly squashed box of *Black Magic* chocolates and a parcel covered in Christmas wrap. A tag on the parcel said *To Rachel, Merry Christmas love from Mother and Father*. There was a homemade card from Jade. On it was a fat robin sitting on a holly tree with juicy red berries and twinkling glitter frost. Inside it said *To Rachie, Happy Christmas and I hope it's not too hot because your chocolates will melt, Love Jade X*. My parent's card was a jolly snowman on skis. I put the cards on the sideboard and looked at them for a long while. Hard tears collected uncomfortably in the corners of my eyes as I thought of Jade. I could see her innocent little face, and the way she would have poked her tongue out with concentration when making my card. How wonderful

Dream Time

it would be just to see her smile, and I suddenly longed for her endless questions and chatter. I went into the kitchen and made a cup of tea and carried it back to the lounge where my parents' letter waited, nagging to be opened.

Murray had fallen ill, and I hadn't seen Luke for some days. The prolonged wet spell had brought on a head cold, while the asthma threatened a bout of bronchitis. He was reduced to quite a weak state, and the Doctor had been called. He thought Murray might have had a small stroke, a mini stroke, he called it. Luke and Bea had taken him to the Infirmary which was the only hospital in Darwin.

I visited the Infirmary while Luke was at work and watched him through the cubicle window. Murray's masked face was fighting for breath. An infusion had been inserted into his left arm through which the nurses administered various drugs. Forced to stay in bed he lay still and fragile; the rasp of his breath cutting through the gentle hiss of the oxygen line. How frightening this must have been for Murray I could not imagine, but Luke and Bea were surely distressed to see him so ill. My own anxiety over his condition rose queasily through my middle and lodged painfully in my heart.

I hurried from the ward fearing I might suddenly be sick on the polished floor. One of the nurses smiled kindly at me and asked if I could come back later. She enquired whether I was a friend or a relative. Her face bore the same expression as the cathedral statues. I gave her the fruit I had brought along and said I was a friend, a very worried friend.

Sickness and nausea had been plaguing me, but I had put this down to the climate. And my memory was playing tricks on me. I couldn't remember important things and had made mistakes at work. Luckily Mrs Clarke thought these were due to my lack of experience, but I realised something was wrong. Outside in the hospital grounds I found a bench to rest on while the nausea slowly subsided. Sitting quietly I found myself becoming confused and desperate.

I concentrated on prayers for Murray's recovery. But the sickness bubbled up into my throat again, daring me to face the worst and mocking me with images of my failed future. I was not only stupid, I was a complete fool. Perhaps my father had been right all along, that I had been born weak-minded and with no hope of ever being strong like him. I couldn't tell Luke my suspicions. Almost certain was the fact I would lose him just at the point of my risking everything.

I tried again to pray. But my thoughts pushed in and dominated my pleas with the same stubborn problem. At university I had seen girls leave their courses prematurely with sad faces while I buried my head further into my books. At home sex had always been a taboo subject, my parents turning off the television set at the merest mention of it, perhaps I now wondered, in order to protect the young and vulnerable Jade. Without doubt would be my parents' abandonment at such news, resulting in a forced separation from my sister. Dry nerves stabbed at my eyes blurring my vision, but annoyingly no tears appeared.

The hospital grounds then appeared to slowly melt away, revealing a bright scene of sun scorched earth. Ahead of me lay a pretty billabong encircled with trees and bushes. A few red kangaroo bent their heads to drink the welcoming water. From the bench I looked through a smoky gaze, gasping in wonder at the silent scene. Like a mirage the billabong gently remained and now welcomed throngs of multicoloured budgies, along with lorikeets and parrots to drink from its well springs. Sunlight reflected on the glistening surface, radiating through the droplets lost by birds in flight. Suddenly Maisie was there, swimming in the water beside a dolphin. It was very large and golden. Tiny myriad fragments reflected back at me as gleaming rainbows, and I was held at once within a golden luminescence. My eyes closed involuntarily with the power of the scene. The mastery of nature and all its beauty engulfed my very being, and I became completely submissive to this living, breathing miracle.

As the vision slowly cleared, peace and calm replaced my former feelings of sickness. After a few minutes I took a small notebook from my bag and diligently recorded the experience. I could recall it to Luke at some later date. Somehow I no longer felt the need to run to the priest or contact the Spiritualists for protection. It seemed as if the beginnings of acceptance were surrendering within me. Maybe, if I no longer fought against Maisie I could become friends with her.

And maybe then she would agree to leave me alone.

It was Luke's birthday, and Flanagan's Bar and Grill shone orange from the bright neon sign, illuminating the dark, muggy street. There were several restaurants along this coastal strip, but Luke liked Flanagan's. Arriving straight from work we were extra hungry. And we were more than ready for a night out, having not seen each other for two weeks. Murray's condition had at last stabilised. He had been moved to a different ward where it was possible for him to take gentle walks in the grounds as long as he was aided. Luke had seen him that lunchtime, and reassured me he was making a steady recovery.

We sat in a quiet corner drinking cocktails while our meals were cooked on a large grill. The restaurant was hot, and I soon finished my drink. Luke ordered a refill.

'Hey it's my birthday,' he said, 'I'm the one who should be knocking them back!'

'Well, with Murray getting better it's a double celebration don't you think?' The red and white tablecloths brightened the candle lit interior. I decided not to tell him about the Maisie mirage at the hospital. Although somewhat relieved about Murray, his brows were knotted and his voice seemed tense.

'How was work today?' I asked, nibbling salad.

'Very busy, we delivered a load of plants to a school in Adelaide River. I'm going back to plant them in tomorrow, but I think it will take a few days to get it all done. Oh, and when I got home, Auntie had baked me a cake.'

'That was nice, she's lovely isn't she? How many candles did you have to blow out?'

'More than I want to admit to. How was it at the hotel?'

'Oh, today was my first shift in the restaurant, so I mostly watched how they work. I did serve some lunches though. Mr Blatto said I did okay, he's the restaurant manager. He calls me Pumpkin for some reason.'

'That's a strange name.' He had eaten quickly, and placed his fork like before, prongs down on the plate.

'Yes, I think it is too. He calls all the girls silly names, I think it's just his way.' I changed the subject. 'Did the nurses say anything else about Murray today?'

'Well, yes. The doctors have said if he continues to improve he can be discharged home for Christmas, but before then they want him to have a practice weekend.'

'That's wonderful news!' I enthused.

He took a mouthful of beer. 'I need to ask you something. We both want you to stay with us over Christmas. What do you say?' It hit me how I hadn't really thought about the holidays. 'Oh yes, thanks for asking me,

Dream Time

I'd love to come!' I said, adding, 'And if I can help out in any way with Murray just let me know.'

'Great, well that's settled then! I was worried you might not want to come for some reason. Dad and Auntie will be delighted.'

The anticipation in my stomach lurched and I crossed my fingers beneath the tablecloth for good luck. Tall waiters in long aprons served elegantly and cleared so we hardly noticed them. I hoped I would be able to do half as good a job at the hotel restaurant. I recalled Mr Blatto's obsequious manner, and how Mrs Clarke had peered at my body as she handed out my waitress skirt and blouse. 'You seem to have gained a little weight, Rachel,' she said, adding, 'be careful not to eat too many sweets now you're working in the restaurant.' And she looked at me again with that squinty-eyed expression.

The evening wore on and more diners arrived at Flanagan's. The background hum of conversations gradually loosened the atmosphere. After several drinks Luke finally relaxed and enjoyed the evening, relaying stories of past birthdays and happy childhood memories. He told me what a good dad Murray had been, how he had always looked out for him, and how he had no idea how he would cope without him. 'He's always been there.' he said, and I wished I had been that close with my own father. In the short time I had known Murray I'd become very fond of him. Secretly I wished I could wipe out the past, and choose a new future.

It was getting late when Luke drove us to a craggy outcrop, as if needing to get as much distance between all that was happening. From this cliff we could see the faint lights of Melville Island twinkling across the expanse of the Beagle Gulf. As the waves crashed splendidly against the rocks below, I gave Luke his present and planted a special birthday kiss on his lips. He was pleased with the years' subscription to *Australian Horticulture* magazine. When he read the card he smiled and said, 'You beauty.' We spread the picnic blanket over the ground and sprawled over it under the diamond studded sky. He whispered words of love and it seemed then the crescent moon could have been made especially for us.

We lay together under the silver stars. Words were no longer necessary, were almost trivial compared to the true meaning locked in our eyes. Our hearts seemed as if corded together with starlight, our bodies cocooned in a force we were unable to break. Luke spoke softly.

'I think I'm falling for you.' Then he drifted into slumber and turned onto his side before I could voice my emotions. I tried to tell his sleeping face, but the words became lost. Perhaps it was weakness that caused it.

I turned onto my back and studied the stars, sprinkled on their dark cloak. I didn't want to lose Murray, but the thought of losing Luke was unbearable. I moved on to an elbow to see his face, relaxed now after all his worries. I smoothed his thick hair from his brow, and kissed his cheek. The last thing he needed was another problem to cope with. Fighting all my fears, I implored Heaven above to help me. But my body was still mocking me, proving beyond doubt how ridiculous I really was. My one dread was something surely even the Angels were helpless to prevent.

Chapter 10

The house stood in eerie silence as I began my morning yoga. The ever present question assaulted my mind, pricking my conscience and demanding an answer. It followed me everywhere now, in the soreness of my breasts and from where my clothes pinched and nagged at the waist. I had to find out, one way or the other, before I spiralled into a pit of despair. I thought about writing to Luke if the news was bad, of how I would be unable to say goodbye and how my heart would break with sadness if I had to go back to England. Until now I had put off reading my mother's letter, worried she might want me to come home after finding out that Kim wasn't joining me after all. But her news was of a different subject, one which I had not yet told Luke.

Belle had died. After an aggressive illness but only about a month ago, she wrote. She heard the news at the butcher's, where she had been surprised to see Belle's mother in the queue. It was the first time she had really spoken to Mrs McTavish, and after all these years she only just recognised her. Belle, it seemed, had talked of me often but much more so recently when she had become so ill, so quickly. Reading about her death plunged my heart into despair. I clutched the letter in my hands, straining to see what my mother had written next. Poor Belle, she had fought so bravely to stay alive and had remembered me even when the cancer had won the battle. She had found her way into my thoughts with comfort at a time when I needed her more than ever. How I wished I had not lost contact, and more than anything I wished she was still alive.

I needed some fresh air to clear my mind, and walked to the Botanical Gardens. It was dry, but the heat had not dropped much. Ridiculous as it was I yearned for rain again, but the clear sky stretched above, promising to be true. A small group of Aborigines spilled out of the gardens as I approached the entrance, stumbling their way home. They ignored me, as though I was completely invisible. Perhaps to them, I was just that.

The first settlers wrote the very same thing about the natives, when they described the continent as *Terra nullis*, or uninhabited. An elderly woman passed me, wincing on worn out limbs. She nearly bumped into me as her thin blanket slipped from her shoulders. She had no need of possessions, carried little and moved on as though displaced. She wandered with her people from suburb to bush all of her life. Similarly the ancient Britain's would travel from place to place, settling in small clans with their own Kings and Wise men. Stories and crafts were also handed down through generations, while the value of the Earth, Sun and Moon were prized above all, without needing science to attest to their wonders.

Like an enchanted forest, inside the gardens all the magic of nature was found. Exotic scents rose from flowering jasmines to delight my senses. Iced sugar blooms hung at

Dream Time

eye level, their insides dusted with saffron. Leafy tracks almost concealed miniature orchids that flowered shyly at ground level. Here, a chanting cicada serenaded a butterfly as it rested on a waxy leaf. Parakeets and native birds sat high up in the canopies, preening and squawking to each other. Inside hollowed trees fruit bats hid in darkness, sleeping before their nocturnal flights. It was cooler here under the palms, and I was able to resolve one thing. I wouldn't see Luke again before I had my answer.

Returning to Monkey Puzzle Street I unlocked the gate. The house standing high on its stilts appeared unfriendly, even sinister. Behind the heavily shuttered windows lay the answer to Maisie's story, I was sure of it. Her visits had become more frequent. Sometimes it was as if I had vacated my body to join her outback. I lost hours at a time and try as I might the time could not be accounted for. But I didn't wish Luke to know about this. She took me to places I had never dreamed of. She showed me craggy coast lines and arid valleys filled with jumping kangaroos. She showed me how she wove and knotted gathering bags, and how to skin animals. All the skills she had learned from her mother. Her journeys were pushing treasured memories away, memories of my sister and our grandmother. Now my mind was stuffed full of new lessons, and my veins ran with fresh blood. My heart no longer beat to the hands of the clock, but to the rhythm sticks that clacked from the distant bush. And every night she sang me to sleep with the word *Yuri*, over and over, her soft voice lingering throughout my slumbers.

Swanbourne Medical Centre stood like a benign haven before me. I found reception and waited while my heart pumped like a locomotive. I rummaged clumsily in my bag for the sample, sweaty fingers nearly dropping the bottle. A helpful woman greeted me from behind the counter.

'Rachel Hardy? Is that Mrs? Miss, I see. Take a seat please; the doctor will call you presently.'

'Thank you.' I said, and quickly made my way to the waiting area. I sat on one of the cool mint chairs. Inside my head the word *Yuri* was repeated. I took a deep breath and felt marginally better although my knees were knocking together.

After some minutes a middle-aged but modern looking doctor appeared. Like the cathedral priest he wore shirt, shorts and sandals. He called my name even though I was the only one there. We went into a consulting room and I sat on a similar green chair.

'I notice you are here on an extended student visa,' he said, 'when does it expire?'

'Next September.' I answered.

'Aha.' he said, and wrote something down on his patient notes. 'Now,' he continued, 'I shall need to examine you, as you are definitely pregnant, probably only a couple of months though. Do you have a note of your last menstruation?' Suddenly my head was spinning and I was about to vomit. I closed my eyes so I couldn't see him or the green chair he was sitting on.

'Rachel?' I heard his voice calling in the distance, 'Are you going to faint? I want you to take deep breaths now, and put your head down between your knees, as far as it will go, that's right. Keep breathing deeply.'

It was all true; I had really done it this time. I stared blankly at the paper in the typewriter, but not because of writers' block. The lounge was in darkness, and all was silent

Dream Time

except for the pounding of my heart. I would have to tell him.

On the table were the leaflets Dr Treadwell had given me. They stared up at me now like a punishment. How to approach Luke about it was terrifying, but the doctor had insisted I must. He had been very kind, allowing me some shreds of respect when I had behaved like an idiot in front of him. Fainting was not so bad, he said, and almost normal for my condition. But when I regained my composure the tears would not stop and he could see I was not able to deal with the shock. I told him of my fears; of going home to face the humiliation of being thrown out onto the street.

'Just talk with the father.' He advised. 'I will see if I can get your visa extended on medical grounds, but I cannot promise anything.'

My hands found my stomach and I thought of Luke. He had enough worry with his father and I felt ashamed, like I had let him down. I wondered if my mother had felt the same way when she was expecting me. I searched the lounge walls pointlessly for an answer but found nothing except Stumpy, on his usual laborious insect hunt. I flicked through the leaflets. They said to eat a healthy diet, and had pictures of meat, fish, fruit and vegetables. They advised as much rest as possible, tiredness being most common in the first few months. Dr Treadwell thought I might be overdoing it at the hotel, and advised me to take some time off. I decided to do so after Christmas, once the busy period was over. The next appointment with the doctor was for two weeks time.

Murray came home soon after for his trial weekend. The doctors said he was doing well; he was walking with a frame, and although slurred, was able to engage in conversation. The nurse said we could bring him back to the ward on

Sunday evening. He called it time off for good behaviour, and said he did not want to go back inside. The nurses were good girls, but the physiotherapists were devils in tunics. And the worst thing of all was the sheer boredom. Murray said it was different when he got bored at home, at least then he could escape to his own garden.

Luke made an effort to encourage him, saying, 'Another week and then you can come home for good.' But it was obvious to me how frail he had become. Now he was shrunken, could not properly grip his left hand, and his left leg dragged behind him as he walked. His clothes hung where once they had fitted, and his hair needed a trim, but thankfully he had not lost his speech. Luke got to work with the scissors, while Bea tried to tempt him with food.

'I've got you some of your favourite crayfish,' she called out from the kitchen, 'I'm doing extra bread and butter to build you up, mate.' Bea bustled round the kitchen in her flowery apron, humming away to herself. 'Rachel's baking a fruit cake,' she continued, 'you know you'll enjoy that.'

On the Saturday Luke went shopping for new clothes, and when he saw them Murray gave a weak laugh at how slim he had become. 'I needed to lose some weight.' he said.

'Bit of a drastic way to go about it, Dad!' Luke smiled at his father and I saw the love in his face for this once indomitable man.

By Sunday Murray was a different person, dressed in his new clothes and relaxed after the sojourn he had so looked forward to. That evening we took him back to the ward but it was difficult to leave him. He struggled onto the hard bed and I saw his eyes moisten. 'We'll be in tomorrow at visiting time.' I reassured him. Murray made movements with his lips, but I couldn't make out any words. He smiled at me as

Dream Time

I leant over to kiss his cheek. Without my usual doubts, I knew his friendship was deep and genuine.

December brought forth the spirit of Barra with aggressive winds and more storms. For once I was excited about Christmas and enjoyed shopping for presents. I had sent some gifts home already, a table runner for my parents embroidered with native flora and a Koala Bear toy for Jade. I hoped they would arrive in time. I hadn't heard anything from my aunt and uncle, let alone Kim, but I posted off their card anyway. Searching the shops I eventually found a mug with red banksia flowers on it for Murray, and some perfume for Bea. I decided to try another day for Luke's present.

I couldn't walk past the cathedral without going in. Against the gathering storm clouds it stood tall and austere. I climbed the wide steps and entered the hushed interior. Moving along the nave I soon passed the empty pews and the ever watching marble stares from the statues. To one side through an open archway was the altar of Our Lady. Here stood the Holy Mother, her gentle features and sky-blue robes painted on and fashioned into the plasterwork that was her body. The tall candle stand to one side of the altar held many thin flames in a bed of golden sand. A box attached to the stand announced: Votive Lights 40 cents each.

I knelt to pray. I had lit three candles, one each for Murray and Belle, and perhaps selfishly, one for myself. I needed extra strength now I was carrying heavy trays at work. Carefully propping up the lighted reeds I choked slightly on their smoke. Musty incense was also wafting on the air, not lending any help to my queasiness. The hard pews were uncomfortable on my knees, so I made my request short, asking that Murray recover as fully as possible, and for Belle to be at peace wherever she was. If she happened to know

Maisie, perhaps she could ask her to leave me alone. Lastly I asked that Luke did not desert me. Because I knew now that I needed him; more than I had ever needed anybody.

A small group of flies tousled with each other in the corner of the window above me. They seemed convinced they could escape but became more and more irritated the more they tried. Eventually they fell exhausted in a heap on the grey stone sill. I felt sad for them, held captive beneath the stained glass. It was probably time I confessed everything to Luke, but the days were running away with me. What the future held for us I couldn't begin to tell. I looked up at the plaster Mary but her face gave me no answers, her eyes only pity.

Driving back to Monkey Puzzle Street automatically I thought of Maisie. I wondered if she would approve of the tinsel garland I purchased on impulse for the lounge. Through the receding clouds a large rainbow appeared and all at once I knew her answer. Maybe she was looking forward to Christmas as well.

Luke swung the truck through the gate and parked up on the drive. I hadn't seen him for a week, and was dreading the evening. Deliberate footsteps crunched their way to the back door. He gave me a casual peck on the cheek as if we were an old married couple. 'Smells good,' he said, 'you splashed out on tiger prawns, I see.' I watched them sizzling under the grill, and avoided his eyes. He didn't seem to notice my clumsiness as I prepared the salad.

'Had a busy day?' I asked, hoping my voice held no tremor. 'How's Murray getting on?'

'He came home yesterday, he's doing really well.'

'Oh, that's great news. Is Auntie with him tonight?'

'Yeah, she's keeping him company. They're going to play cards; she reckons it will get his brain going.'

'Hey, that's a good idea.' The words came out a little too loudly.

He took hold of my hands and made me put down the cutlery. 'And how are you?' He asked.

'Much better for seeing you.' I said quickly. He helped himself to a beer from the fridge.

'It's a wet one today, that's for sure.' I nodded agreement. It wasn't raining yet but my body was soaked. I wiped my face and returned to the grill. The yabbies were done. My news would save until we had eaten.

Luke carried the dishes out to the sink. We spoke at the same time, and I hesitated as he went on, 'I've just remembered, I need to borrow something.'

'What sort of thing?'

'Well, it's a bit of a secret, to do with Christmas.'

'Oh.' I smiled but my legs were like jelly.

'It's supposed to be something personal, like a watch or an earring. Have you got anything like that you could lend me?' He looked anxious, as if worried I would say no. I suggested my tortoiseshell hair comb and told him to look for it on the dressing table. 'But Luke,' I said firmly, 'I really have to speak with you.'

'Okay,' he said as he made his way towards the bedroom, 'be back in a tick.'

I reached for a towel to dry my hands, and suddenly a loud buzzing rang through the house. It took me a couple of seconds to realise it was the doorbell. Outside darkening clouds were giving a false appearance of dusk, and I didn't recognise the shadowy figures as I approached the front door. The evening stillness and gentle cicada song was harshly interrupted as I pulled it open. The towel I was still holding dropped to the floor. Before me stood my cousin Kim, looking taller and blonder than I had remembered, her face contorted into a wild grin.

'Surprise!' she shrilled. Behind her was my uncle, as stout and grim faced as ever. 'We've come to collect you for Christmas Rachel.' He barked.

Chapter 11

Uncle Sid sat awkwardly beside Kim on the threadbare sofa. He appeared red faced, and glared angrily at us both. I had introduced a startled Luke as we entered the lounge, he just appearing with the tortoiseshell comb in his hand. Both my uncle and cousin appeared annoyed as Luke shook their hands roughly and said, 'G'day.', his face falling when Sid explained why he had driven to all the way from Brisbane.

'I can't come with you, Uncle; I'm very sorry.' I stated plainly. 'Luke has already invited me to stay with him and his father for Christmas.'

'I see.' Uncle hissed through clenched teeth, his blood pressure seeming to boil up even further. Kim crossed her legs delicately and sat quietly chewing gum. She played seductively with her long golden hair, twirling it into tight spirals and letting it go again. I could see Luke looking at her out of the corner of my eye.

'I see your leg is better Kim,' I said, 'and I'm rather surprised you didn't try telephoning before coming all this way.'

'Now look here Rachel,' my uncle almost shouted, 'your mother is very worried about you.'

I lifted my chin in defiance. 'Well, she needn't be, because you can see for yourself I'm perfectly okay. Is this why you want me to go back to Brisbane? This isn't really your idea is it, its Mothers'.' Kim stopped chewing and put the end of a lock between her teeth, while Uncle drew in a long breath.

'Alright, I'll come clean with you.' he said, 'I had a call from your parents, and they're less than happy with you being here alone, especially over Christmas.'

'But I won't be *here*, Uncle. I've already told you I'm going to stay with Luke and his father.'

As if I hadn't said it he sailed on, 'Come back with us now, and perhaps we can talk about you returning here after the holiday.' Luke had disappeared into the kitchen to make coffee, and I hoped he could hear my protests. I stood up and crossed my arms.

'I'm sorry, but I'm not coming with you. It was you who sent me up here in the first place, and now suddenly you want to keep an eye on me. The only reason you're here is because of my parents.' My already shaking legs were now quaking beneath me, and the earth felt as if it was about to subside. 'I'm staying right here-and that's that.'

'Well,' exclaimed Kim, suddenly bouncing into life. 'There's gratitude Dad. Stay here for all we care, you scrounging mongrel.'

'Kim!' Uncle's voice snapped, but she stood up and flounced off into the kitchen.

She held the door open so we could hear her say, 'You'd better watch out for her Luke, she's the sort of dag that stabs her family in the back.' Luke walked past her into the lounge, and placed the tray carefully on the table.

'What's going on here?' he demanded.

Uncle Sid stood up laboriously, panting in the humidity. I thought he might burst. 'You tell me mate.' He held out an open hand. 'I'll have the keys to the station-wagon please Rachel.' I retrieved them from the sideboard drawer and handed them over. 'Come on Kimmy,' he said, 'let's find a motel for tonight.' His eyes were grey with fury. 'I don't know why we bothered to ask you over here, I always knew you were trouble. We'll drive home tomorrow; you won't be seeing us again.' They walked off without a goodbye, out onto the veranda, down the front steps, back to the waiting car.

I turned to Luke, and watched him clear away the coffee nobody had touched. They didn't even say Happy Christmas, I observed sadly. I heard the engine start up, and the sound of the station wagon driving away. Luke went out on the veranda looking after them, and suddenly announced he was also leaving. I was sure he must have believed Kim's spiteful remarks.

'Please don't go,' I said, 'if you let me explain it will all make sense, I know it will.' I looked into his face and searched for the kindness I needed now, more than ever.

'I've got to get back to Dad.' he said, 'I'll call you.' He followed the same route they had taken out the front door, and drove off without waving back at me. It wasn't like him at all. In that moment I had lost him forever, all because of Uncle Sid and the meddling Kim. I leaned over the veranda rail, craning to see through salty tears as he drove away. I stood there numbed for a long time, and then the rain broke. Like poisoned barbs it hit my skin, but wasn't able to wound as deeply as their words. The weeping turned gradually into mild hysteria. It was stupid and ridiculous to lose Luke now when he remained ignorant of the real problem threatening our relationship.

That night I couldn't sleep as the wind battered the house in punishment. It rattled the doors and windows and whistled through the deserted loft. I hadn't heard the forecast and hoped Trevor the Weather hadn't announced a Red Alert. The rain fell in thick curtains and crashed from the roof, exploding against the hard ground. I tossed and turned, imagining strange feelings where the baby lay inside me. I had stood up to Uncle, had somehow found the strength to defy him, but now everything felt hopeless. I drifted in and out of fitful slumbers. Now completely alone, I was left with my ghost for company. I began to gather some crumbs of comfort from her.

Finally the night morphed into daylight. Held captive in my fevered bed I applied sheer willpower to prevent the sickness. Eventually I plucked up the courage to move, padded out to the kitchen and made some weak tea to settle the nausea. I switched on the radio as I passed through the lounge, and hastened back to the bed that was my island. At least the storms had moved on. My mind had worked overtime through the dark hours, and by morning my fears had found some perspective. It was time to face facts, time to make plans for the coming baby. I made a vow there and then that whatever happened I wouldn't let this child down.

I was almost grateful to Uncle; strangely without him I would never have met Luke or Murray. If I had stayed in London I might never have fallen in love. Love, I began to appreciate, was scary. I would have to find the courage to contact Luke as soon as I could, tell him my news and talk it through like adults. After all, he was the baby's father and he had a right to know it.

Dream Time

I could see a sunlit glade through the window, and the nausea rose up again. Mulga's little house was calling to me, and the garden was suddenly a haze. The sunlight made mirrors on the damp vegetation, and on this cue an insect orchestra began a melody to a choir of birds. The scene then became as in the dream, a fenced yard of red dirt full of Aborigines. They were singing, softly at first, but then chanting so fiercely I was forced to bury my head under the pillow. I stayed like that until the chanting hypnotized me into slumber.

Somewhere in the distance a telephone was ringing. The hope that it could be Luke forced me into consciousness, but as I sprang into life I hit my toe on the doorframe. I limped to the phone and lifted the receiver. Instantly I heard Mr Blatto's voice say, 'Rachel, is that you Pumpkin?'

'Oh, hello Mr Blatto.' I winced as I rubbed the sore foot.

'Pumpkin,' he drooled, 'can you come in tonight to help with evening service? I need a good waitress.' His voice rose and fell in a way someone else might have considered attractive.

'I'm sorry, I can't. I'm not very well.'

'Not well, not well?' Poor little Pumpkin, I will have to come to see you, I bring your favourite cake from the kitchen, yes?'

'No! Thank you anyway, I have to go now, I think I'm going to be sick.'

'Sick?' he started again, but I quickly hung up. I guessed if he really wanted to he only had to look in Mrs Clarke's filing cabinet for my address. I felt guilty to have cut him off, but was far too queasy to ring him back. I made my way to the bathroom and heaved myself over the toilet. Then, staring up at me from under the rim was a bright green tree frog. It had Mr Blatto's wide mouth and his round, bulging eyes. I yelled out and jumped, falling back against the wall. The tiles were cool against my hot, moist skin. I wanted to cry but I was laughing. The more I thought about Mr Blatto the more I dissolved into hysterics. My tiny visitor had forced the nausea away, and I soon felt well enough for breakfast.

I stayed in that day except to walk around the garden, leaning over Biffs' fence so I could pat Ringo's head and scratch his old, itching ears. He looked up at me and closed his big brown eyes as he slowly relaxed into the massage. I left him sleeping in the shade and wished I could join him. The chanting was still in my head, urging me to sleep, to lie down in the tall grass near Mulga's house. I made an effort to walk in the opposite direction, hoping it might break the spell.

The temperature was 35C, with humidity at 80% I heard the radio say earlier. Dark clouds were beginning to build up in preparation for the next downpour. I took the steps down to the storm shelter, opened the creaky metal door and as if for safety went inside. Nothing had changed except an orange dust covering the contents, probably due to the strong winds. I checked the bed for creepy crawlies and sat on the edge of it, looking out of the open door. I kept thinking about Luke, and how I was now surely under the same curse as him. Belle had died, and Murray had been gravely ill. Coincidence, or was it all part of the punishment, the same punishment that had been growing within me, secretly mocking me, ultimately controlling me.

I'd slept most of the morning but I couldn't shake off the drowsiness. I closed my eyes; aching now from being forced to stay open. Lying on the bed I tried to ignore my throbbing toe. I could just have a little sleep. The clothes drying on the line made a distant swishing sound, while the stale smell of damp earth assaulted my nostrils. And now behind heavy eyelids a cellar door was looming above me.

The damp stench in my nostrils was coal dust, clinging to everything and hanging in the air on thin shafts of light from the pavement window. Sitting on the 21st step, I wait out my sentence of neglect within the vastness of the blackened room. My candle has burned nearly to the end so that I am no longer able to hold it in my hand. I place it spluttering on the step beside me. I can hardly see a thing, but could just make out my peg-doll, Sally. She had wool for hair, a crookedly drawn face, and a pretty blue dress made from a hanky, kept in place with rubber bands. As the light from the candle grew dim I picked her up and put her in my lap.

A thud and the cellar door is flung open. I scrambled up because surely it must be time to get out. I had to shield my eyes from the glare of the hall light, and realised then it must have been evening. At least I hadn't been forgotten entirely. But the silhouette in the doorway didn't belong to my father. The stocky figure began descending the stairs, his feet slipping clumsily on the damp stone.

'I know you're down here, you insolent girl,' he said, the voice slurring the same way my father's did, 'come and say hello to your Uncle Sidney.' Involuntary I hid in the gloom. Halfway down the steps he stopped to light a storm lamp. In an instant the place was illuminated, although the corners of the room remained dim. Uncle spotted me standing there alone, but his eyes followed the noise of rats scurrying to the edges of the room. I didn't dare move, but from the corner of my eye could see the grim array of old paint pots, worn out brushes in jam jars, and my father's glinting axe.

Uncle reached the bottom of the stairs and was very angry. His wolf eyes glared at me with impatience. 'Come here Rachel!' I did as he asked, knowing there was no escape while he blocked the only way out. He grabbed my arms and shook me like a rag doll, and Sally fell to the floor. His words hissed through broken teeth. 'Naughty girl, give Uncle a kiss.' I smelled the drink on his breath, the same smell I'd breathed in so many times from my father's lips. I called out for my mother as a baby bird cries even when it must know it has long been abandoned.

Suddenly a rat startled him as it scurried over the dusty shelves. Taking the chance I wriggled free and kicking out hit him squarely on the nose. I dashed up the stairs like a wild thing. 'You little bitch.' he shouted. Then the horror struck home how he might have locked the door behind him. But the storm lamp outlined his hunched form below and I saw the open hall ahead.

Then I was out of the dungeon, past the dining room and the jeering laughter. I heard the clink of glasses as I crossed the flag-stoned hall, and just reached the handle to pull the door open to freedom. Then I ran as hard as I could, although weak with hunger and fear. I ran to the only person I knew, Belle. Her bedroom was at the back of the block of flats. I couldn't disturb her parents, so I crept through the gardens and up to her window. After an age she heard me, let me in and listened patiently to my shameful story. She fetched a flannel from the bathroom and wiped my tearstained face. Then she tucked me up in bed like a secret mother and promised to wake me early so I could slip home unseen.

I lay there at the edge of despair, unable to sleep and not daring to think I would escape further punishment.

I didn't know Uncle particularly well as he and Aunt May were always busy in their Public House, *The Gloved*

Hand. They visited once or twice through the year when my parents invited them over for an evening meal, but on those occasions I was usually put to bed early. I would hear them all downstairs, laughing and talking in unintelligible conversation that became more raucous as the evening wore on. Sometimes they would visit with Kim on Boxing Day, but only stayed a short while despite my mother's protests that she hardly ever saw her only brother. Kim and I were then supposed to play together while listening to their comments on how much prettier and brighter she was than me.

The next morning Mother woke me as usual for school. She announced that I looked a sight, but didn't mention anything about the previous evening. A few weeks later Uncle Sid left for Australia, and as time went by I must have forgotten the horror of that night. As for my father, he probably had more than his usual quota of booze that particular night. Over dinner the next day it seemed he'd completely forgotten about shutting me away in the cellar.

Chapter 12

The trapped paper stared back at me from the typewriter, reflecting my expression. Pulled uncomfortably between the past and the present, I struggled to bring my thoughts out from the dark tunnel of yesterday. I had remembered things. Things that were perhaps best left covered with the sands of time. But the dense fog clouding my memory for so long was now lifting, only to be replaced by inner turmoil. My fingers hovered over the keys and then dropped into my lap. A heavy sigh ruffled the paper. Why did my heart feel like a washed up shell? I didn't want to be left alone to splinter into fragments. Past days swam together until I was unable to tell them apart.

The blank paper rolled before my eyes like a movie, again and again revealing the reason for my abhorrence towards Uncle. I wondered where my Guardian Angel had been that day. Had it been she who opened the door for my escape, like the ones Belle had spoken of? Perhaps she had returned as my protector when I arrived in Darwin. Something had prevented Mulga from putting the fever on me, the way he had done so to Luke. I rose from the chair,

Dream Time

suddenly needing a drink. The kitchen was musty, and the steam from the kettle only added to the pressing heat. I took the tea mug back to the table. What if the clock incident was part of *her* wrath towards Mulga? One question kept coming back, the craziest one of all. Was Maisie my Guardian Angel, or was she my destroyer?

The nausea was thankfully absent today, but so were any other signs of life. Even the tree frog had escaped from the toilet, while Stumpy was nowhere to be found. I made a deliberate attempt to continue my thesis but found I had stupidly typed the word LUKE. Tongue clicking, I shook my head and reached for the ink eraser. I managed to get rid of the LU before my mind turned to the rubbing out of so many native names. Not just names but whole tribes that had been lost through the years, perhaps even Maisies'. Regional dialects had gone and people scattered away from the cities, into the bush. How much folklore had been rubbed out and forgotten?

Now the weight of Luke's absence felt like bereavement, and I couldn't imagine a remedy for living without him. My head lay heavily on my arms, sharp elbows pressing down on the table. I rocked my wretched form to the flickering beat of the fan, unable to dream, unable to think of anything except him. I thought about his towering frame and his unexpected soft, sweet kisses. I remembered how he had trusted me enough to tell me things he had never told anyone else. He was my friend, and I had lost him. The fan squeaked out its rhythm like a broken bell, and all was darkness and exhaustion.

It was some time later when I noticed the figure standing silently at the end of the table, a tortoise-shell hair-comb in his hand. For a moment I thought he was just another figment of my imagination, and not like Luke at all. Then he stepped forward noiselessly like a ghost, placing the comb down carefully before me.

'I've been to see a friend of mine, a clairvoyant.' he said, the words equally weighted as if the recollection of this event greeted him with unexpected surprise. Unsure of what to say and not entirely sure what a clairvoyant was, my mouth simply opened a fraction further.

'First though,' he continued, 'I want to say I'm sorry.' I couldn't shape the words I so desperately needed to say. The dull, offbeat ping of the fan created a continued distraction, marking out time, urging my response.

'What are you sorry about?' Finally the heavy words hung lifelessly in the charged atmosphere. He moved closer to me.

'I'm sorry I walked out of here like that. I suddenly felt desperate to find a way to keep you here, to stop you leaving for England in a few months time. And since talking to this lady, I'm sorry about all the stuff you've been through in the past.' My head was numbed by his words.

'What do you mean?'

'I mean, well, this lady told me things. She's a psychic.' he said, 'She knew Mum when she was younger, but she moved out to Katherine some years ago. That's where I've been for the past few days, I had to get away from here and think things through.'

'I see.' My words faltered, as I didn't really see at all. 'What about Murray? Who's been looking after him?'

'I asked Auntie if she could take care of things for a few days. She was happy to help out. But let me tell you about this lady in Katherine.' He sat down heavily on one of the dining chairs. 'She's someone who knows things Rach; she can tell what has gone on in the past.' His voice had softened, and when he spoke my name my eyes were forced to look into his.

'I took your hair-comb, and she held it in her hand. I wanted to get you some answers about Maisie, for a Christmas present.' He paused and looked away. 'She told me things, things that happened to you when you were very young.' He appeared upset, moved. He screwed up his face, little pleats appearing around his mouth, his rough fists clenched on the table before me. 'I didn't know . . . ,' he almost whispered. I placed a hand on one of those impenetrable fists, sensing the anger trapped within it. This lady had told him things, things she had seen. She must have seen the baby, and he'd come back to say his last goodbye.

'Please tell me.' I urged.

Slowly he told me about Frances, the psychic lady. He was young when she had been friends with his mother, and consequently she knew him and Murray quite well. The two women came from quite different backgrounds, Frances being been born in Darwin, while Ruth had come from Shropshire. They met one day in the park, while Luke was playing on the swings. Ruth was on a bench reading the paper, when Frances sat down beside her. 'Is that your boy?' She asked. 'You mustn't let him play on the slide.' Ruth looked over and could see Luke climbing up the slide steps.

Worried by this strange warning, she went over to him with Frances following, and they both called for Luke to come down. He took no notice and carried on climbing, but when he reached the top step it gave way under his feet and he tumbled off the slide into the arms of his mother. He was only shaken and not hurt, but cried so much they went off together and bought ice cream to calm him down. The two women became firm friends from then, and Ruth was never in any doubt that Frances possessed the gift of inner sight.

He held my hands in his. 'She told me about your father, the way he locked you up for hours at a time until you were fainting with hunger and how your parents drank and ran you down in front of people. And she told me about your uncle, and how you managed to escape from him.' Truly astonished, I gasped and nearly choked.

'She had no right to say such things!'

'I don't follow you. Did Frances get it wrong?'

'No, not wrong, but what she said about Uncle I've only just remembered myself. I've never forgotten how I was locked in the cellar, but until now I had no recollection of any details. Yesterday I remembered terrible things. But I don't know if there is worse to come. When I'm alone it comes flooding back, like it needs to be released.'

'I hope you don't think I was prying; she only told me those things because I told her how I felt about you.'

Before he could say goodbye I sat up straight and summoned up all my courage. 'Did she tell you about the baby?' I said.

'What baby? You mean Maisie's baby?'

'Our baby Luke, I've been trying to tell you for some time.' Like a cowering dog I looked away and waited for the blow of his words, waited for him to take back the feelings he had begun to pledge all those weeks ago.

He took my face in his hands and I was forced to look at him. Realisation slowly crept across his face and his eyes betrayed what I read to be horror. I wriggled free, expecting him to storm off again. I thought I had prepared myself for the worst. Then I felt his big hands on my shoulders, his rough fingers tilting my still reluctant gaze into those ocean eyes.

He held me gently and I heard him say, 'We're going to have a child.' I wanted to run away from him but he caught me in his arms and was spinning me round and round, laughing and weeping with a joy that replaced all recent angst. I was falling, and he had caught me. At last I could let go of that fear. I kissed his happy face and pressed him closer against me.

'Don't cry,' he said, but my tears were unremitting, like the relief of summer rain.

* * *

It's foolish to hold on to burdens when there are too many of them to carry around all your life. This was my second visit to Doctor Treadwell. I waited in the room with the lime chairs while hope and excitement hummed a soft tune through my mind. When I was called I glided into the consulting room with a smile on my face.

'You look radiant Rachel.' Dr Treadwell said, 'I take it you've had a word with the father.' He looked at his notes. 'Luke was it? Yes, I think I know the family.' He consulted his notes some more and continued, 'You're eligible to apply for an extension to your visa after the birth, and once the confinement is over. In the meantime you can start applying for full resident status if you wish to stay in Australia. Luke and his family may wish to sponsor you. You've got a lot to think over, so take your time over it.'

'Yes, I will doctor.' I said.

'Get plenty of rest and no more heavy work at the hotel.' He added, 'And do have a very happy Christmas.'

I took the opportunity to walk to the town next day. The outside of The Drover Hotel appeared unchanged, but as I entered the staff entrance everything felt different. The once jolly kitchens were now stressed, the happy-go-lucky staff tired and irritable. I made my way down to the

Housekeeping Department, and Mrs Clarke's office. I had prepared a typed letter of resignation and watched her scrunch up her face as she read my reason for leaving.

'I see.' she said, in her usual crisp tone. 'So your uniform was the right size after all, it was you who was gaining weight.' I had to agree it was. 'Well,' she continued in a softer tone, 'I'm very sorry to see you go, *very*. If you ever need any work in the future or a reference, I would be only too pleased to oblige.' Her kindness surprised me so much I couldn't resist the urge to hug her. 'Please keep in touch, won't you Rachel?' she said, 'And will you bring the baby in for everyone to see?'

'Of course, I promise.' I wiped my eyes, and made for the restaurant to see Mr Blatto. I found him polishing wine glasses that were obviously not up to his standard.

'I never have to do this when you're here.' he said reproachfully.

'I'll be back soon,' I said, 'but I'm sorry to say I'll be leaving after Christmas.' I told him about the baby.

'Pumpkin!' he almost screamed, 'Now you really will be pumpkin shaped, no?' He laughed so much he had to sit down on a banqueting chair and wipe the moisture from his face with a serviette. 'I will tell the others,' he said when he had recovered, 'they will be very sorry to lose you, but very excited about your news, like me.

It had been fun to work with such a good bunch and at such an exciting time of year. I had enjoyed every minute, but especially the buzz of the restaurant compared to the lonely turndown shift. Time flashed by as each session burst with mini drama's in the kitchen, and mega drama's from Mr Blatto. He huffed and puffed, issuing orders to all and sundry, only calming down when the coffee was finally served. I had been lucky to work with such a good crowd and

I would miss them, but the future was beckoning. Perhaps it was my Guardian Angel who whispered that real joy was possible, even for me.

The radio was playing *Windmills of your Mind*. Earlier thoughts of doom abandoned, I typed furiously at my thesis, fingers flying over the keys like so many tiny hammers. The music was rudely interrupted by the whine of the phone. It was very early for a call, but I turned the radio down and lifted the receiver. My heart sank when I heard my mother's voice, as I realised this was an opportunity to tell her about my pregnancy. She was drunk and her mood was not good.

'I've waited up half the night to talk to you,' her words slurred together. 'How dare you upset Uncle Sidney?'

It had rained recently, not much, but enough to coat everything in the garden outside with a shimmering of silver. It might have been sprayed there by visiting fairies eager to illuminate the slender cord of each cobweb, every fat dripping mango, and all the slender blades of brittle grass. I tried hard to listen to her as she ranted about my inexcusable behaviour. But most of her voice was drowned out by the warm rays of the rising sun, sifting over the garden and through the house to rest finally and securely on the hardwood floor.

'And what about this boy, Luke is it? What do you think you're doing living-in-sin? For God's sake girl, just what were you thinking?'

It seemed pointless to argue. 'I'm pregnant.' I told her.

'What did you say?' The voice stoked up to fever pitch, and off she went again, incandescent with rage. I tried to listen to what she was saying, and would have heard most of it if only the lorikeets had not started their morning song, heralding in the new day.

There was something about going to the doctor to 'get rid of it'. And somewhere in her continuous screech the assurance I would not see Jade again. But this only just reached me, as the cicadas began their timely intermezzo while two courting gulls chased each other noisily up the street.

'I must go now.' I stated as calmly as I could. I placed the receiver back on its resting arm and cut off the tirade of abuse.

I longed to explain things to Jade. I felt sure she would understand the way children are often able to. I didn't wish to carry the wound her loss would inflict. I felt sure my parents wouldn't harm her, but I still yearned to protect her. I turned the radio up hoping Noel Harrison's song could extinguish the sting of my mother's threats. The song had almost finished.

> *Like a carousel that's turning, running rings around the moon,*
> *Like a clock whose hands are sweeping, past the minutes on its face,*
> *And the world is like an apple, whirling silently in space,*
> *Like the circles that you find, in the windmills of your mind.*

Chapter 13

I sat back on the sofa cushions and listened. 'When I was a young man I dreamed of being a policeman like my father. As far back as the first settlers my forefathers belonged to the military.' Murray was telling me about his past. 'I served my country in the Second World War, but when I came home I realized I wanted to break the mould. My war left a raw hole that needed to be filled.'

He had lost mates the same as Luke, but more deeply, he lost respect for those in authority, including his own father. He took to going out night after night, brusquely pushing past his father in the kitchen as he polished his duty shoes. His mother would glance at her husband and ask him to 'Have a word.' The reply was always, 'Give him time, he's been through a lot.'

'I used to come back home three sheets to the wind wanting to stamp dust all over my father's gleaming shoes. They seemed to deserve more attention than I did.' He stopped and coughed for a while. 'When I went to Agricultural College to study landscaping, a wedge grew between me and my father. Sadly this was never bridged.'

On the cabinet, his father's face stared out powerfully from its frame. Murray picked up the picture with his good hand, and told me, 'It's the only picture I've got of him.' He fell silent as if thinking of his childhood, of his hopes and dreams, and of his regrets in life.

'And your mother?' I said. 'Have you got a picture of her?' He moved with a shaky gait towards a cabinet in the corner of the room and rummaged around inside. He held up a picture of a vibrant young woman, long hair spilling down one shoulder and eyes that made me want to smile.

'Frame's a bit dusty, she's only seventeen there, just a child really.' he said, and wiped the picture on his trouser leg. I took it gently from him, and stood it beside the proud policeman. Murray nodded approval, and squeezed my arm. The evening was clear and fresh, but so near to the fall of darkness I felt suspended in a strange time all of our own. Luke dozed peacefully nearby in a large armchair, while the fairy lights from the tree beside him dappled his body with a rainbow of colours. This had been without any doubt my best Christmas ever.

We had risen to a hot, dry day and had opened our presents in the shade of the porch while sipping home-made ginger beer from Bea. A true friend, she always came over for a festive lunch of cold meats, salad and fresh rolls. In the afternoon we played cards, and later Luke and I tried to play charades, but mostly fell about laughing. Luke loved his present, and I was pleased I had used my earnings to buy him a boat trip for two into Kakadu Gorge.

Murray gave a toast over dinner to 'The Little Guy,' while pointing his glass at my belly, and Bea insisted she would have to start knitting some cotton vests. Luke gave me a little squeeze whenever he passed me, and kept asking if I should be sitting down. At one point I was overtaken with dizziness because of excitement rather than my condition.

'You've made an old man very happy,' Murray said with tears in his eyes as he toasted us both after lunch. He added unsteadily, 'you two would have made Ruth very proud.'

I took my family cards and gifts, a cream shawl with brown and orange flowers from my parents and Jade's chocolates-and shyly placed them with the others in the lounge. There had been no further calls from my parents and they probably didn't realize I was staying at Luke's over the holiday. Even so, I felt as if they had washed their hands of me forever. Murray said I was not to worry about it, the same thing had happened between him and his father, and as far as he and Luke were concerned I was now part of their family. As soon as my rental agreement ran out at Monkey Puzzle Street they insisted I was to join them at Acacia Avenue with no arguments, because it was all settled.

That evening I joined a sleepy Luke in the big armchair and snuggled into his arms. If I looked at the Christmas tree and screwed my eyes up like Mrs Clarkes' the fairy lights took on a magical glow, and I made a wish in case dreams really did come true. But it was impossible not to think about home, especially Jade. After our meal we had shared round her box of *Black Magic* and Bea caught me fumbling for a hanky. She placed a beefy arm around my shoulders and gave me a mumsy squeeze. It was kind and sensitive of her but even so I flinched in her embrace. Why was it that I longed for the attention of my imperfect parents when I knew I would never receive it?

If only Mother had a heart like Bea. She must surely have had some feelings for me even if she never showed them. Bea ignored my flinch and kissed my head. 'Don't be sad at Christmas time darl,' she said, 'save that for some other dull day.'

Bea turned on the TV, and we watched the Christmas episode of Coronation Street. It was odd to see snow and Christmas trees, and England felt further away than ever. Luke had taken to chewing his nails now he had given up smoking on account of the baby. I guided his huge hands to my stomach and could feel him loving the child inside me, as much as he was nurturing our own love.

When the episode finished Bea turned the channel to a programme called *An Australian Christmas Special*. The opening act was a carol called *Three Drovers*, performed by three singers dressed as swagmen.

> *The black swans flew across the sky,*
> *The starry lustre blazed on high,*
> *And still they sang Noel! Noel!*
> *Those drovers three, Noel! Noel! Noel! Noel! Noel!*

The end of the carol was punctuated with explosions from outside. We went into the garden and looked up at the sky. Natures' own firework storm lit up the heavens with streaks of blue and white ribbons. The lightning ripped through the sky like scissors through black silk. On and on it went, flashing like a neon snake, out and over where the ocean lay sleeping. Luke said it was the true beginning of the wet.

Maisie was telling me things as I became lost in the wonder of it all. Away from the town, out-back away near the Daly River something was stirring. Gudjewg, the Spirit of the wet, was ready. Deep in Kakadu Gorge, Golomomo the crocodile was preparing for the mating season, churning in and out of the water, rolling and creating great waves. His

Dream Time

dance was as old as time itself. But the Crocodile people of Kakadu were gone forever, a long time extinct.

The white man had profaned their sacred places, powerful artefacts had been taken to sell, and strangers now entered the caves of their ancestors with eyes and souls that could never understand. These places were the link for the Crocodile People to the Dreaming, but this link had long been lost. The bones of the dead, the wall paintings and sacred objects had been taken to warehouses for profit. These relics had acted as title deeds to the lands of the Crocodile People. Now the peoples' source of life was lost forever, meaning they could never return to Kakadu, not even in Spirit form.

She was showing me how it felt to be forgotten.

The lightning slowed to an occasional pulse of silver as it travelled northwards. This spectacular end to our Christmas deserved our keen applause. From inside the house the words of the song *Santa never made it to Darwin* floated out into the night air.

But now Barra the Wet Season Man was here and he had some pretty impressive plans of his own.

* * *

Darwin town was closed up. Shops, offices and municipal buildings were all on holiday. This was a time for families and friends to catch up with each other, to rest and recuperate. Bea was away visiting her cousin in Bendigo. Luke wanted to go fishing for mud-crabs with his mates and asked if I could stay with Murray for a few days while he was gone.

The house became a warm, nurturing chamber with Murray fussing over me as much as I fussed over him. He continued to tell me stories about his past, of Ruth, and of Luke's childhood. He told me about the years he spent in the army during the war, and of the Torres Straight islanders who had loyally enlisted but had not been recognized as citizens, even following their bravery. He had a particular mate he had fought alongside in the battle to protect the north end from the Japanese. His name was Warrun, but he was called Warren. He used to take Murray fishing back then and that was the main reason he had taken Luke fishing as a youngster. The time since Christmas had gone by so quickly I hadn't realised it was nearly New Year. We were expecting Luke home well before then, but even so I missed him like he was never coming back.

One afternoon a letter arrived from Miss Green. I opened it and read it to Murray. It said:

> Dear Murray,
>   Hope you're all well up at the top end. I'm writing this from hospital, because in the middle of December a car hit me as I was crossing the road. I was unconscious for some time but now I'm starting to feel like my old self. I've got a broken pelvis and a fractured leg, so I'll be here for some time yet, but should be recovered enough to come back up north in March.
> Hoping you had a good Christmas.
> Your friend,
> Daphne.

Murray took the letter and held it to his chest. 'Terrible news,' he said, 'poor Daphne, knocked down by some fool of a motorist. Probably drunk.' he added. This news was shocking, and it joined my list of casualties, but Miss Green couldn't possibly be a target for the so-called curse. She, of all people, surely had to be exempt.

That night before I fell asleep I remembered Luke's present, the information about Maisie from Frances. She had written the word *benevolent* and insisted Maisie was looking after me. There was also a connection between her and the dolphin shield, but Frances was unable to see what it was exactly. One thing she was certain of was that I was being prepared for something, but just what that was remained hidden for the time being. My dreams contained hundreds of dolphins flying through the sky, swimming past clouds and scudding over treetops.

I woke in a sweat to find the bedclothes tangled around my legs. I was trapped and Maisie was before me. Strangely still, it looked like she was crying. I couldn't help staring as she floated there in the shadows, and I tried to tell myself she was a trick of the mind that would soon disappear.

'Dead baby,' she said, and her face frowned as the smoky form began to disperse. I struggled free, jumped from the bed and turned on the light. I was alone. Surely this must have been another dream? But those words, what did she mean by them? My hands found my swollen belly and I remembered her last dream. I needed to know if she meant to harm me or my child. I walked past Murray's room to the bathroom. It was a dream, it had to be, but all the same it felt more like a threat than before.

I turned on the cold tap and felt the soft water run through my fingers. Suddenly I shuddered as I remembered Luke. He was away somewhere on the Daly River with Vince and Dave. Could Maisie be warning me about him? Had something awful happened, the way it had happened to Miss Green? I scooped up the cool water and splashed it over my burning face. I was starting to panic, and couldn't catch my breath. I slumped onto the toilet seat, and put my head down between my knees the way Doctor Treadwell had shown me.

But now Murray was calling from his room, 'Ruthie, Ruthie help!' Shocked into action, I ran to his bedside, to find him almost on the floor. I struggled with his dead weight, and managed to haul him back onto the mattress. He lay back heavily on the bed. 'Help,' he said again, his eyes wide with fear. I took a minute to get my breath.

'What happened?' but he could hardly speak for terror. 'W-warrior,' he finally spluttered, 'Aborigine warrior. He's come to get me Ruth.'

I tried to soothe him. 'There now, there's no one here except us. Go back to sleep Murray.' I tidied the sheets and made him as comfortable as I could. Then I drew up a chair and stayed beside him until the morning. We both moved in and out of fitful slumbers, with Murray occasionally muttering, 'No, don't let him take me.'

The following day still Luke did not return. Murray continued to sleep as if drugged, and refused the food I offered him. I struggled to get him to drink, and later that evening called Dr Treadwell. By the time he arrived it was gone 10pm. 'Lead the way Rachel.' he said. I showed him into Murray's bedroom and waited while he did his examination. Several 'Aha's' later, he looked up and took the stethoscope out of his ears. He ushered me out of the room and closed the door behind us.

'I think he's had another smaller stroke.' He lowered his voice before continuing, 'this was to be expected you know.' I must have looked a sight from lack of sleep and worry. 'Now; what about you, young lady? Are you on your own here?' We went into the kitchen while Murray slept, and he made me sit down while he made some tea. I told him about the situation, and of how worried I was over Luke's safety.

'He should be back from the fishing trip by now.' Beyond tears, my tiredness had grown into stupor. It threatened to engulf me if I didn't get some proper sleep.

'I'll tell you what we're going to do.' The doctor said crisply, replacing his teacup in its saucer with a clink. 'I'm going to get Murray into hospital, now don't look like that Rachel. You've done a bonsa job keeping him hydrated and comfortable, but now he needs to be where he can be monitored. As for Luke, I'm going to call the Police so they can keep a look out for him.'

'Oh, thank you!'

'These delays happen all the time, and remember Luke knows this area well and all the risks involved. I'm sure he's okay, I'll bet he's on his way home right now.' I could see him acknowledging my doubtful expression. 'What I want you to do right now is get some proper sleep.'

I could hear him calling the hospital as I fell on to the bed. I thought *I'll never sleep now, it's been too long*, and sure enough suddenly felt wide awake. But later the doctor woke me as he sat on the edge of the bed. He reassured me he had put the word out about Luke's delayed return home. He said he would accompany Murray to hospital, and would be sure to look in on me the next day.

When I finally awoke it was early morning and strong winds were assaulting the house. I got up and went in search of food, my stomach finally relaxed after the worrying vigil with Murray. I found we were right out of milk and suddenly felt extremely annoyed. What surprised me was how angry I felt with Luke. More than that, I was furious with him. Why had he left us alone to go and do a bit of silly fishing? That was reason enough to be annoyed, but to not come home when he must have known how hard things were with Murray! I slammed down the mug I was holding and broke off the handle. There was my temper again, I was ashamed to admit. It was I who was being unreasonable. Luke could have been injured in the outback for all I knew. Even, heaven forbid, lying in some creek as a crocodile's supper. I put the broken handle in the mug and hid it carefully at the back of a cupboard.

I usually looked forward to the New Year. It held the promise that life could change, that good things come to those who wait. It was a time of resolutions, and of making the most of whatever one had. I resolved to do whatever it took to make it work with Luke, but now I had to make the baby my main priority. This feeling had started since my sleepless night with Murray.

As a child New Year sometimes included a visit from Uncle Sid and Aunt May. The four adults would sit squashed up on the sofa drinking and giggling all night. I was able to creep down the stairs unseen, and watch them through the banisters. I understood now that Aunt May had flirted with my father, every now and then touching his knee or smoothing back a lock of his Brillcreamed hair. My mother had appeared oblivious to May's attentions which was probably a blessing. She would stumble off to the kitchen and usually spilled her drink. My father refilled her wine glass while she passed round nibbles made from Fanny Craddock recipes.

My mouth watered as I sat on the hard stairs, while I hoped none of them heard my rumbling stomach. After Jade was born they used to leave me to sit with her while they went out together on the town. When we were alone I would put on the record player, carefully play my mother's Beatles records and dance with Jade round the room. She enjoyed this more as she got older, and squealed with joy when we tried to do the twist. When Sid and May emigrated my parents reverted to staying in at New Year, thus ending my little bit of fun. At a younger age Grandma joined us for Christmas lunch but she usually fell asleep in the afternoon and was driven home by teatime. These few people were the extent of my family. It never occurred to me I might have more relatives elsewhere.

By the time Doctor Treadwell called again the weather had turned to gale force winds and lashing rain. He made a mad dash from his car to the porch, and waited patiently while the water cascaded off his clothes and onto the deck. Inside I took his drenched coat and hat, and hung them up to drip.

'I've just heard,' he said, 'the police have found Luke. He's staying at a mate's house near the Adelaide River. The truck crashed in the storm, but no one was hurt, and he's making his way back to Darwin as soon as he can arrange some transport.'

'Thank God he's okay, I've been worried sick.'

'He tried to call, but the storm had blown down the phone lines.' I took in the news like food to a starving man. 'And Murray has stabilized, so don't fret about him, he's sitting up and eating well.'

It seemed the panic was over for now. The doctor did an examination and reassured me the baby was doing well. 'Expect Luke any day.' he said as he redressed in his still sopping coat, to brave the weather once again.

The evening brought with it rolling thunder, hail, and more gales. Around midnight Bea burst in through the door to find me alone at the kitchen table. She greeted me with a bosomy hug.

'Happy New Year darl!' Her smile widened as I squeezed her back.

'Happy New Year Auntie; boy, am I glad to see you.'

She looked round the place and declared, 'Well, where the devil is everyone?'

Chapter 14

Luke came home later on New Years' day. Shocked to find his father in hospital, he soon became distant, brooding. We visited him every day in hospital until the strangeness of it all became our reality. Bea helped out cooking meals and doing chores at the weekend. It seemed like Murray had been right to fear the warrior. He'd chased him down and had got to him in the end.

I had to get away for a while and walked the rough track to Fannie Bay. I found the long expanse of golden sand with rocks just large enough to provide a seat. The waves slapped against half submerged boulders in their languid fashion, but this did little to relieve my pain, or my guilt. Dark thoughts ebbed through my mind and reflected back at me from the dense ocean below. Still distressed, I forced myself to breathe deeply filling my lungs with the raw salt air.

It was difficult to take it in, that Murray was dead.
Even when said out loud the words echoed back at me calling me a liar. The enormity of it had sent the fun of Christmas to a distant hazed memory. He had been gone a

week already, and Luke was inconsolable. At the Infirmary the doctors said it was another, but much larger stroke. It came out of nowhere and just as he seemed well enough to come back home. They said it was a very serious condition, one that he might not recover from. Luke had nodded as if he understood, but between us unspoken words said *he will be okay; he will get better, like he did before.*

We stayed with him night and day, taking turns to snatch some sleep in the day room. Now and then he opened his eyes, looked up and smiled weakly. But near to the end he lapsed into a deeper gasping sleep, and the nurses drew the curtains round to give some privacy. They warned us it wouldn't be long and brought us sweet, sickly tea. We held his hands and I prayed he would get better, but that night he slipped away from us like a falling feather. The nurses washed him, clothed him and placed a flower on his chest. Like a chrysalis he lay emptied; his true essence now taking its final journey. Silently I kissed his cool brow and said goodbye to my friend.

A nurse said most people die in the early hours, somehow trying to reassure us, but no words could fill the void where this man had been. We hobbled home crippled with grief, plagued by guilt. Surely we could have done more to save him? For a short while we were closer than ever, clinging desperately to the life force in each other. But empty confusion and night walking afflicted us both. We met on those nightly travels to the bathroom or the kitchen, and clung tightly together. His hands on my swollen belly, Luke turned his reddened eyes towards mine. I didn't know if he wished he could forfeit this new life for the return of his father. Such thoughts accompanied my maddened dreams.

By day his pain hardened and flared out at me from his once soft eyes. Hunched and wearisome he loaded up the

Dream Time

truck and prepared his return to work. This was a way to serve Murray but I could see it also tortured him. Returning home he forgot he was gone, that his father would no longer smile and wave from the porch. It sometimes felt as if his death was just a dream, but for Luke it was a living nightmare.

He stood under the shower for a long time, his eyes closed. It was as if he needed the water to soothe away his heartache. The weight on his shoulders never budged because understandably he carried his loss everywhere. I couldn't reassure him, but I stayed on and went quietly about keeping house. Instead of my studies I poured over recipe books that must have been Ruth's. Now Bea helped me tempt him with food the way she had done so recently for Murray. Thank goodness she was there, solid as a rock and the only one who could make him smile.

A respite from the recent rain allowed another escape to the shoreline. But on this rugged edge I was left feeling small and vulnerable. The gulls began scavenging noisily at the waters' edge in a search of morsels. With surprisingly little effort they hovered for minutes over the waves, looking eagerly down into the bobbing water. Further out it was time for the deadly jellyfish to procreate along with numerous other unseen creatures. The eternal cycle of life lent to me a tiny fragment of hope. I imagined the baby like a butterfly, its soft flutter reminding me of love.

The wind washed over my senses and slowly the torment inside my head dispersed. The ocean beckoned me to her foamy edge where she kissed the warm shoreline. I dipped my toes in the water, and waded out to my knees. Here her swelling body rose and fell like music. I pulled my hands through the healing liquid. She was the life force of the planet, the wellspring that nourished us all. She belonged to everything that lived and was the font of all creation. Perhaps it was her song that guided us home; perhaps she alone was able to rescue our souls eternally.

* * *

Luke wanted to visit Frances before the funeral. Katherine was the best part of a days' drive away. I wasn't keen to go and worried she might tell me things I didn't wish to hear. But a weekend away did sound like the tonic we needed. On the way we dropped in at Monkey Puzzle Street to feed the fish. After being away for so long the old house was unfamiliar but I could see my typewriter in the lounge through the kitchen window. I knew I would have to return to complete my work.

Luke saw my expression as I closed the gate. 'Don't tell me you miss living here?' he said.

'Of course not,' I said, 'there's just something about the place.'

'It's haunted Rach.' he said as he turned the key in the lock.

'I still want to know why, and I'm worried about Miss Green.'

We walked to the truck. 'I'm sorry; I'm not myself,' he said, 'loosing Dad-it's brought back memories of when Mum died. Greenies' accident is probably just one of those things. But yes, I do want to know more. Let's hope Frances can shed some light on it.'

Soon we were out of Darwin and onto the red dirt of the Stuart Highway. It was only 7am, and the road was deserted. Luke sped up as if to outpace the rising sun.

Dream Time

Murray was safe in the hands of *Ferryman's Funeral Care*, and lay wax-like in their Chapel of Rest. He was unaware of the strange vacuum we occupied, the timeless space between his death and our future. The fetid stench of dead kangaroo came up on the wind and assaulted my nostrils. I would have preferred Luke's cigarette smoke.

'Road kill.' he commented, squeezing my knee reassuringly with his free hand. At least he was beginning to relax. He was wearing Ruth's wedding ring on his smallest finger and it dug into me as a reminder of his loss.

Every now and then after Murray's death it had seemed I was able to feel more alive than ever. Perhaps it was the life growing within me and the gradual realisation of its presence. But the words 'dead baby' kept coming back to me, no matter how hard I fought to push them away. Luke was rubbing his eye, the one he had hit when the truck crashed.

Unbelievably this had occurred at about the same time I had seen Maisie that night. The three men had been on their way to the pub after fishing all day. It was dark, the wind was up and they realised they were driving straight into a storm. From nowhere a huge owl flew into the windscreen. Dave slammed the brakes on, but was unable to stop the truck sliding into a tree. Luke hit his head so hard against the doorsill the skin split above his eye. Head wounds bleed copiously, and his was no exception. Vince bandaged him up but they couldn't get the truck started and ended up walking the rest of the way.

He stopped rubbing his eye and chewed for a while on a fingernail. The road stretched ahead into the distance with no beginning and no end. Only the occasional road sign marked our progress.

'Like being in a time warp isn't it.' he said, as if reading my thoughts.

I was suddenly relieved we were going to see Frances, and smiled back at him. Too much had been happening, and I was tired of feeling confused. I needed to know if the baby was in any danger, and just prayed Frances could come up with some answers.

We made it to her house by early evening, and found our host waiting on the front porch. I was surprised to see she used a wheelchair, and wondered how she managed. Luke had never mentioned this, leading me to suppose that she too had suffered an accident.

'Hello friends,' she called out, 'come in and dump your bags.' The hall was cool and smelled of fresh flowers. 'You must be Rachel, but I feel as if I know you already,' she said as I settled on a porch chair. 'I'm so sorry to hear about Murray. I told you on the phone, Luke, how I've got such fond memories of both your parents.' She wriggled in the chair. 'It's God's will that they be together now.'

'The funeral's next week,' Luke said, 'I still can't believe he's gone.'

'It's a hard time for both of you, even with your happy news.'

'Murray was really excited about the baby.' I said.

We ate sandwiches and drank fizzy lemonade while the two of them reminisced over the past. During the conversation I learned Frances had fallen off her roof and broken her back some years ago.

'Strange how you saw my fall coming, but not your own.' Luke teased her. Frances gave a twinkling laugh.

'Some things in life,' she said, 'we're not able, or supposed to avoid.'

'Aren't you angry about it?' I said, certain I would be if my legs no longer worked.

Dream Time

'Don't get me wrong, I had my times. But after the fall I realised what I was really here for. I quit work and set up my school.'

'What do you teach?' I asked.

'Art, mostly, but also colour therapy, and henna hand painting.'

'Did you know there was an Aboriginal artist at the house I rent?'

She rested her hands in her lap. 'I think there is a very strong presence at the house, but it's not clear who it is. It could be the warrior or the artist-'

'What about Maisie?' Luke said, 'where does she fit in?'

'She seems to be more attached to Rachel.' Frances pushed back a wisp of her auburn hair. I noticed it was quite grey underneath.

'And the baby, does she mean to harm it or me?' I responded.

'I don't think she's capable of harming anybody.' she said.

'But you can't be sure.'

'Come on,' she said, 'let's go inside and talk about this over something stronger.' In the open plan room I noticed many paintings hung from the walls. Frances wheeled up to a particular collection.

'These are my favourites,' she said, 'don't you think my students are a clever bunch?'

Luke brought some beers from the fridge. Frances drew close and placed a hand on mine. I noticed again how she wore several rings on her fingers.

'Rachel, you look worried and believe me I understand why. Let me try and explain as best I can.'

Luke took a gulp of beer. 'Before you start,' he said, 'let's make sure you know all the facts.' He told her about the crash caused by the owl, of Murray simultaneously seeing the warrior again, of my own visions of Maisie, and of her threatening words. She listened to everything with her head bowed as if meditating.

Finally she spoke. 'You may know the white owl is the familiar of ghosts in some Aborigine cultures. They call him *Mook Mook*.'

We exchanged glances as she continued, 'The way I'm seeing it, because Murray was so frightened by his first stroke the warrior came to help him when he was about to have the second one.'

'But he was terrified of it.' My voice squeaked with concern.

'I want to assure you Murray did not die from seeing the apparition. Sadly, it was his time to go, and the warrior came to guide him through it.' He's not letting me see much but I still get the feeling he's connected with Maisie.' She stopped and slowly interlaced her fingers.

'Are you saying these events are linked together?'

'They must have been Luke. As for Maisie, there is a further connection between her and the baby.' Alarmed, fear crawled at my stomach.

'No! I thought you said she can't harm us?' My voice shook. Luke sat next to me and held my hand. In the distance I could hear the laughing, mocking squawk of parrots. Frances undid the brakes on her chair, and her rings clinked together as she moved.

'One thing I can say is your baby will be a very special boy.'

My mouth dropped open. 'You know it's a boy?'

'I think I can be bold enough to say I'm sure of it.' Her lips quivered as she continued, 'I got the word *chosen*, as if the child will have a special purpose.'

Dream Time

I leaned back against Luke. 'What do you make of that?' I said.

He squeezed my hand and answered, 'Isn't it amazing, we're having a son!'

'I'm sorry I told you so roughly,' she said, 'but I feel it's important you know.' Frances drained her glass and suddenly appeared fractious. 'Now you two, it's getting late and you must be tired.' It was only 9pm. 'Try not to worry about the things we've talked about. They're merely possibilities and only what I'm picking up at the moment, you understand. Why don't we sleep on it and we can talk some more in the morning?'

A muggy dawn brought grey skies and the promise of further rain. I had hardly slept, and my head felt muzzy and sore. In the distance silent birds swayed on branches and kangaroos dozed under silvery gums. Time was still, frozen, and I was reminded of the house on Monkey Puzzle Street. Rich ochre earth lay spilled like blood as far as the eye could see. Houses and wind turbines dotted the landscape and telegraph wires sliced through the big sky, separating and dividing it. What lay under us? Had I unwittingly trampled and desecrated sacred ground?

Out here it was possible to see where once nothing had resided but the Song. The out-back seemed nothing but a barren waste ground to those who knew no better but natives still honoured this land. They could travel through it as gently as a whisper, making the lightest of impacts. They visited every rock formation, every tree and every animal. The land welcomed them with food and shelter, providing billabongs and bush tucker. They had no need of crops or herds, all they collected served their requirements.

Women dug for honey ants and roots with specially crafted sticks. Reed and grass nets woven by them were used to catch kangaroos, emus, and the occasional duck. Some baskets were so tightly crafted they could carry water or honey without leakage. Men used spears to catch fish and other fast moving prey. Some spears were designed with an axe-like attachment for chopping firewood or for construction of shelters. Tiny children learned to track animals as soon as they could walk, using silent hand movements to remain hidden. When differing tribes met, songs and dances were exchanged as well as food and goods. The valuable red ochre of the north was one of many currencies used.

We joined Frances on the humid porch for breakfast. She had pulled her flame hair into a topknot, and wore a flowing jade dress that matched her feline eyes. On the table lay a plate of fresh fruit and a steaming jug of coffee. She shared out some fruit for us.

'I hope you slept well,' she said, 'I meditated for a while and tried to get some more answers.'

'Any luck?' Luke said, pouring the coffee.

'Hang on a tad,' she said, then drew a long breath and closed her eyes. She opened them to find us looking at her. Lowering her gaze, she continued, 'They still don't want me to see very much, like the whole thing's got to be a secret.' She sighed and my heart sank. 'I did pick up a few things though,' she said, 'it goes back to the word connection.' I glanced at Luke, but he remained silent.

'You asked yesterday, about the painter?'

'Yes Mulga, we think he put the fever on Luke, and he tried to do it to me but was only partly successful.'

'Well, I'm not sure that he did, he doesn't seem to be part of the connection.' She raised a finger. 'Apart from the fact that he worked near to the house, in the back garden was it? The only other thing I saw was a man with a scared face.'

'What sort of man?' Luke said.

'A white man, possibly in his twenties but he could have been older. I only saw his face and the scar, probably because that's all I'm allowed to see.'

I leant forward. 'I've written down the details of my dreams and I'm sure there was a man with a scar in them, do you remember Luke?'

'Now you mention it, yes. Wasn't it one of the men where she was held captive? You could look it up when we get back.'

'Okay, maybe we're getting somewhere at last.' Frances clasped her hands together and her rings chinked like little bells. 'But these are only possibilities, you understand. I cannot guarantee any of this to be fact, but it may help in some way. She dished out more strawberries and juicy melon slices.

'Did you dream at all last night?' She asked, and I didn't like to tell her I hadn't slept. 'There will be one more dream for you, Rachel.' She wiped her hands on a serviette. 'I must tell you before you go, this will be the last dream from Maisie. Whatever you see try to believe it won't harm you or the baby. That's something I want you to remember.'

I put a hand to my mouth and looked at Luke. I felt his strong arm around my shoulders. 'After that,' he asked, 'will it be over?'

'The nightmares will be over.' She almost said the words through her teeth. 'It's necessary for you to have this last dream so you can be released from something, but what that is I cannot say. I'm so sorry I can't be any more help. But please keep in contact, and call me if you're worried about anything at all.'

As we pulled into Acacia Avenue that night the yellow wattle shone cheerfully in the headlights. Even the rain hadn't dampened its soft, golden glow. Luke put his jacket round me as we ran through the drizzle. It felt good to be home. He kicked off his shoes and smiled his old smile. I hadn't seen him like this for weeks.

'Half expected to see Dad in his chair.' he said.

I gave him a bear hug. 'It's going to be strange for a very long time, isn't it?'

'I just wish he could've hung on to see the baby born,' he said grittily, 'but I guess it just wasn't to be. Like Frances said, his time had come.'

'I'm hoping he'll still see the baby from heaven.' I replied. He kissed my forehead.

'However weird life becomes, I'll never regret the day I met you.' he said. We cuddled up on the sofa, weary after the journey. I looked over at Murray's empty chair, wishing he was still with us, trying not to think of all the things we had yet to arrange. We were going to be busy, because the funeral was only five days away.

'Do you believe all that stuff Frances said?' Luke suddenly wanted to know. I thought about it for a minute.

'You know, I'm just not sure. I got the feeling she was keeping something from us.'

'Me too, but why would she? Unless she got it wrong about the baby being a boy.'

'Well, we'll find out soon enough!' I laughed and snuggled up closer to him. 'When the funeral's over I'll make some notes and see if anything comes out of it. Sometimes that happens when I write things down.'

The gate at Monkey Puzzle Street creaked open, and I walked the steep incline to the back door. Luke was busy sorting out the funeral with Bea, and I was back to working on my thesis in the solitude of the old house. At around five o'clock every evening Luke called by to pick me up, taking me back to his house for the night.

That particular day Ringo barked non-stop, urging me to look over Biffs' fence in case anything was wrong. The dog was balanced on a tree stump and was yapping at a cat in a tree. The feline was high up, perched on one of the branches as it calmly washed its paws. Below Ringo was becoming delirious with rage, his shrill barking straining more and more. I couldn't stand the noise any longer and propelled a fallen mango in the cats' direction. After a few more mangos it duly took off. A few minutes later Ringo was much quieter, with just the occasional grumpy woof to let everyone know he was still on his toes.

I retreated into the house to escape the stoking heat. Thankfully a downpour was beginning but was so noisy on the tin roof it was impossible to concentrate. Perhaps it was going to be one of those days when nothing got done. I made a hot drink and waited for the rain to subside. I thought about looking through the keyhole into the locked room in search of Stumpy, but decided against it. Instead, I stood in my favourite place on the veranda and drank the warm tea. My belly was starting to show a sweet little bulge, but it was unreal to think there was a son growing inside it.

Bit by bit the rain eased off, and I took a walk round the back garden to stretch my legs. The washing I had hung out earlier was drenched, and the fishpond was in danger of overflowing yet again. Slowly a hard ray of sunlight escaped from between the clouds, illuminating the pale back wall. Something huge was stuck against the paintwork. About the size of a telephone handle it was bright pink, the shape of a lozenge and had long waving antennae. As the sun began to dry it out its long filigree wings spread open. Gossamer and fairylike, they shimmered with all the colours of the spectrum. All at once I was suspended again in time, lost in wonder at this strange creation. I began to shrink, and was left feeling no more than a tiny fragment in the vastness of this unique world.

Luke had taught me it took eight minutes for the sun's rays to reach our planet. I wondered how long it would take to reach a farther star, one on the outer edge of our solar system. In that moment I could see Murray had landed on such a star. He added to its brilliance his own special light, twinkling down on us unseen by day, but shining with a timeless iridescence through our sleeping hours.

Finally the huge insect took off in graceful flight. After a near miss with the washing line it rose upward into the sky until I could see its rainbow wings no longer, no matter how hard I strained my eyes.

Chapter 15

I took a firm hold of Luke's arm as we climbed the steps of Christchurch cathedral. Inside the vacuous space and at the end of the main isle was Murray's coffin. The Australian flag had been draped over it in recognition of his army service. A simple spray of red banksias, yellow wattle and white myrtle adorned the lid, their green foliage falling over the sides of the casket as if he were urging them to grow.

We sat at the front of the church and waited for Bea to arrive. This solemn occasion produced a heady atmosphere which wasn't aided by the strong smell of incense that drifted through the air. Luke was tense, and tried desperately not to chew his nails. Then from behind a gloved hand squeezed both our shoulders. Instantly relieved to see Bea, I realised I'd been holding my breath. Minutes after her arrival the church had filled to bursting point. It seemed as if everyone who had ever known Murray had turned up. Old mates from the army, friends and neighbours, school friends he hadn't heard of for years, and his colleagues from the Municipal Parks and Gardens. The organ struck up and we tried to sing the first hymn, the words catching on the raw emotion in our voices.

The priest with the freckles stood at the Altar, his hands raised up.

'Welcome,' he said. 'My name is Father Craig. Welcome to this final meeting with our dearly departed Murray. Today we come together to celebrate his life before committing his body to the earth.'

From behind us, I could hear Bea weeping softly. Luke was looking down at the hymn book in his lap. My misted sight turned Father Craig into a peach blur, while my grief pushed his words to a background hum. He described Murray's life; his young life as a happy typical boy, his adolescent struggle taking a career choice of agriculture and gardening, and the service he gave during the war. He spoke of Ruth's untimely passing and of Murrays' own retirement from work for health reasons. How he had made so many friends at the Parks Department and his true happiness in this occupation. He finished with Murrays' love for his family and friends, most especially for his devoted son and business partner.

A single teardrop fell from Luke's bowed head, silently hitting the book in his lap. I squeezed his hand and he clutched so tightly my fingers burned. I craned my neck to see beyond the altar and my eyes found the plaster Madonna in her arbour. Even at this distance her gaze seemed to pity me. I knew it wasn't possible for her to reverse time, to allow Murray to come back for a few more weeks, but I wished for it anyway. I hoped she could take away the dull ache that had settled in my stomach along with the crushing pressure on my shoulder blades. I had been here before and was sure that in time it should fade as life swept it aside. Buried but not forgotten; sleeping in the far corners of my mind, until some memory ignited the pain of his loss again.

Some honeybees had flown into the church and they buzzed round the flowers on the casket. Murray would like that and maybe he'd even called to them, loving all living things the way he did. At last the organ struck up for the final hymn, *Abide with me.* The congregation stood noisily, and various coughs and splutters were heard at the back. Then we sang as hard as we could, filling the church with our cracked voices, trying to do justice to his memory, trying to remember him laughing at life. The last verse finished and the pall bearers approached the casket. Between them they carried Murray out of the church, through a line of servicemen and gardeners, and down a ramp beside the steps. Carefully they placed him inside the hearse, ready to be transported to the Crematorium. This was the part I was dreading. And it was too late to ask him anything now. If he knew any secrets about the family trophy it was certain these had died along with him.

A long way away in England, spring flowers would be just about to emerge. Creamy pink magnolias would be in full bud and pink and white blossom would soon hang like confetti thrown across leafless branches of hawthorn and wild plum. Luscious green pastures would become dotted with tiny white lambs and wild hedgerows would glow with primroses and crocuses. The juicy leaves of the first daffodils would surely be showing above the frosted earth in my parents' garden. I wondered if I would ever see them again. Or perhaps like Murray, they had left my life forever.

Frances called a few days later and spoke to Luke. She had sent a lovely arrangement of flowers, but for obvious reasons couldn't get to the funeral. She told him Murray was at peace, that his soul had been freed to exist in another and much kinder realm. He was with Ruth at last, happy and young again, she said. The undertaker had given Luke Murray's ashes that day. He placed the small urn gingerly on top of the cabinet that housed his family photographs. We kept looking at them and weren't really able to comprehend this had once been his robust dad. How very strange it seemed that in the end we're all reduced to such a small amount of dust.

We talked about the funeral and the people we had met that day. Some of them joined us after the crematorium service. At Luke's house Bea had been busy earlier that morning preparing refreshments. Quite a few turned up, had obviously not met in years and spent a long time chatting together about days past. It didn't matter that most of them hadn't kept in contact with Murray. They hadn't forgotten him; rather it was as if the passing of time made their memories even fonder. I passed round plates of sandwiches and sausages on sticks. A surprising amount of sherry was consumed, and everyone left happy, if sobered by their own personal loss.

Miss Green's card was one of many surrounding Murray's urn. Inside she had written how sorry she was about his death. She was slowly getting better and would come to see us as soon as she got back. We gradually returned to a daily routine, but it was difficult to concentrate on anything. In the evenings we took out the family photographs and Luke talked me through them. Doing this I could tell what freedom he had experienced as a child. Then, his parents had known almost the entire population of Darwin first hand, Murray meeting many of them as a landscaper or tending private gardens later on in life. Ruth didn't work as such but helped out at a junior school in the lunch break. She often came home to tell Murray, 'We'd better watch out for so and

Dream Time

so in a few years time, for he was out of control now, and only heaven knows what he might turn out like later on.'

One evening after we'd eaten Luke brought out a special album. Inside were some snapshots he'd taken in Vietnam. There were only five small pictures of Luke and his mates. Instantly I recognised Dave among the smiling faces. Luke pointed out American soldiers in a particular shot. They had stripped to the waist because of the intense humidity, and were trying to relax between operations, he said. Most of these young men had been killed or badly wounded by enemy fire and grenades. He could remember all their names, what they liked to eat and some of the funny things they did. The pictures were from another world, most of it hot thick jungle. In one photograph tall palm trees and huge hills loomed behind ten cheerfully waving soldiers.

A different group were standing in a large tent-like structure with no sides. This was his base camp, called Balmoral. He said there it was hotter than the worst wet in Darwin, and when the rain fell, it truly was torrential. He'd never seen anything like it, before or since. Men got foot rot and everything from pencils to cans of beer had to be tied up with string so the wind didn't blow it into the mud and slime. He told me how the war had started, and how the Johnson Administration in America began the military conflict by sending in ground forces and ordering air strikes. He had been called up for National Service in 1967 and following basic training was sent out with his unit to camp Balmoral.

'Around 50,000 Australians served in that war and over 500 lost their lives.' he said. 'I became one of the casualties after an enemy attack put two bullets in my shoulder. But I was one of the lucky ones,' he said, raising a shaking finger and resting it lightly on two of the figures in the photograph.

'These guys didn't make it,' he said, through tightened lips. I swallowed hard and sat forward in the chair while he continued, 'there were others who were killed by friendly fire, either by accident or because some poor guy had lost his marbles with the pressure of it all. Back then, and even now I've no real idea of why it had to happen. I wish I could tell you what, if anything, was achieved by any of it.' I sat back in the chair, and shook my head in disbelief. I didn't like to ask any more about his shoulder.

'I remember this photo was taken on the day of the raid. I was with my mates in the canteen playing cards, drinking grog and listening to the Seekers on the radio. Funny how it's so clear, like it was only yesterday.' For a second I thought of my own memory of the cellar, how I could see every detail, hear every sound and smell every odour.

'The enemy came in from nowhere, Rach. Suddenly the camp was under attack on all sides. The Commanding Officer radioed for help when he realised we were outnumbered, but the real damage had already been done. Within seconds of the first shots I was wounded. My face hit the mud and I thought; this is it, it's over for sure.' He paused, and I had to ask the question.

'What happened then?'

'One of the bullets just grazed my heart, but I still felt it beating away. I was pumping blood out through the wound, my energy faded, and I ended up unconscious.'

I saw him laying there in the filth, asleep in the middle of an explosive chaos. Pretty soon he was rescued by a MASH unit helicopter, and taken to a medical base for surgery. The bullets were released, and when he woke up there was Dave in the next bed along.

'He was making a play for a nurse, even though he was stuck in bed with his leg in plaster.' Luke laughed as he thought about it. Dave had taken a bullet in the bone, smashing his femur apart.

They got through the next few weeks together, talking things through over a smoke and having what laughs they could while the damage mended. After what seemed an age, Luke was allowed home, but he couldn't find the will to leave Dave. Once on board the chopper he started to panic as he remembered the enemy fire and suddenly he couldn't breathe. He needed Dave by his side as he had always been, but his leg needed further surgery and he just wasn't ready to fly. An American soldier sat next to him said, 'Hey buddy, don't you want to go home?' But by now Luke had begun to shake and feel sick, and he passed out right there in the yank's lap.

He was sedated for the plane flight to Darwin, and swore from the minute his feet felt the ground he would never fly again. He had memories from Vietnam he would never forget, but the strongest was the day they were ambushed at Balmoral. That was the day the slush turned to blood, and the day he lost his mates. It was the day he had survived, along with his best friend Dave. It was a sad fact how for centuries man had been continually at war in one place or another and that so many lives are still lost to that cause. Luke placed the photos reverently back in the cabinet. He fetched a couple of beers from the kitchen and wordlessly passed one to me. I saw tears in his eyes but didn't know what to say. Nothing could bring those mates back again. All we could do now was to try and remember them with the love and respect they deserved. I raised my beer bottle.

'To Murray,' I said.

'To Dad, may he rest with Mum.'

Sarah Starr

In the lounge at Monkey Puzzle Street the ceiling fans squeaked and the wood floor groaned as I walked across it. Several of my Yoga postures were becoming uncomfortable, and a few of them were impossible. I needed to modify my routine to accommodate my thickening belly, and sat on a chair for some. Though truly it was too hot to exercise, write or even eat. Sweaty fingers slipped off the typewriter keys and next door Ringo barked intermittently at some animal, or perhaps just because he felt like it. Work on my thesis was nearly finished, but I had several books I still wished to study on the ancient Aboriginal culture.

Stumpy was around today and every now and then would dart under the locked door to get to his own private pantry. It had been so long since anything weird had happened, I felt as if the past was a crazy dream in itself. Murray's death had brought me up short and I could no longer dwell on what had happened in the house. I couldn't fret about Maisie or the warrior, and if I was in the garden I no longer worried over Mulga or his little house. Life was almost normal, and that suited me down to the ground.

I stopped typing to answer the phone. It was Mr Blatto on the line.

'Hello Pumpkin,' he sang, 'just ringing to say how are you?'

'Hello Mr Blatto, I'm fine, thank you.'

'Now listen, Pumpkin, and no arguments please. All of us here, including Mrs Clarke, wish you to come to the hotel in a couple of weeks. We have got a little party for you, because we didn't have time to say a proper goodbye, and because we miss you.'

I was flabbergasted. 'How very kind, I don't know what to say.'

Dream Time

'Just say you will come on 6th March. Please bring Luke with you, yes? We will see you at 4pm.'

'I can hardly believe it's nearly March.' Bea's flowery housecoat was pink and cream making her look like a huge strawberry desert. She held her breath as she dusted round Murray's urn. She was still doing household chores for Luke at the weekends, because she said we had enough to cope with. She enjoyed dropping in on us, and fussing over us in her own caring way.

'It seems as if Christmas was yesterday, doesn't it? Be a darl and put the kettle on would you love?' she said, bending over the sofa and plumping up the cushions, 'I'll make a cuppa when it boils.'

'Okay Auntie.' I buzzed off into the kitchen. Luke was due home from work, and I had been busy baking. When he arrived we sat round the kitchen table, drank tea and ate the still warm cookies. Luke told us about a special project he'd been working on the other side of town. Conversation fell silent for a while before he said, 'You know, I've been thinking about Dad's ashes.'

Bea pulled a face. 'It's not too soon is it?' she said without looking up.

'I don't think so.' he replied. 'It's not right having him on the cabinet when he loved the outdoors so much.'

'It seems to me he would have wanted them scattered somewhere special Luke.' Bea responded.

'Somewhere that's wild and natural.' he said, gazing into his teacup.

'Somewhere near to Darwin?' I ventured.

'Oh, yeah.' They said together.

'You see Rach, I've got your boat tickets for Kakadu Gorge. Maybe we could use that trip for it?'

'Wow,' I said, 'would we be allowed?'

'Well, I've made enquiries and they're happy for us to do it provided we scatter the ashes in the water.'

'When did you want to do it?' I asked, finishing the last cookie crumbs.

Luke scratched his chin. 'I've already booked it for next week, you see, I haven't told you it's the same place we scattered Mum.'

'Why didn't you say? Then it's the perfect place.' I thought for a minute. 'Isn't it strange how I got you those tickets?'

I borrowed a book from the library about the Gorge. In it was a fable about the Rainbow Serpent, known to Aborigines since time began. I read: A long time ago, when the Dreaming was very young there lived a serpent. But this was no ordinary serpent because she had beautiful rainbow colours along her body. Back then the world was bare and under her cold flat surface the Rainbow Serpent slept. One day she awoke and pushed her way up to the exterior. Then she travelled through the land, leaving her mystical winding tracks behind her. She would sleep when tired, leaving her imprint on the ground. This created the rocks and hills and the landscape of the continent. She travelled far and wide and then returned to call on the frogs to come out. The frogs had bellies full of water, making them slow and sluggish, but the Rainbow Serpent tickled their stomachs and made them laugh. Then the water flowed from their mouths into all the tracks and hollows she had made. This created the lakes and rivers, and woke up all the animals and plants. They followed her across the land, settling in many different places. To some, the Rainbow Serpent remains a great creator and brings the wet season every year. During this time all forms of life multiply, and rainbows form in the sky. However, as the Serpent is also the protector of the land and the source of all life, she can also become an aggressive force if sacred sites are not respected. Drowning can be administered as a punishment to those who don't respect the land. Some believe the Rainbow Serpent lives today, her rainbow colours still resplendent beneath a waterfall deep in Kakadu Gorge.

The small boat drifted off from the craggy shore, and we were afloat on the gorge. I was aft, cradling Murray's urn and its precious contents. I kept one hand on the rudder but had to twist my body to steer it. Beside me sat a large wreath of wild flowers, arranged lovingly by Bea. Luke was at the stern rowing in a steady, relaxed fashion. Any conversation created an echo within this hollow and the occasion seemed to dictate that we be as quiet as possible. The rock walls of the gorge rose up on either side, intense heat concentrating in the dish-like formation.

The boat rode deeply through the still, cool water. I was tempted to put the urn down and drag my hands through the river, but I also knew about the alligators. And although to most the Rainbow Serpent was just a fable, I for one didn't wish to disturb her. Luke pointed silently to a sleeping alligator over by the waters' edge. I nodded to him, and he smiled back. He seemed more resigned with his loss today and pleased we were taking this trip. Real confirmation had been given to us when we saw the name of the craft was *Miss Ruth*.

Luke had driven us to the gorge early that morning. I'd packed a picnic to eat further down the river. On the journey some of the tracks had been flooded because the Adelaide River was high on her banks. All the recent heavy rain had creeks and ditches running over when weeks before they had been dried mud beds. When we arrived at the northern entry station we showed the ranger our boat passes. He informed us we had chosen a good day to come, though to watch out for short, heavy bursts of rain.

I kept a watch out for crocodiles although Bea and Luke assured me they weren't as dangerous as the saltwater cousins. We continued to glide along the river, Luke watching and waiting for the right spot to scatter the ashes. The water was as calm as silk floating on the breeze, and ran for miles like a wound cut deep into the earth's crust. The life blood of the planet flowed towards it, winding its way in from the mighty ocean. Miles above us birds of prey circled for lizards or small birds to catch.

The water parted silently before us as Miss Ruth's bow cut a steady course. A small crocodile swam alongside us for a while, its long nose and eyes comically the only part visible above the water. Wispy grey clouds gradually blew in over us and the temperature dropped a few degrees. We pulled on our Macs in time for the first few spots of rain. Like the usual cloudbursts it proved to be sudden and very fierce. The downpour was so heavy it was as if the heavens were pouring another river straight on top of Miss Ruth. The huge drops hit the surface of the water with increased force; splashed and rocked the boat like a frenzied cradle. I held on and steered with all my strength but Luke was unable to move the boat to the waters' edge.

Rain flowed from our hats and jackets into the boat. I tried to bail her out with a picnic cup but she became even lower in the water. I realised if this carried on she was very likely to sink. Luke was shouting something at me but I couldn't hear his voice above the thunder and the rain. I suddenly felt cold, damp and sick. A rising fear gripped me. I could feel the water around my legs, and the gorge sucking the boat into its jaws. I could drown and lose the baby, and my throat constricted in panic.

I remembered the Rainbow Serpent and thought we had done something to displease her. Rocking hysterically from side to side, it was clear Miss Ruth was losing the battle. I screamed something as Luke made a wild effort to pull on the dancing oars. Slowly, laboriously we started to move towards the bank, all the while bailing out the rain. By the time we landed on dry ground the storm had almost stopped, but needles of rain stung our raw faces. Falling out of our valiant craft we landed on the hard rock ledge and pulled Miss Ruth safely aground. We remained collapsed for some time, exhausted by the rain's aggression.

Then all at once the sun reappeared, started to dry us off and gently warmed our chilled bodies. I opened my eyes, looked up, and there it was. The biggest, widest rainbow I had ever seen, hanging above the gorge right over us. Luke turned to me with fresh tears in his eyes.

'This is the spot.' he said. I handed him the urn and we watched as Murray's ashes swam from it and merged with the river. The flowers though somewhat bedraggled followed right after.

We stood on the ledge holding hands, watching the river guide his remains to their resting place. It seemed then like Murray was smiling down on us from the top of that huge rainbow. I said a silent prayer of thanks. In spite of our ordeal it could've been true the Rainbow Serpent was also smiling on us, and I asked for her blessing for whatever lay before us.

Chapter 16

The party at The Drover Hotel was in full swing, and provided a welcome diversion. Mrs Clarke, Mr Blatto and several colleagues I'd worked with were there. Music poured from the restaurant speakers and the kitchen staff had made a cake. They'd all clubbed together and bought me a pram. It was dark cream, the same as the baby clothes Mrs Clarke gave me. She seemed genuinely happy to see me and quite obviously had a ball shopping for such a small creature. Her eyelids fluttered more than usual as she peered over her glasses and fussed over me. Mr Blatto was his usual raucous self, but thankfully kept his references of anything resembling a pumpkin shape to a minimum. Instead, he did a lot of teasing the other girls, who he also referred to as vegetables, including *Squash* and *Rhubarb*.

Overcome with their generosity and kindness I was forced to sit down and was spoiled by everybody. I was given tea and cake, lemonade and ice cream, and then more tea. *Squash*, whose real name was Julia, waited on me hand and foot, and wouldn't hear my protests. At eighteen she was the youngest and thought the whole baby thing to be very romantic. Her friend Maxine was similarly excited about the coming child as her sister was due very close to my date.

Luke arrived about an hour later to join us and was treated to the same routine with many added jokes about fatherhood. He lapped it all up along with wine and gateau, and we stayed unintentionally for a further hour. Even then we were only able to escape because dinner service was about to commence. We both promised the waving throng we would return with the baby when he, or she, was born.

That evening I sorted through the presents and practiced pushing the pram in the lounge. Luke had a go but after all the wine collided with the kitchen door and had to pack it in. We both got the giggles and ended up collapsed on the sofa, Luke whispering 'Pumpkin,' repeatedly in my ear. The party had been wonderful, and I would never want to forget it or the kindness everyone had shown.

During the afternoon Mr Blatto had pulled me aside, a serious look developing over his puffy face. I wondered what on earth was wrong and asked if he was alright.

'Oh yes, I am fine Rachel. But I wish you to know, that is, I have a friend in Melbourne.'

'That's nice.' I said.

Mr Blatto straightened himself. 'This friend,' he continued, 'he has the same surname as you.'

'Does he?'

'He is living in Melbourne, but his family came here a long time ago. From England they came.'

'I see.' But I didn't really. Hundreds of people from England had done the exact same thing.

'Do you mind if I give out your address to him? He is looking for family tree? How do you say?' He tapped his head as if trying to knock out the correct expression.

'Oh, I see what you're saying now. He's probably trying to find possible relatives. Well no, I don't mind at all. What's his name, I mean his Christian name?'

'Oh. His name is Ray.'

April finally arrived and with it came the most glorious weather. Now the days rolled by with soft sunshine, blue skies and gentle breezes. Temperatures dropped to a manageable 24C, with not a drop of rain anywhere to be seen. My rental lease came to an end. But before I left Monkey Puzzle Street I felt compelled to check the mailbox for one last time. Sure enough, at the very back of the rusty tube lay a crumpled envelope.

The letter had been sent some weeks earlier from England, and on opening I found it was from my mother, with a smaller note enclosed from Jade. I didn't delay in reading them hungrily, there beside the gate. Mother had been harsh she said, and hoped I would be able to contact her. She wanted to know how the pregnancy was going, and if I was planning to return home to have the baby. She had exchanged words with Uncle Sid, and it seemed he had also softened slightly towards my plight. There was no message from my father, but Jade's small note on *Winnie the Pooh* paper made up for it. She simply said *I miss you Rachel, please come home soon, Love Jade X.*

I tried to digest the contents as I took a final walk through the garden. By now I knew every inch of it; every leaf and branch, every sound and every smell. I touched all the trees that had so faithfully given me shade, said goodbye to the fish and bowed in respect before the remains of Mulga's little house. I stood before the rough foundations and saw what must have been a daydream.

In my mind's eye a small dark man sat before me cross-legged on the ground. He held a paintbrush in one hand and another between his teeth as he worked with colours mixed on a small piece of bark. In front of him lay a picture full of intricate dots and squiggles. Ancient secrets lay hidden behind his eyes, while his face carried the most peaceful of smiles.

The daydream dispersed as soon as I remembered the kitchen clock. Months had passed since it crashed to the floor, its hands frozen at ten past nine. The day I fought like a banshee with the cockroaches was now like a distant memory. The never ending insect song, the bleating of frogs and possums, and the long weeks of insistent rain might never have happened at all. But how all this had pushed me to the limit, almost to insanity I couldn't forget. Neither could I halt my gratitude for the change it had created inside me. I realized how much I would miss it.

The back door squeaked as I opened it. I tightened my hold on the letter and put it safely in my bag. I walked around the quiet rooms. Luke had taken my luggage to Acacia Avenue the previous evening so I only needed to post the house keys through the front door. Miss Green was due back from Adelaide in the next day or two. I'd left everything clean and had stocked the fridge with fresh milk and bread. The last quest was my farewell to Stumpy. I searched the house for him before realising he was probably behind the locked door. Without thinking I tried the handle.

The door opened immediately, swinging wide to reveal a beautifully furnished bedroom, obviously Miss Green's. From above me Stumpy dashed out into the corridor, stopping outside on the ceiling to take a rest. Sunlight flooded the room giving its contents a golden translucency, making everything appear unreal. The now almost forgotten shield was laid out on the bed and underneath the true shaft of a warriors spear nestled into the pillow. I reached out and touched the satin counterpane and felt the very solid bed. Surely this time it was not my imagination. As well as the bed the room contained a dressing table, two chairs and a wardrobe, all with ornate carving. Marble table lamps solidly adorned the bedside cabinets. I noticed the room smelt of lavender.

Terrified the warrior might appear I dashed from the room. Perhaps Maisie was able to keep him away from me. I saw my hands visibly shake as I locked the front door. I hastened down the drive and heard the gate make its click with the upright post. I glanced back nervously at the house, past the mango trees where the fruit bats had entertained me for so many evenings. Beyond the foliage I could see the veranda and my favourite resting place.

Then all at once I saw him. There, where I had rested so many times, listening to the radio or sleeping in the evenings. He stood at least 6 feet tall, and I could just make out a victorious grin now he'd at last managed to be rid of me. His feather matted hair and dark skin had white paint daubed over them. Otherwise he was masked by the dolphin shield I had seen just moments ago. Why had he come instead of her, and where was Maisie? What was it his black eyes saw as he looked out, far away into the distance? I strained my eyes as his form slowly dissolved, the shield going last of all. I took out a tissue to wipe them. When I looked again, he was gone.

Very soon Daphne Green would return here, and I wondered if I should warn her she might find a surprise waiting.

* * *

Dream Time

'This is real English tea, Daphne.' Bea stirred the leaves around the pot, and replaced its lid and cosy. Wearing her orange housecoat she made a vivid contrast with Miss Green's pastel clothes.

'What a treat, thanks Bea. And it's so nice to see you all, thanks for letting me come over after the time you've had.'

I offered her a biscuit. 'And yourself,' I said, 'are you fully recovered?'

'Well I must admit I still get pain in the leg, but I'm lucky to be here, really I am.'

The table fell silent until Bea continued, 'Exciting news about the baby isn't it, who would've thought it? It's just the happy future we need after losing dear Murray.' Her face betrayed her fondness.

'Luke will tell you he was one of my oldest friends,' said Daphne, 'People used to say such spiteful things about my artist and the way I helped Aborigines. Murray always stuck up for me when he heard those remarks.'

'I didn't know him for long, but I thought he was a lovely man.' I said, glancing at Luke.

'That's for sure, we all miss him.' he said.

Bea poured out the hot tea. Luke straightened himself in the chair and addressed Daphne. 'I don't like to ask this but have you ever seen a ghost at your house?'

'A ghost?' she echoed, 'no; course not. Whatever makes you say that Luke?' She sipped her tea but put her cup down when she realized we'd gone quiet. 'What's the matter?' she said, 'Don't tell me you've seen ghouls and things that go bump in the night.' She chuckled to herself, and I joined in with a giggle.

'It's not funny really, I don't know why I'm laughing,' I said.

'Let me explain, Greenie,' Luke began, and relayed mine and Murray's encounters.

'It doesn't seem fair on top of what these youngsters have been through.' Bea added.

'I've never seen or heard any ghost, Aboriginal or otherwise, and I've certainly never seen a shield.' Daphne insisted, her face serious. 'I do remember Luke became ill one day just before the last wet, I thought he'd had too much heat. And I found my bedroom door unlocked when I got home, but the house had been left in a clean and tidy condition. Thank you for that, Rachel.'

Her voice had become crisp. I wished she would go, and felt foolish after confiding in her. I thought she was about to leave but to my surprise she took Bea's offer of another cup of tea.

'Don't you believe us?' Luke asked.

'It's not that Luke; I just won't have anything said against my artist, or any Aborigine, so let's leave it at that shall we?'

I could see Bea looking at me as if to say, *don't say anymore; there's no point in upsetting her.* My tea was suddenly cold and sickly. Luke looked over at me and raised his eyes to heaven and I blinked back acknowledgment.

'Now, there's something I want to tell you,' Daphne said, 'but it has nothing to do with the supernatural.' She lowered her voice slightly. 'I think I mentioned to you Rachel, about looking into my family tree. Well, while I was in Adelaide I found out some very strange things, perhaps even stranger than your ghosts!' She grinned in her nervous fashion. 'It seems, although I've got more research to do, but it seems that mine and Luke's family are connected.'

* * *

By July I felt quite huge and walked like a waddling duck. Large but in good health, I was supremely happy. After finding mother's letter all those weeks ago I'd eventually written back, and also enclosed a note for Jade. Since then we'd spoken on the phone several times, and Mother had made an effort to be civil. My little sister was very excited about the baby and wanted me to fly home immediately. I told her I was too big to fit into the plane seat and though reluctant she accepted this excuse. All three of them wanted to come out to visit us after the birth. I was enthusiastic over this news, but nervous at the same time. Perhaps they thought the news of this visit was what I needed to hear.

Life at Acacia Avenue had become cool and mellow. My thesis was finally finished and this I packaged in plenty of brown paper and string and sent it off to my course tutor in Essex. While Luke was at work Bea popped in for a cuppa, and in the afternoons I tried to take a short nap. Luke had made Murray's room into a nursery decorated in peach and lemon. He glued an alphabet freeze round the walls and we bought new furniture, including a white cot. I couldn't pass by without going in and luxuriating in the splendour of it all. I could almost feel Murray's approval seeping out from the wallpaper and I hoped his love would be able to reach the baby while it slept in its cot. The unborn child kicked regularly and so hard and strong I thought he must surely be a boy.

It no longer bothered me if I passed my degree or failed. My new family was my new career and my only priority. Perhaps in the future my life might include a teaching job. Luke was happy I was with him at Acacia Avenue, and he had his own plans to expand the gardening work. He wanted to develop a creative role while broadening the foundations of the business. I was confident in his ability, and felt the details would come to him in time.

My own time was getting nearer and I flopped on the sofa more and more. Movement was laboured now due to my immense size. My back ached continually and all my joints felt sore. Up several times a night, I tried desperately not to wake Luke. He was so patient, so loving to this whale of a body that needed continual food. I hadn't seen Maisie for months and wondered what had happened to her. But I was resolved to remain calm and an inner resignation overtook me.

One day in August Luke dropped home for lunch. He'd finished work early so was able that afternoon to tidy his own garden. I was relieved to have him nearby. My back ached more than ever and my belly throbbed with sharp spasms. The baby was due any time soon. I settled down in a big armchair and put my puffy feet on a stool.

Luke had positioned it so I could see out of the patio doors into the back garden. I watched him as he worked round the shrubs, deftly clipping them back with secateurs, bare arms shining in the sun. The chair cradled my enormous middle like a hammock. Here I was relaxed, safe and secure. Minutes later the hum of the lawnmower sent me into a deep, distant sleep that took me back, way back, to a time long forgotten.

> It's dark now and I'm shut in the small hut for punishment. I've been hit and starved and I'm hot as fire. Outside someone is calling me. Not Maisie, but my real name Moree. I know the voice comes from one of the women in my hut. She's not from my tribe but from a neighbouring one in Arnhem Land. She's digging away the

ground from under the door. 'Come on,' she says under the gap, 'help me to dig. We're going home, I'm getting you free.'

Now I am running, running very fast even though the child within should slow me down. Now I'm hiding behind a fat boab tree, and I hold my belly. I'm frightened, and I'm angry. I've been held in the metal hut for days, longer than some of the men. My family's been killed with the stinging stick; it was the scar-faced man who murdered them. But I'm running some more now, running back to my people but it's a long way away. I don't know where I am, but I know how to get home when it's dark by the stars. Soon the sun will get some rest, and I will move by night.

The girl who set me free has gone ahead because now I'm too slow for her. She's young and strong and I hope she makes it back to her people. I'm moving as fast as I can but the baby is slowing me down. I stop to rest under a tree.

Its morning and I'm a long way away from the white men, the metal hut, and the hate they tied us up with. My unborn child is heavy and it pulls on my back. Now the sun is coming again, so I must hide. This country is wide open, it's raw like my mouth, its' as hard as my belly. I have my digging stick to make a hole in the ground. A long time goes by before I find the frog. I hold him up and drink from his bladder. He goes back in the ground, while I try to run.

I have to run faster than ever because the white men have found me. They're chasing me on horses and they're coming for me. They're a long way off but there's nowhere to hide. They whip the horses to run faster and come towards me in a cloud of red dust.

Soon they are upon me, and I can hear the horse's breath. A whip bites my face and I stop running. I put a hand to my cheek to stop the blood.

'What about killing two birds with one stone?' One white man says to another. I don't know what this means, but I know the word 'kill'. I try to run again but one of the horses is blocking my way. The man with the scar points the lethal stick at me. It explodes like a bush fire. I'm thrown to the ground and I can feel the baby slowly die. Blood comes out of my side and drips onto the raw earth. I hold up one of my arms, the other is wrapped around my belly. Something inside me appeals to these men to help me, to help my baby.

The scarred man gets off the horse he has almost ridden to death. He walks up to me and says, 'Filth.' I don't know this word but I feel the hate behind it and I don't understand. He takes a knife from his belt and with one hand holds it to my throat. He grabs my hair and I feel something else from him. It is fear. Not little wasp stinging fear but big crocodile biting fear.

I don't care why; I only know I'm no longer scared. I feel the knife cut my throat and my life slowly ebb away. Suspended between life and death the stars are reaching out to claim me, offering the secrets of all eternity.

Dream Time

I must go to them with my baby. I have to take him back to my ancestors. Only they will know what to do.

My eyes sprang open and I sat forward, the birth muscles contracting the same second in a vicious grip. In slow motion I saw Luke running for the house. And I heard myself crying out; a deep primal cry that came from the depths of my soul. It was the same noise women had sounded from ancient times, the roar most of us are born to. Pain burned from my shoulders to my knees and engulfed me as the contraction twisted like a vice. I closed my eyes to see her face was still there. Then Luke was holding my hand. I smiled weakly, tears of terror running down my face.

'I saw her in the dream,' I panted, 'the dreadful last dream.'

'Shh now, I'm here. Don't worry about it now, push it to one side. Concentrate on your breathing love. We'll time the contractions together.'

• 169 •

Chapter 17

If it were possible to taste heaven on earth then I was in paradise. And I was falling in love all over again. In my arms lay my sleeping baby, as peaceful as an angel. His tiny hands shivered and stretched ever so slightly as he dreamt.

'Sleep now, my darling.' My words were whispered. Luke lifted him from me and placed him gently in the hospital cot. The window was ajar allowing a drift of sweet morning air to flow into the room. We remained unable to move our adoring gaze from this tiny, perfect creature. Exhausted, I soon fell into slumber while Luke kept an eye on our precious bundle.

'What shall we call him?' He asked when I woke. The tea trolley had been and we sipped from the thick hospital cups. I looked over at our beautiful child and heard the same name in my head.

'What about Yuri?' I asked.

'That's unusual, but I like it. What does it mean?'

'I don't know,' I confessed, 'but I've got the feeling it's what Maisie wants.'

'That's good enough for me love.' He kissed my forehead and I stretched my aching legs. I closed my eyes again.

'Sleep now,' he said, 'I'll keep a look out for the little one.'

I snuggled down in the bed. Luke had been with me throughout the birth and the midwife even let him cut the baby's cord. Yuri was pink and wrinkled at first, but his skin seemed to plump up right after his first feed. He had briefly opened his dark eyes which matched his dark hair and skin. This did not seem strange to me, and I thanked God repeatedly for giving us such a wonderful gift of joy.

Later that day I recalled the horror of the last dream. Like a switch it had started the labour and brought Yuri into the world. Luke listened quietly as I told how this new life had birthed following such a vivid nightmare.

'Dead baby, she said all those months ago. I guess she tried to prepare me for the last dream, but I thought she was threatening *our* baby.'

'He looks fit and healthy to me love; I don't think we need worry on that score.' Luke joked, but I noticed a line of concern etched across his brow.

In those first days the doctor came to see Yuri for some routine tests. He checked his limb reflexes, the sucking strength against his smallest finger and he looked into his eyes with a special light. He stood there for a long time seemingly lost in his own thoughts. Then he looked into Yuri's eyes, again using the light. I was preparing to get ready for his next feed and struggled getting off the bed. My belly was still large and strangely floppy now that Yuri had vacated it.

The doctor gave me a tight smile but remained silent. He left the room with just a nod in my direction. I didn't take much notice and went about feeding the baby. My life had been transformed by his arrival, outside that my thoughts didn't need to trouble. Afterwards we lay cocooned together on the hospital bed. Luke was due to visit soon. I made a mental note to tell him about the doctor. I wondered why he'd reacted like that. I thought about Yuri's eyes and slowly concern crept over me. But surely there was no cause for alarm, if there were anything wrong he would've said so. I flipped through the charts on the cot in an attempt to satisfy my anxiety. But I only found Yuri's temperature chart; the doctor had taken the others away. Then I suddenly saw something.

Time of birth: 09.10, on 07.08.1974. An icicle shot through me. The same time as the clock that fell off the kitchen wall! Somewhere outside I could hear the slow, whining buzz of a lawnmower. Right then I needed Luke's embrace. I needed his common sense and his calm words. I knew he couldn't be far away but even so became breathless and Yuri whimpered as he picked up on my panic.

I hadn't felt this vulnerable for some time and I didn't like it. While Yuri had been nestled inside I'd found a new confidence, and the belief that life was worthwhile at last. My outlook had grown, had stretched as much as my body to accommodate this new life. Like bowerbirds we had hovered and fussed over the embellished nest for our young. But my fear of Maisie was back. Her power threatened to defeat me and all reason was washed away.

As I tried to push it elsewhere the memory of the last dream flooded over my joy, seeped into me with the greyness of possible flaws inflicted upon my child. I rocked him gently in my arms and wept, hoping my tears held the soft healing of the wet. He began to cry, a tiny helpless tune I was unable to comfort. Now the noise of the mower was louder than ever, a background of mechanical clatter that did nothing to silence us.

Luke found me tear stained and desperate, useless and wretched. He listened to everything while he rocked little Yuri asleep. I was left feeling crazed while he went to find a nurse but at last Yuri was sleeping. His little arms twitched very slightly as if he were dreaming. An overwhelming tide of love gripped my heart as I looked over at him.

'It's the baby blues Rach, apparently quite normal.' Luke said on his return. 'The nurse said not to worry about it.'

'Are you sure everything's alright?' I said.

A tap at the door revealed a different doctor wearing a suit. He looked older and carried an authority that only comes with experience.

'Rachel, Luke, my name is Doctor McGee.' He began, and shook both our hands in turn. 'I was coming to see you this afternoon anyway. I just want to have another look at Yuri's eyes, if I may.'

'There's no need,' I said, 'he's had them checked today already.'

'If I may, I need to make sure. The doctor who looked at them earlier was a little worried about them.'

'Why, what's wrong?' Luke said as the doctor made his examination.

'Sorry to wake you, little one,' he said as Yuri complained.

He placed the special torch back in his pocket and sat on the edge of the bed. Frost gripped at my throat and I searched for Luke's hand.

'I'm not certain, but from what I've just seen there may be a problem with your baby's eyes. I don't want to alarm you, but feel it's only fair to prepare you.'

'Prepare us, for what?' Luke said his voice rough with annoyance. My hands reached for my heart.

'I'm sorry, but there's a possibility Yuri may be blind.'

* * *

The hawk circled high in the sky, lifting its wing tips to catch the thermals, scanning the ground with it's almost X-ray vision. It was a good day and every cloud had its perfect place. Mulga knew Hawk Dreaming, knew that big fellow in the air could see everything, from the huge leafy tree canopies to the tiniest insect crawling on the dry earth, even the smallest lizard shading itself below the coarse spiniflex grass.

He spat onto some ochre powder and mixed it to a paste with a gnarled finger. He was old now, and not as swift as that Hawk fellow. But he could still hunt, catch fish, maybe even spear an emu on a good day. Today he was in the garden. He knew this garden well. He came here to find peace and quiet to do his work. He could paint anywhere really, but sometimes he liked to paint on the ground in this place.

It belonged to a white woman. White woman: name of Green. Mulga thought that was very funny. He called her something of his own. He called her Kora, meaning companion. They would sit together and talk in the garden about his people, about her world, and how these two things could perhaps one day exist in harmony. They didn't speak of sorrow, cruelty or dishonour. Or how a race of people had been robbed of all it had. How ignorance and misunderstanding had fuelled an arrogance that lasted until this very day, or how the white men could have got it so wrong when they had the books and education. Rather, they spoke softly and laughed in fondness as they found a way to bring a positive element to the problem.

But there was no need for words that day; instead he set to work in quiet solitude. He was alone with his thoughts and his canvas of tree bark. He was painting a very large piece, arranging the dots and lines to reveal a big fish. His canvas stretched out in front of him, the paints a little way off under the shade of a tree, each one covered lovingly with a small leaf.

Behind him stood the small stone built house. When it became too hot, he would lie in there on the cool earth. He would look up at the palm roof but saw through it to the majesty of the big sun, the tall trees, and all the sky beings. There was no hunting to be done here. This place was for painting, talking and for thinking. If big talk and big thinking with Kora could help his people, then that's what he would do.

Mulga examined his work, mixed a new colour of vibrant blue, and took the reed paintbrush from his mouth. There was still much work to be done.

I walked through the house on Acacia Avenue, my hot feet sizzling on the cool floors. Yuri was clutched to my confused, guilt ridden body. Tenderly I put him down for his doze, pulling the mini mosquito net over his cot. The blurry figure beneath the net gurgled and stretched his little arms.

'He's got your eyes.' Bea had said when I brought him home. Did he really see with them, perhaps me as a fuzzy blur through the netting? I sang softly to him, not a lullaby but a tune I'd heard on the *Evening Falls* radio show. I rocked his cot and hummed the gentle tune willing him to sleep, but above all willing him to see. I knew how his problem might take us away, far away from here, in the quest for a solution.

Doctor McGee had been frank about the options we could take to help Yuri. He advised us a special test was needed to establish his sight capabilities and to rule out any possible defects.

'He needs to see a Paediatric Ophthalmologist.' he said. 'There is one you could visit in Brisbane but you could see a team of experts at the Melbourne Ophthalmic Hospital. Here Yuri can have his retinas tested and this will give a better diagnosis. It may be advisable though,' he said, 'to move to Melbourne permanently.'

August was drawing to a close, and with its passing our resolve to move south became ever stronger. Although it exposed my vulnerability I posted a letter home explaining the situation. The long shadows would be nearby now, in England. Trees that reclaimed their leaves in May would now boast a full resplendence, cool canopies giving dappled shade in the high summer heat. Garden blackbirds might be rearing their second brood, kept busy foraging the earth for worms and grubs. The mornings might've turned cooler though, with sparkling dew necklaces hanging from silver cobwebs and hedgehog prints in the soil making Jade laugh with delight.

Tomcats that couldn't sleep would probably be yowling for mates under bedroom windows, and late into the night the occasional fox might join in the din. Soft seed heads

Dream Time

usually blew in through windows on warm breezes while fat bumble bees foraged for the very last drops of nectar. Already the fields would have given up their harvest of grain, vegetables and fruit. All dreamed the autumn would last forever, knowing the darker months ahead were also the colder days of snow and struggle. I felt the arrival of my letter could make the season even colder.

Daphne Green called by to show us her research. She spread her papers on the kitchen table and pointed to the top of the page and the name Frank Jarvis.

'He was an officer aboard the First Fleet.' she explained. 'He married one of the few real ladies that came over on the voyage, Jane Blythe, and they had three sons.'

Luke read out their names: 'Tobias, Jacob and Nathaniel. Tobias, Rach; the one I told you about!'

'That's right Luke.' She nodded. 'Your family line comes from him. But it seems during the voyage Frank got one of the convict girls pregnant. I discovered this because she cited him by name as the father, and here he is on the birth certificate.' She drew out a photocopy and placed it on the table. The name of the mother was Lily Green, and the baby's name was Thomas.

'Lily brought him up as Thomas Green,' she continued, 'and I'm descended from him. He had a sheep farm near Alice Springs.' Luke quickly sat down as the shock hit home.

'Strewth,' he exclaimed, 'it might be distant but we really are related. Get the kettle on Rach, I think we could all do with a cuppa.'

'Would you like me to find out more about your line, Luke?' Daphne asked as we supped the refreshing liquid. 'And we must keep in contact, even if you move down south.'

'Thanks Greenie, anything you can find out will be a help, I'm sure.' Luke said. She smiled encouragement and collected her papers together.

'I'll write to you from wherever we are.' I promised.

'And I'll be in touch. Look after yourselves, all three of you, I'll let you know what I find.'

Yuri had fed and was asleep in the nursery when Frances phoned. She listened intently to my news about the baby but remained oddly silent.

'Are you still there?' I said thinking we had perhaps been cut off.

'Oh yes, I'm here Rachel, sorry. My congratulations on Yuri's birth, and I'm so very sorry to hear he might have a problem.' She paused for a while again. 'I'm just trying to tune in, um, trying to see if I can give you any messages to ease your mind.' Another pause, 'Ah,' she finally continued, 'something wonderful is going to happen.'

This was too much. Insensitive didn't describe it and I reiterated my worries, adding in our probable journey to Melbourne through the desert.

'If Yuri is blind, or even partially sighted, we will also have his problem.' I almost snapped the words. 'He'll need constant care for the rest of his life.' I reminded her rather cruelly, that she should know, after all she was disabled herself.

'I know, you're right and I really am so sorry. And I apologise if I'm being clumsy again. I see so many things but haven't got much of a way with words. All I can say is that it's not necessarily how things are going to turn out. Remember all the strange things that happened at the house?'

'Well, yes of course I do.' And I relayed to her the third dream, and hoped she had been right about it being the last.

'You've witnessed a part of Maisie's life, events she wishes you to be aware of,' she said, 'when you dream you become a time traveller allowing you access to things that might seem irrelevant now. But somehow, what happened to Maisie will tie in with your future, with your destiny, if you like.'

'I don't want to lose Yuri!' I almost choked on the words.

'I don't think you will lose him at all. Haven't these experiences brought you and Luke closer together?' I thought about it for a minute.

'Well, I suppose it's a miracle we met at all really. I never thought I would ever find anyone.'

'So who's to say a miracle won't happen to Yuri?' Her voice held an excitement I couldn't understand.

'You mean he's not blind?'

'I mean he might be blind, but he may be cured.'

A feeble ray of hope probed my heart. 'Frances, I'm concerned it might have been Maisie who caused this problem. And I dreamt about the artist recently.'

'Maisie is pure love,' she insisted, 'it's impossible for her to hurt you or anyone else. The artist, yes the dream about the artist happened because you are entering the next stage of your journey.'

'But he was painting a shield like the one I saw, and you said he had nothing to do with the equation.' I protested.

'He's had nothing to do with the haunting, but one day you'll discover that all things are connected, even if by the most tenuous of links. You mustn't give in now Rachel, and please don't give up hope. I can't stress how important that is.'

'I've found a house in Melbourne.' Luke announced. It was a Saturday, and Bea was due to pop in at any time.

'That's good news but we haven't sold this one yet.'

'We don't need to do that Rach,' he said, 'it's a house *swap*.' He smiled broadly, obviously pleased with this arrangement. I felt a tingling of doubt and was sure my expression showed it.

'Are you sure it's legal?' He sat back in the chair and looked down at Yuri, asleep in his Moses basket.

'It is if you get it drawn up by a lawyer.' He pulled out a picture from his shirt pocket. 'There,' he pointed, 'what d'you think?' The picture showed a house not dissimilar to his, nestled cosily in the corner of a leafy lane.

'Gee, it looks lovely,' I said, 'but are you really sure about moving? It means leaving all your friends and Auntie as well as your home.' It struck me then how much I would miss them so terribly. 'Don't you think we should think about it a bit longer?'

'Rach, for goodness sake, there's nothing to think *about*. You and Yuri are my family now. We're going to Melbourne to find the best doctors we can to help our boy. I've got enough saved to fund the trip. We'll get by until I find a job, and, 'he paused to embrace me, '-and we won't give up hope, like Frances said.'

'Do you think he'll be okay?' I said, glancing at Yuri. Luke kissed me gently and we held onto each other as hard as we could.

'When all's said and done a man needs a purpose to fight for. Mine used to be Dad and the business, now it's you and little Yuri.'

'Is it as simple as that?' I searched his face for an honest answer. He looked at me with his true blue eyes and opened them wide.

'It's as simple as that.' he said.

'I love you so much,' we said it together and laughed. Yuri woke from his nap and gurgled happily, as if he too approved of our plans.

Chapter 18

Life at Monkey Puzzle Street and the dreams that had haunted me were becoming a distant memory and my records of them lay forgotten in my bedside drawer. But one night as I lifted Yuri from his cot I realised I had dreamt about Belle. Yuri suckled while I struggled to remember the details but all I could recall was Belle's happy, smiling face. It might be she was alive in a different way. I thought about those early years we'd shared as friends and the comfort I'd taken from her when I'd been so afraid. Thinking about her and listening to Yuri's sighs brought such peace that I fell asleep sitting up with Yuri still snuggled against me. When I awoke Luke was stirring and the early morning birdsong had only just begun.

A busy day was before us; Luke was to visit the solicitor to finalise the swap agreement on the houses and I was to stay at home with the baby and sort out the final packing. We were due to meet our friends that evening for a farewell party. Luke had hired a room at the Kicking Horse bar in town. We planned to take Yuri for the first hour after which Bea was due to collect him. Dread descended upon me

Dream Time

when I thought about everything that needed doing before the leaving day. Luke brought coffee to drink in bed and assured me everything would go as smoothly as clockwork. 'Thinking about how you'll manage things is far worse than actually doing them,' he said.

'I'll just have to take your word for that.' I said, but knew he was probably right.

Sure enough the morning passed more smoothly than I'd anticipated. Yuri slept peacefully for most of it while I packed away all but the bare essentials we would need to survive the last week. The furniture and large boxes would follow us by road train but because of our various planned stops on route it was likely to arrive at Melbourne before we did. We were taking almost everything we owned, there just wasn't enough time to sort through Murray's possessions. Luke gave Bea a keepsake of a family photograph from one of his albums. I got it framed in town and added a crystal vase I knew she was fond of. She promised to visit us during the next wet season reminding us it would be the perfect opportunity to catch up with her cousin in Bendigo.

I was nervous about the evening ahead, knowing people would naturally be inquisitive over Yuri's eyes. I felt emotional enough and full of maternal hormones. I really didn't feel inclined to answer the inevitable questions that lay ahead. But it only took one look at Yuri to remember how lucky we were. He was such a beautiful baby I was sure everyone would love him just as much as we did.

We arrived early at the Kicking Horse and settled Yuri into a cool, quiet corner in his basket. The bar was empty but even so tight anticipation seemed to fill the air. The jukebox was quietly playing Elvis Presley's *Blue Swede Shoes* and the bar staff were busy filling little bowls with peanuts and crisps to put out on the tables. Luke bought soft drinks saying he might progress to the stronger stuff later.

Pretty soon people started to arrive and they all came over to meet Yuri. Everyone turned up including Dave, Marty and Vince from the Daly Tavern. Even Dr Treadwell popped in for a quick drink and wished us the very best of luck. He added we must let him know how things went at the hospital.

'Doctor's orders,' he joked.

Mr Blatto and Mrs Clarke came with one of the chefs and several housekeeping and restaurant staff. Mr Blatto arrived with his usual flair and carried a cake almost as big as his body. On it were the words *Good Luck in Melbourne* in large pink letters. The top of the cake was decorated with little sugar flowers and a sugar lawnmower. The chef, still in his whites ceremoniously sliced it up.

We stood round chatting and eating pieces of cake and nobody mentioned Yuri's eyes. Instead he had plenty of cuddles and bounces on knees. He seemed to enjoy the whole thing, surpassing himself with cute gurgles and hiccups. I'd brought along a bottle of milk which was duly warmed and fed gently to him by Vince. For such a rough and ready bloke he looked positively broody through the whole experience.

Daphne Green popped in to wish us well, and we promised again to stay in touch. She gave us a small painting of an eagle Mulga had finished very near to his death.

'Thanks Greenie,' said Luke.

'Yes, thanks so much Daphne,' I said, finding it hard not to call her Miss Green. We kissed and hugged her goodbye, knowing how very precious his work was to her.

'You know we're family now.' she said as she was leaving.

Dream Time

People gave us their best wishes for Yuri's health. They were very sweet and kind, and offered to help in any way they could. Mrs Clarke got tipsy and blamed Mr Blatto for buying doubles of vermouth.

'Ziggy Blatto,' she said as her eyelids stuttered, 'you're impossible.'

'I don't know what you mean,' he replied, 'you usually can drink me under the table.'

Biff turned up with a crate full of beer for the trip and Bea came to collect Yuri. She told us he'd got far too excited and probably wouldn't sleep.

'It'll take me hours to get him off,' she complained. We thought she was really hoping so in order to have as many last cuddles as possible. He was to stay overnight at her house giving us as long as we needed to enjoy this last night out with our friends. As the evening wore on Luke discussed the intricacies of the journey with Biff. He, it seemed was an expert on the route and gave us instructions to drive flat out to get there as quickly as possible.

'We can't do that Biff; we've got Yuri to consider.' I butted in.

'She's right Biff,' said Luke, 'we're not in that much of a hurry old mate.'

Biff nodded, and thought for a while. His eyes appeared moist. 'I really wish you didn't have to go at all.' he said.

Eventually we said our goodbyes and left for home. I didn't need to tell Luke how this night would be cherished in the months ahead.

There's something curious about packing everything up and moving on. When forced to do without the so-called necessities life becomes simpler, even easier. But the enormity of the trip itself pressed down on me and became heavier every day. Luke was also leaving the home that held all his memories but at least now I was sure he was ready.

The dry season was nearly over. Trevor the Weather gave his forecast for settled warm weather, mild winds and the usual high of 24C. I turned up the volume as the DJ played a track by *King Crimson*, and found some of the words echoed my frustrations.

> *I'm on the outside; looking inside,*
> *What do I see?*
> *Much confusion; disillusion, all around me.*

My conversation with Frances had left me puzzled and every day I struggled to understand it. I turned her words this way and that, but still no answers came. Perhaps it didn't help that Yuri needed to be fed every three hours. Looking after a small baby left little thinking time. Luke had taken the truck in for a full service before the Big Push, as he called it and I decided to take the baby into town.

I put Yuri in his pram and walked down the street. I followed my usual route until I reached the Botanical Gardens. I wanted to stop at the point where Murray had been remembered. His old boss from the Municipal Gardens had paid for a plaque with the simple words: *In memory of Murray, our dear colleague and mate, now gone from this Earth and dearly missed.* Emotion welled up in me as I read the inscription and at once Yuri began to bellow from the pram.

I picked him up and told him we would never forget Grandpa Murray, and that a part of him would always be there in our hearts wherever we were in the world. The palm canopy overhead swayed and rustled allowing a twinkling of sunlight to dapple the stone memorial. Small bush orchids were just beginning to erupt from the surrounding moss, heralding new life with their hidden beauty. I bent down and took a pebble from the flower bed and placed it into the pram.

'We'll take this with us to Melbourne and call it the Grandpa Stone.' I told Yuri. Immediately he stopped crying.

We reached the steps of the cathedral later that afternoon. Leaving the pram on the sidewalk, I took Yuri into the church and sat in my usual seat. Here, at least, everything appeared to be timeless. The silence was rarely interrupted, but today tiny noises seemed to assail my tired nerves. Like waves the familiar pungent incense crept up my nostrils and down into my lungs making me want to choke. I laid Yuri on the pew behind me and placed a kneeler beside him to prevent his sliding off. I knelt, and looked into the blue eyes of Our Lady.

As before the plaster Madonna was looking down on me, her blood red heart emblazoned on her breast and her arms outstretched as if to scoop Yuri up and make him well again. The days were running away like rain and suddenly I needed extra time, an extra month just to see everyone again. I wanted to stroll through the streets in these cooler days, able at last to soak in the place that had welcomed me home. I was leaving Yuri's nest and felt a heavy weight descend again onto my shoulders. The baby sensed my angst, became fractious and needed soothing.

I prayed this last time, asked for her help to cure him or at least to give him some partial sight. Then I rose, walked to the small table in front of her and lit a candle for my little boy. Together we were about to leave on the most challenging journey of our lives. But taking up our roots I hoped to grow stronger and brave enough to overcome any obstacles I might find. I would take that courage and use it to plant new seeds in the spent soil of my being.

The light was dim and it probably wasn't so, but as I stood back from the candle and looked up at her I fancied she was smiling down at me.

Everything possible was packed and the crates were stacked in the lounge ready for collection the day after our departure. Bea was on hand as usual to make sure the removal men had the correct instructions. Above everyone in Darwin, she was going to be missed the most.

I kept one of my history books out for the journey and started it while Yuri was asleep. "Known to locals as 'The Track', the Stuart Highway runs some 1,900 miles from Darwin to Adelaide. It took John McDouall Stuart three attempts to cross Australia from south to north but he finally succeeded in 1862. A qualified surveyor and keen explorer, Stuart was born in Fifeshire, Scotland. He graduated as a civil engineer from the Scottish Naval and Military Academy, and arrived in South Australia in early 1839. Here he worked as a surveyor, but also undertook several expeditions into the outback before his huge journey began in October 1861.

At this point he had barely rested for a month following his second attempt to go north. Taking a party of several men but stubbornly refusing to use the Aboriginal knowledge of the environment, Stuart and his companions travelled armed in case they met native Australians. They took packhorses and rode out into the bush, in itself affording more miles of travel per day but with the complication of these large animals needing regular water in the parched interior. There had for some years been a supposed inland sea, or lake. In this search they were unsuccessful, because Stuart and his party didn't understand the ability of the interior to flood depended on the season and the rainfall.

Thus all they found was a dried up desert bowl, simply because they were there at the wrong time. Along the way it is extremely likely they would have come into contact with Aboriginal tribesmen, resulting in the inevitable native deaths from the white men's guns. The horses became exhausted and most of them expired during the harsh crossing, where temperatures could exceed 45C at the centre of the continent. Stuart himself became ill and had to be carried on a stretcher by the other men for some distances. Eventually they reached the north coast, finally linking the top end to Southern Australia.

On their return to Adelaide in January 1863, a procession and large banquet were held in Stuart's honour. Apart from this, he received hardly any recognition for his efforts from the government at the time."

I closed the book and sighed. I hoped our own travels wouldn't prove to be as formidable. There were only a few days left before our departure.

Chapter 19

We arrived at John Flynn's memorial on the second day of our journey. I'd read about Katherine the night before and found the history of the region most absorbing. I flipped my book to the appropriate page.

"Approximately five hundred kilometres south of Katherine the road splits in three; one road leads back to Darwin while the other two lead off to the east and south. Aptly named *Three Ways*, near to this spot stands a memorial to John Flynn. The founder of the Flying Doctor Service, and Superintendent of the Australian Inland Missions, Flynn studied theology as a young man in Melbourne, and took up Missionary work in South Australia in 1911."

It was getting late and we decided to stop overnight at Tennant Creek, a short distance away. I climbed down from the truck to stretch my aching legs. Then I took Yuri round the back and changed his napkin on the tail flap. I had him covered over with a mosquito net to stop the biting flies. When the net was off I held him in one arm while the other arm waved them away. Luke took his hat off and poured

Dream Time

precious water over his head. The heat in his skin made it steam. It was sure to get even more intense as we drove nearer to the desert.

Bea warned me Yuri would quickly dehydrate so I gave him water from a little bottle between feeds. The truck was loaded with large square water containers and Luke had planned the journey so we could stop to refill them. The time spent driving lengthened each day but if that meant a decent shower and a night in a bed it was worth every kilometre.

Luke pointed to a huge rock on top of the memorial. 'It's one of the Devil's Marbles Rach, it should be in your book.'

'Let's see, yes here it is: "A group of spherical rocks hugely important to the Aborigines." It says someone in the local authority thought one of them would look rather good on the memorial, they took it from a sacred site and the tribe in question are negotiating to get it back.'

Indeed it was stunning, massive. As if suspended, it looked down on our tiny forms below. The edifice did afford us some shade but I wished it could roll off and go right back to where it belonged.

A car was approaching from the south, a Holden Humpy. It drove right up to us in a cloud of dust and almost hit the truck. The door opened and a figure sprang out. Equally grimy as his car, the man's eyes darted from a weather worn face. Luke moved in front of me and I held Yuri close.

'You from the Top End?' he said.

'That's right mate, from Darwin.' Luke replied amiably as the stranger walked forward, kicking up little clouds of brown dust. His skinny frame loomed over us.

'Don't want to stick around here too long in this heat; it'll dry you up to a crisp.'

'We're just about to leave.' I said, stepping out from behind Luke. 'We stopped to stretch out legs.'

'We're headed for Tennant Creek.' Luke added.

'Yeah? So you're staying at the Creek: why didn't you say? The name's Flintlock, by the way.' He spoke in a more affable tone. Luke shook hands with him while I went to the back of the memorial in the shade. Yuri had almost dozed into slumber. From behind the rock I shuddered as I heard Luke give him our names. Flintlock's voice rasped as he continued.

'I'm on the way to Mount Isa myself. I'll be away for a couple of days, why don't you stay at my place tonight? Ask anyone in the Creek for Flintlock's house.'

I reappeared from the memorial to protest, but was too late.

'I don't need payment, wouldn't hear of it,' he told Luke, 'my door's always open.' Finally he addressed me. 'Ah, little lady,' and his leather features folded into the most remarkable smile, 'you and your baby please make yourselves at home.' Leaving Flintlock behind, once again we hurtled along the track.

'What sort of a name is that anyway?' I asked Luke sullenly. 'We don't have to go to his house do we, he gave me the creeps.'

'We could at least take a look at the place, Rach. If it turns out to be an old hole we'll find somewhere else to stay, how's that?'

'Fine, okay then.' I said, without meaning it.

'Don't you know Aussie hospitality by now Rach? We can't turn him down.' But something about the man didn't feel quite right. I held Yuri close, smoothed his face and breathed in his sweet baby smell.

The Stuart Highway cut straight through Tennant Creek like a river in full flow. The town built up either side was reminiscent of the old Prairie towns I saw as a child at Saturday morning cinema. The truck swept into the main street as if it were a stagecoach escaping from the Native Americans. I almost expected arrows to fly towards us but snapped out of it when Luke pulled up outside a roadhouse.

'I'll just go and ask for directions,' he said, obviously enjoying this adventure. He soon returned to say we needed to drive to the other end of town. Darkness had fallen, and as we approached the timber building our headlights lit up a sign. It said: 'R. Flintlock, Guns for Hire or Sale.'

The front door was unlocked. Tentatively we stepped into the hallway and through the adjoining opening. Inside the main room a harsh electric light illuminated a treasure trove of guns, ammunition, papers and general rubbish strewn over the meagre furniture. Yuri began to whine, quickly working up to a full strength bellow. I worried his eyes might hurt from the glare of the ceiling bulb. I sat down on a crooked chair and tried to feed him while Luke explored the rest of the place.

My attempt to settle Yuri was in vain. He kicked and screamed until I was certain he must be ill. Luke was unsuccessful in finding any food, there being only whiskey and cough sweets in the kitchen. He took the crimson-faced Yuri from my arms.

'What's up little man?' he said raising his voice above the din. 'This isn't like him at all, he's usually so docile.'

'There's something about this house, he doesn't like it.' I said.

'Are you saying it's haunted, like Greenies' house?'

'I'm not sure what I'm saying, but something about it feels very odd.' My ears were ringing from Yuri's cries.

I noticed a wall covered in photographs and had to take a closer look. Some of them were extremely faded. I gestured to Luke.

'Come and look at this, can you see it?' In the raw light I was drawn to two old pictures. One looked like a much younger version of our host stood with some other men. They were all carrying guns. Luke winced as Yuri's screams reached fever pitch.

'It's no good love, we'll have to leave.' he said.

'Not just yet, look at this one.' The second picture looked even older, torn and dirtied. It showed a group of Aborigines tied together by their waists, their hands tied behind them. The man in the first picture was in it but the photo was old enough for him to have been Flintlock's great grandfather. Another man near the back of the line was using his gun to force the natives forward. He had a scar that ran visibly down his cheek.

'What d'you make of that?' Luke squinted at the photograph.

'Stone me!' he shouted almost as loud as the baby. He handed the screaming Yuri back and took a closer look at the picture.

'I don't like the look of it love; we'd better go back to the roadhouse right now.'

The morning found us weary after a restless night. I packed up our things and we headed off further down the Track. Yuri had stopped crying as if by magic the moment we left Flintlock's place, and slept better than both of us. Consumed by the photographs we laid awake for hours. Beside Luke my mind worked overtime while my body remained motionless. Whoever the men in the picture were it was obvious they had captured those Aborigines.

'For some sort of cruelty or for lynching,' Luke said. He whispered the words so not to wake Yuri.

'Why do you think he's got those pictures in his house?' I said as quietly as possible.

'I thought the same as you did, about the resemblance to Flintlock. What if that really is his relative?'

'In a way that's academic.'

'How do you mean?'

'Because, it's the man with the scar that interests me Luke. You remember what Frances saw.'

'Course, you think it's the same man who killed Maisie?'

'Well, I've been thinking wouldn't that account for Yuri's outburst? It might even explain this connection Frances spoke of.'

'There's no other way round it love, that outburst was a reaction to something. He's been as quiet as a mouse ever since.' It might've been the exhaustion of the day finally got to him, but I didn't think so.

As we talked the long night hours ticked by. Luke agreed we should report the experience to Frances as soon as we got the chance. Eventually I slipped into tenuous slumber. Disturbing thoughts drifted through my consciousness as I lay half awake. The dreams might well have stopped but weird things were still happening, not just to me, but now it seemed, to all of us. I resolved to write to Frances the next day, and felt myself slip into sleep at last.

Luke had phoned Frances before we left to tell her about the Big Push. She told him we were doing the right thing. I asked him if she meant Yuri was going to be alright, but she hadn't made that clear. She wasn't able to say what might happen one way or the other and it was unfair to expect her to do so. But she was sure that the move was right for us. *One door closes to allow another to open* she told him. I hadn't forgotten what she'd said about miracles. She promised one day to make it to Melbourne but we knew how difficult that would be.

Now we were alone again on the road and the excitement of discovering this land was tinged with foreboding and trepidation. I held Yuri close and he snuggled happily in my arms. He fell in and out of a heated sleep. Whatever happened now, I had to remember Yuri was special. Frances had urged us to trust he was no ordinary child, but a special gift from God.

As we drove away from Tennant Creek I wanted to tell Luke to turn the truck round and go back to Darwin. Maisie no longer bothered me as much as the possible problems ahead. We raced toward the Territory border and I knew it was too late to go back. I looked over at Luke, then down at Yuri. We should've been on the biggest adventure of our lives if we hadn't got these worries. We were driving into the abyss, praying we might find a cure for our child on the other side. The truck slid along the Track like a butcher's knife following a bone. The road stretched ahead like a scar impaled deep in the flesh of the living earth.

Deeper into her interior we drove. The soil changed to light ochre and vegetation became sparse. Huge termite mounds took the place of gums and fat boab trees. Far away in the distance wandering camels shimmered like a mirage. They roamed free in the desert and flourished there. The sun burned with the same cruel heat every day, our dripping bodies melting under its glare. Yuri exhausted me, needed all my time. I used a battery fan continuously on his body but it did little to keep him cool. Whenever we stopped I sponged him all over with water; that he loved. The heat made his eyes weep and crust over and they too required regular bathing.

But the lack of comfort in the cab did not distract us from our goal. At times I could see how travel alone can free the soul as discovering new places brought us fresh exhilaration. We started our days as early as possible and stopped to rest at midday if we were lucky enough to find shade. Then Luke boiled up tea in the billycan and we dozed together on the picnic blanket. Waking refreshed we were able to travel longer into the evening.

The extreme heat of the day contrasted with a sudden fall in temperature after dark and meant we had to search for thicker clothes and blankets. The truck, although reliable and able to traverse the route, was nonetheless a bone shaker. At the end of a day's drive our spines felt they'd been crushed by a steam roller. The constant flies were more than just an annoyance. The nearer we got to the interior the longer teeth they grew and we both had to wear hat-nets for any peace.

If Luke was driving after dark we'd watch out for the bright lights of road-trains. One of these monsters could drive you right off the road. Those times one came up behind us Luke drove onto the scrub while we waited for it to speed past. Road-trains were one vehicle not to argue with, he said. I remembered how I'd mostly despised the rain in Darwin only to find I now longed for just a drop of it. Some days we were lucky enough to find a small billabong with a bit of surrounding scrub. Here we rested and cooled off. Luke took Yuri still clothed, for a paddle. He adored the feel of the water and squealed with delight as he splashed his feet in it. I joined in his glee and remarked how he would make a good swimmer one day.

Days went by and we passed through Alice Springs. Headed towards Coober Pedy the truck sped by *flat out like a lizard drinking,* Luke called it. We crossed the dried up Finke River south of Alice and drove through the breathtaking MacDonnell Ranges. Kangaroo mobs bounced through the plains in clear view, searching for new forage or fresh waterholes. Shy emus we sometimes spotted through the trees, and on one rare occasion we saw a male with five chicks. The mountain ranges stretched east and west from Alice and I read in my book "were full of cliffs and gorges, waterholes and wildflowers." I asked that day if we could visit Uluru. To see it would surely be the journey's greatest thrill. Luke said we were making good time and confessed he had always hoped to see it himself.

Hours later we approached the holy ground surrounding the monolith. Luke stopped the truck here to view its magnificence from a distance. There seemed little point in getting too close anyway; the immensity of Uluru would only have been lost. We sat on the hot earth and regarded the vast rock. It was illuminated by the sun and paid homage to by the clouds. Its vast bulk rose from the dusty scrubland and naked, fire-eaten trees. It possessed something indefinable, yet so powerful that pilgrims had continued to congregate here since its eruption. In the centre of the earth it is the rock of timelessness; the rock of all wisdom. No words were necessary while I watched, as if outside my body, the ever changing hues on natures' finest monument.

I knew then how I was connected to everything as in turn, it was connected with me. I wasn't limited or encaged by my physical body but a part of all I beheld, the trees, the earth, the sky and the stars. Just as the rain in Darwin had washed my soul clean with its healing water, now the earth was sending to me its own blessing, rejoicing in my eagerness to understand her and all the life she was mother of.

She was trying to show me the very pattern of life, a pattern as ancient as the journey of my own soul.

Chapter 20

Flanked by two great deserts we travelled south and followed the rail line, the next destination Coober Pedy. A herd of brumbies galloped away in the distance sending up smoke signals that melted with the heat haze. Impossible as it seemed, it had become hotter than ever. Miles of sand passed before we crossed the Northern Territory border and in South Australia it was more of the same. Luke soaked cotton handkerchiefs in water to place over our heads. I sponged Yuri as we drove along, enjoying the cool puddle it made in my lap. Wearing no more than a napkin I kept him covered with the fly-net constantly. I was looking forward to staying at Coober Pedy, I'd read in my book how the people there lived underground.

It was mid September and I'd nearly finished reading it. We stopped for a morning stretch and I continued with the chapter *Origins*. "As far back as 60,000 years ago the first humans began their long journey of migration from Africa. One band of Homo sapiens ventured into Europe while a second wave migrated eastward, eventually crossing the sea from South-East Asia into Australia. It is thought at that time the continent was far wetter with more forests and inland lakes, providing in turn more food. Over the centuries the natives learned to read the land, discovered specific areas they called Holy Ground where they obtained teaching and wisdom. This teaching took place in the third language, in the unspoken resonance of light. They learned through stillness, and by quieting their inner narrative. Thus, over time wisdom began to flow inward. This huge bank of universal knowledge was activated and shared among them in the form of stories, songs and dances."

Yuri appeared healthy and thriving but the arduous conditions made him hot and tetchy. I hoped he was too young for it to have a lasting effect on him. Luke said because he was so small he'd only sleep and feed where ever he was. The driving probably lulled him to sleep in the absence of a cot but I reminded Luke the jolting also woke him and made him cry.

We reached a flat landscape dotted with humps of earth. 'Nearly there love,' Luke said, 'I'm buying you a decent meal tonight.'

The soil mounds weren't only from dugout homes. Most of them were from the shafts of the 250,000 opal mines. Here I saw hardly any vegetation and could detect no other life. For a moment I thought we'd found the end of the world. The inhospitable temperatures above ground were in excess of 40C during daytime. Contrasting icy nights meant life in dugouts was the only option for survival. Luke headed towards an underground motel called predictably *The Opal*. Our room was air conditioned and I bathed and clothed Yuri in luxury before his evening feed. Luke went out up-top for a while, he wanted to refuel and explore the place before we had to leave the next day.

Yuri slept soundly in his Moses basket while we ate supper in the deliciously cool restaurant. But in this relaxed environment my anxiety over Yuri returned. I guessed the closer we got to Melbourne, the worse it would probably become. The manager Rory Smitz waited on us. He told us how he'd arrived in the 50's but never made it back to the States. I assumed he'd come to work the opal mines but he told us 'I was at the Joint Defence Facility near Woomera, we were running nuclear trials back then at a place called Maralinga.'

'Sounds slightly dangerous to me,' Luke remarked. He drained his last drop of beer.

'Well, we seemed to come out of it okay but a few of the natives got fried in the fallout.'

I was horrified. 'You mean you actually let off bombs? Didn't they evacuate the locals?'

'I remember they had to force them to leave but I guess some of them came back too early. They just didn't understand the danger.'

He took our sweet order over to the counter. I recalled as a youngster how my parents had been terrified of nuclear war. They knew the Russians would aim for London above anywhere else in Britain. I reminded Luke how I'd been more worried about being trapped under the stairs than dying in such an event.

'How does it feel down here?' he said. 'You couldn't get more closed in than this.' I realised at once I'd not experienced any such anxiety in this subterranean chamber.

'That's strange,' I said, 'I hadn't even thought about it.' We celebrated this along with our so far successful Big Push. We'd driven almost the whole length of the Track and were due to break off along the Barrier Highway any day. Luke made a toast to Melbourne and we tapped our glasses together. Rory came over to clear our table. 'You say you came through Tennant Creek?' he asked. 'Did you have a chance to visit the old Mission site, just outback from there?' We confessed we hadn't, knowing nothing about it.

'It wasn't mentioned in my guide book.' I added.

'You would've found it interesting,' he said, 'it's been made into a museum, but the chapel's still there.'

I gulped, nearly choked and put a hand to my mouth. A silent movie ran through my mind of Maisie, sitting on the hard red earth with the small church behind her. Yuri, bellowing at the photograph of captured natives, and the man she had called Scar Face, the captor of innocents. Luke was looking at me as if the same thoughts had flashed across his own mind.

'Let's take a look at the stars.' he said quickly.

Outside the temperature had dropped and I shivered; something I hadn't done for months. The stars were all out, resplendent in their glory. The ribbon-like Milky Way stretched above us across the night sky. I wondered if Maisie as well as Murray looked down and saw us from one of those stars. All at once a silver thread shot through the heavens.

'A shooting star!' I exclaimed.

'That's beautiful.' Luke said, and slid his arm gently round my waist. 'Come on love, let's go back inside, we mustn't let the baby get chilled.'

The Track stretched out ahead, a never ending band of grey that would eventually lead to a full explanation. Today it led us to Port Augusta, a vibrant town with lots of shops and a harbour full of boats. Luke stopped the truck at a roadhouse and we hurried into the shady reception area. Jim, the manager passed the keys over the counter. He regarded Luke with a quizzical eye.

'Are you alright mate, you don't look so good.' he said.

'I've got a bit of a headache,' Luke admitted, 'think I'll lie down for a while.'

The room was cool and Luke soon dozed off. I sorted Yuri out and took a nap myself. I didn't wake until evening and saw they were still both asleep. But after a shower I was concerned as Luke hadn't woken. I shook his huge frame and saw his bloodshot eyes.

'What's the matter love?' I said.

He groaned and reached for some water. 'I think it's a migraine Rach, I haven't had one for years. I think there might be some tablets in the truck compartment. Can you find them?' I dosed him up and left him to sleep it off. I was worried but Jim said he got them too and all I could do was to wait for Luke to feel better.

'It might take a day or two,' he said, 'mine usually last that long.'

Morning came and Luke wasn't much better although he did manage to take a shower. Jim said he would keep an eye on him so I could take Yuri out for a walk. I carried him a long way through the town and then along the quayside. It looked out to the beautiful Southern Ocean. The beach was long and the white sand appeared fine and soft. I made a mental note to take him along the shore if Luke was still ill the next day. Cargo boats offloaded supplies at the port and cormorants perched on fence posts. Far too small to appreciate it, Yuri dozed in my arms as a pang of sadness stabbed at my heart. This was one of many scenes he might never be able to see.

The recent drive had left a slight dizziness which worsened if I looked out at sea. Wild bitter dust remained in my mouth no matter how much I rinsed it away. And my bones ached, yearned for an answer. Although silent, the desert had been strong and wise. It alone knew the secret of survival. I rested on a bench and breathed in the clear sea air. Yuri was on my lap and seemed more alert, perhaps sensing the activity around us. I read from my book how the Adelaide to Alice Springs plus the east and west railways converged here bringing many travellers. I saw how it bustled with people of all ages, while cheery workers joked on the wharf.

It was a real tonic to be away from the drilling heat and the pesky flies. The suns warmth and the cool breeze began to refresh my soul. I heard gulls and was reminded of Darwin's shore. I walked for a while and found a small piece of green near a play area. Here it was possible to rest in the shade of some buildings. The ground seemed relatively soft compared to the seats in the truck. I'd brought the picnic blanket in my bag and spread it out on the ground. I wrapped the baby in his shawl, tucked him in the crook of my arm and looked up at the true blue sky. I thought of Luke and of how selfishly I needed him to be strong enough for all of us.

Yuri gurgled and blew bubbles while I told him how beautiful he was. My back burned but at least most of our journey was over. The baby listened to my voice, his arms twitching as I explained we were nearly at our destination. Later, the road would turn eastward towards Broken Hill and then we were in New South Wales. Once Dada was up and running again, that was. From Broken Hill we had to turn south towards Mildura in Victoria, and from there it was more or less straight through to Melbourne.

I'd brought my book along and read a few lines before I stretched out on the blanket.

"The Great Victoria Desert lies on the west side of the Stuart Highway, while the Simpson Desert lies to the east.

They form part of the great artesian basin that extends throughout the middle of the continent. Aboriginal travellers avoided the Simpson Desert as it was so arid; however they did visit its western edge, where natural warm springs flow. Every so many years heavy rain flows into the middle of Australia, collecting in the so-called *Dead Heart* that is Lake Eyre. Mostly this lake is a barren salt flat, but when it becomes flooded thousands of birds arrive to breed and long dormant flowers erupt from the soil as bright and colourful as any jewel. The dead heart becomes a living thriving thing of beauty, fruiting into bloom only to wither back into desert as the drought returns. Very few, if any, witness this phenomenon, but some are gifted enough to know when it will happen."

The text made me sleepy and without meaning to I fell asleep. I'd been watching for clouds in the sky but only noticed the occasional gull floating effortlessly above the branches of an overhanging tree. Yuri was happily sucking on his fist. I could hear his thick baby whispers as I drifted away, further and further back into the desert wind.

> A tall warrior approached the riverbank. He didn't walk so much as glide over to the waters' edge. This was the first time he'd been able to fill his water bladder for ten days. He'd arrived at the Finke and the river floods were just beginning. He drank and filled the bladder, then sat on the bank to give thanks. New life was all around him, birds flocked to the water and plant life grew abundantly. He watched the brightly coloured parrots and budgerigars as they swooped to drink in their dance of celebration.

He was on his own journey. He'd witnessed strange goings on at the eastern coast, events that struck the very roots of his civilisation. He'd seen pale men and he'd heard strange words. Now it was time for him to return to his Elders and relay all of this. His father, the wise man, would know what to do.

He laid his spear on the ground and reclined, resting his head against the gathering bag of roots. There was no need to search for food here as he could see it was a place of plenty. He was surrounded by trees, bushes and birds. Later, he might be lucky enough to catch a small marsupial out on its night hunt. At the very least he knew there were fish aplenty and bush fruits ripe enough to eat.

Pretty soon he would be back with his own people in the north. He would follow this river through the Central Ranges and on past Uluru. After this he would head east for a while towards Mount Isa and finally north again to his country. Meanwhile he enjoyed watching the Black Cockatoos as they communed in Red River Gums on the opposite bank. Any confusion in his heart since seeing the ghost men began to melt because he trusted his Ancestors to protect his people. Help might come from the fierce giant Gorrorelli who was powerful enough to frighten anyone away.

I heard Yuri's whine and stirred from my slumber. I realized I was in the park and hoped I'd not slept too long. The baby needed feeding and was about to become fractious. He suckled under the shawl as I recalled the dream. Convinced I'd seen the same person on the veranda, otherwise it was a mystery to me. Still, I had felt his strength, the conviction he had to help his people. Like the desert wind he had flown away, and I remained in confusion. Perhaps I was to be haunted forever, and he had simply replaced Maisie. Or was it that we live only to dream; our earthly experience being just an extension of the other world behind that veil? Beyond the park a large black cormorant alighted on the quay wall. It watched me for some time before turning and flying off. I drew Yuri close and kissed his soft, nectar brow. Slowly my heart relaxed under his spell. I began to understand, thought I saw a possible message in this dream. I saw the traveller's apprehension, but when he drew strength from his ancestors this surely lead to his empowerment.

As I walked back to the roadhouse I felt stronger than before. It was no exaggeration to say the dream had bestowed me with unexpected courage. 'Come on, little man,' I said to Yuri, 'Let's go see how your Dada's doing.'

Luke was on the mend but we stopped a few more days before heading off. I told him about the dream and also wrote it up in my journal. The enforced respite benefited us all and Luke seemed to possess fresh vigour even after the migraine attack. A part of me didn't want to leave, in those few days I'd become attached to the place. Jim prepared light snacks for Luke's sickly tummy while I'd explored with Yuri. We talked over the final leg of the journey and hoped our combined strength would be enough for what we faced in Melbourne.

The time to go suddenly arrived. I fed Yuri in a quiet corner of the bar while we had breakfast. Luke paid the bill and thanked Jim for all he'd done for us.

'Is Rachel very religious?' I heard Jim say, 'Only I've seen her go into the church most days.' Luke gave a half smile as I glanced at him. I snapped my gaze back to Yuri. It was true I'd been to the church while Luke was laid up, one day I even went twice. Perhaps it was a habit I couldn't break, but I didn't really see how it hurt anyone. Aside from a place to pray, it provided a cooler, more peaceful place to think. I lit candles for people because I liked to do it, and could sit and watch their hot tongues for hours. Jim signalled for Luke to move closer.

'You've got a real beauty and a bonza boy there mate.' he said, failing to keep his voice down. Luke looked over with real pride and I felt myself colour up.

'I'm still pinching myself Jim.' he said, and I blushed even deeper.

'Let's hope all those prayers get your kid sorted out,' continued Jim as he shook Luke's hand. 'God's speed mate, have a safe journey to Melbourne.'

We drove away from Port Augusta, both of us reluctant to leave. Now completely recovered, Luke was nonetheless driving more gently. Intermittent feelings of anticipation and sheer panic bubbled up from my stomach. Less than two days away lay Melbourne and after arriving there was our appointment to take Yuri to the Hospital. We left the coastal road at Wilmington and picked up the Barrier Highway to Broken Hill. Turning off to Mildura we travelled north a short time before we rejoined the Track to Robinvale. The Murray Valley Highway soon took us to Swan Hill. The truck rolled along beside the Murray riverbank. Luke suddenly braked and gave me such a kiss I knew beyond doubt of his love. We jumped down, boiled the billycan and made steaming tea. It was beautiful by the waters edge, Yuri beside us and the world seemingly for a moment, was ours. I nestled my body into Luke's arms and shared my new courage. He held me tight.

'Have I ever told you how much I love you?' he said.

'I love you too,' I said, 'with everything I am.'

He searched for something in his pocket and told me not to look. Eyes closed, I felt him thread a ring onto my finger. When I looked I saw a beautiful opal, as soft as a cloud but with the turbulence of the deepest ocean.

'Oh, Luke-it's beautiful! Thank you.'

'I nipped out and got it at Coober Pedy.' he said.

We might have stayed there forever wrapped in each other's embrace, hearing Yuri's enchanted gurgles and squeaks. 'Don't you want to see our new house?' he said eventually.

'Oh very much,' I assured him, 'but can we stay for just a little longer?' Finally, after more than 3000 kilometres across the continent we had reached Victoria. Here the land was warm, lush and soft. But it promised a kindness I doubted it could honour.

Chapter 21

It was the end of September. Melbourne, we discovered was a large and vibrant city, with parks and leafy suburbs and I thought not unlike Croydon. However a large part of me continued to miss the dirt track feel of Darwin.

We moved into our new abode, a cosy house in Queens Park Crescent, a grand name for such a small road. On the outskirts of St Kilda, it was only a short drive to the sea and we were nicely tucked away from the main thoroughfare. Perfect, Luke said for a growing child. With no front garden to speak of a white picket fence separated the front door from the street. In this space two fig trees sprouted from ceramic pots. The main door opened onto a useful hallway, and leading from this was an open plan living room, playroom and kitchen. To the left of the house were the bedrooms and bathroom. The kitchen opened into the back yard and garden, a clever design of raised beds, grass and crazy paving. I loved it at once, and soon settled into the new neighbourhood. Only a couple of weeks passed before Luke was taken on by the Parks and Gardens Department, working mainly as Murray had in landscaping and garden design.

But the first priority was to register Yuri with the local doctor. Dr Treadwell had sorted out the appointment for the hospital specialist in October, but we hoped this date might be brought forward. Our general doctor was called Neville Breville, which we both found comical. Doctor Breville had a thick mop of greying hair and shoes that squeaked. We tried desperately not to giggle as he led us to his consulting room. To a small extent our amusement took the edge off the nervousness.

'He's a great little guy,' the doctor concluded after examining the recently fed and therefore very relaxed Yuri. We beamed with pride but I knew there must be more to come. Dr Breville put his ophthalmoscope on the desk and placed his finger tips together, as if he were about to pray.

'It must've been a long haul for all of you driving down the Track,' he began. Then his face became serious. 'But I'm sure you've done absolutely the right thing coming to Melbourne. Truly there is a problem, but it may not mean complete blindness. You do understand I'm not qualified in this specialty.'

'Yes, we've got an appointment with the specialist at the end of October.' Luke said.

'Let me make a note of that.' He scribbled the date on Yuri's notes. 'Now I hope they find some sight when they examine, but I can't say if it will ever be improved. No, I'm not going to raise your hopes by saying such a thing. But I will say this,' here he paused annoyingly while he shuffled some papers, '-um, I'd say you have a much better chance of a solution from the Melbourne Ophthalmic than anywhere else. You know it has an international reputation?'

'Can't you tell us anything else?' I said.

'Well, I think your appointment there is a few weeks away? I can't really comment further until he's been seen by the consultant. But he stands a much better chance at the hospital.' he repeated, just in case we hadn't taken this in.

'Do you mean a better chance of seeing or a better chance of coping with blindness?' Luke said, his voice quavering.

The doctor paused and pressed his fingers together even harder, making his knuckles whiten. 'Well, I would say, perhaps both.' he concluded, and a rather triumphant look lit up his face.

After the surgery Luke took me for a coffee at a pavement café. 'He didn't really tell us anything, did he?' I said. He'd brought out the hot drinks while I nursed Yuri. He searched through my bag for the baby's bottle.

'No love, he didn't.' Luke agreed. 'But he did say he'd try to get that date brought forward, though it won't make any difference because Yuri's too young for treatment anyway.' He sipped the froth on his coffee. 'It's all very well telling us to be patient, but if we have to wait until he's two or three before they can treat him-well that's like a flaming lifetime away!'

'Steady on love; here take your son.' He took Yuri and gave him his feed.

'I don't know what to think,' I said unhappily, 'but you never know; there's got to be something the doctors can do. After all, it's Dr Elkhart at the hospital who's got the real expertise so until we see him we will just have to be patient.' Luke drank his coffee and gave a sad nod. He was overtired and anxious about this strange new world, the world of hospitals, appointments and of continual grief. I squeezed his arm and he kissed my fingers.

'She'll be right.' he said, and gave a brave smile.

Dream Time

Life settled down into its predictable routine of food, work and sleep. Yuri was going longer between feeds, and continued to thrive beautifully. The summer delivered days of glorious dry weather and I was able to visit the park most weeks. I hadn't contacted my parents or anyone in Darwin as I wanted to wait for Yuri's appointment. Then I could let them know the verdict we were all waiting for. I told myself Yuri would see as well as normal children. But if I thought about it too much a terror gripped at me and I doubted he really was sighted after all. At night I held his little body and was consumed with guilt for allowing these thoughts to enter my mind. I kissed his tiny unlit eyes and knew I could never love him any less whether he could see or not. There were times when we cried together, clinging onto each other somehow aware we must face the unknown as one unit. And the days continued to merge together as we moved slowly forward to the date ringed in red on the calendar.

There were crates to unpack and this took up most of my time. Bit by bit I saw our new home form around us as each piece of furniture found its place and every item was safely put away. As I took the wrapping from each object I felt Murray giving me the strength to carry on and the determination not to cave in. I put all his old paperwork in a cupboard and closed the door. One day, when Luke was up to it, it could be gone through and sorted out.

At last the fearful day came. The three of us waited in the Outpatient Department to see Doctor Elkhart. Yuri had been fretful that morning and hadn't taken his feed. I thought it possible this was a reflection of my recent suspense. He quickly picked up emotions, especially if Luke felt the same. The waiting room was thankfully comfortable and cheerfully noisy, full of children playing and crying babies. But Luke wasn't comfortable and I was certain before too long he'd have to go and buy some smokes. Happily we were called before everyone else and went willingly into the consulting room like lambs to a slaughter house. It wasn't the axe but the consultant before us, aided with a crisply dressed nurse.

'Come in, come in,' he said, in a lovely fatherly way. 'Nurse will just take Yuri off for some routine observations, don't worry he'll be back with us shortly.' While Yuri was gone he asked us about our general health, about my pregnancy, the health of the baby and what our expectations were for his future. He'd received a letter from Dr McGee, outlining the examinations done following his birth. The nurse brought Yuri back in a cot, and Dr Elkhart tested his eye responses again.

At length he explained how Yuri might have a very rare inherited disease. His pupil responses were so sluggish they might as well not be there at all. He asked if either of us knew of any blindness in our families. We'd had this question from Dr McGee and couldn't tell him of any, but it was not altogether impossible. Ruth's family history was mostly unknown and my parents never discussed such things with me.

'Not to worry,' Dr Elkhart said cheerfully, 'the problem could have come from generations back.' We followed him to a special room, the nurse pushing Yuri in the cot. He was to have a test called an Electroretinogram. This produced a graph indicating the retinas response to light. 'Yuri's eyes are cosmetically normal other than a slight involuntary jerkiness to their movements.' he told us. This, of course, we had seen on countless occasions for ourselves. We returned to the waiting room and sat in hopeful anticipation. Since his birth I'd prayed every waking moment for a positive outcome.

Perhaps the doctors had all made the same ghastly mistake, and he really was sighted after all.

We were called again; the crisp nurse showed us where to sit while Dr Elkhart showed us the graph he'd just taken. 'In a normal eye the graph moves up and down as it records the response of the retinas.' he said. 'Now look at Yuri's graph, can you see how flat it is?'

'It's flat as a pancake.' Luke said.

'I'm afraid it's as I thought, and more than conclusive. It's the disease I told you about.' The words hit me like so many knives, wounding the very depths of my soul. I looked helplessly at Luke but couldn't speak, as if any further utterance would only cause more damage.

'I'm so sorry; it's an incredibly rare disease.' The doctor said as kindly as possible. We looked at our baby with blank faces and were unable to register the weight behind the flimsy terms. Dr Elkhart said he was going to send us for counselling and advice regarding Yuri's development and care, leading eventually to his ongoing educational needs. He would see us all again for a review in six months time.

There was no operation available. There was no cure for this condition.

I found Luke's hand and knew his grief matched my own fathomless despair. Weeping we sobbed our pointless questions at the doctor.

'I'm so sorry.' he said again. 'I know this has been a great shock, even if you had thought it possible. Take as long as you need.' Yuri gurgled from the cot and blew happy bubbles. They left us to be alone together but the nurse soon returned with two mugs of sweet tea, seemingly the proven panacea for misery. I realised we needed to prove we were able to cope long term with his blindness. Surely this couldn't happen to our perfect, beautiful Yuri. The words I'd heard had to be lies to wound and maim us, to leave us lifeless, wordless, and unable to digest this reality.

The reality was our sheer helplessness, and the cruel truth that no one could ever help Yuri to see.

* * *

Now the sun didn't feel so good, sleep didn't bring rest, and food lost its taste. Luke's warm embrace didn't give comfort, flowers didn't smell sweet, and little Yuri became unsettled. Luke and I nursed our wounds and knew their pain would last a while longer.

Yuri was getting bigger, thriving and learning all the time. At nappy time he stretched and kicked trying to reach the boundaries of his physical abilities. He needed to feel and hear as much as possible, this would provide the baseline from which he could exist and learn and he needed us to help him. In November we attended our first session of family counselling. It was held at a large clinic in a neighbouring suburb. Here we met other families, some with blind or partially sighted children, but a few with a blind parent. An amazing two hours of discovery followed and included stories, tears, laughter and fun. Some of the children at the session were school age, and so confident and happy it filled us both with a fine new valour. Yuri was made a fuss of by everyone there and lapped it up. All of them urged us to be positive, and while keeping him safe to let him be as independent as possible. We came away looking forward to the following month's meeting.

One particular day when the world seemed even kinder two letters arrived on the hall mat. As I consumed the contents a faint ray of hope began to shine once again within my heart. Somehow life has to move forward, I told myself.

Dream Time

Negative events can change us but even in the very midst of despair real fortitude is rarely completely extinguished from the human spirit. Phoenix-like we're able to rise up from the ashes, letting our passions smoulder and burn within us once again.

I took the letters into the kitchen and sat at the table. One had been redirected from Darwin, while the other was local. The one from Darwin had originally been sent from England, was very battered but had somehow survived the long journey. It said *University of Essex* on the envelope and I opened it gingerly to reveal the certificate within. I saw *Modern History Degree, 2:1, Pass with Distinction,* and instantly welled up. It felt like a million years had passed since my arrival at Uncle's with the sole intention of finishing my degree. Today this piece of paper confirmed what I'd dreamed about for so long. In the past year my entire life had changed. I'd experienced more than I could have imagined was possible. Australia was my new home and Luke, Yuri, and Auntie Bea were real family.

I wiped my eyes I wished Luke was home. Then I opened the other letter. It said:

> Dear Rachel,
>
> You don't know me but our mutual friend Ziggy Blatto may have mentioned me. He passed on your Melbourne address from memory so I'm hoping this letter will find you.
>
> I've been tracing my family tree and believe we may share the same ancestor who arrived here with the first fleet in 1788. As we both have the same surname there is a possibility we might be related, even if only distantly.

I would be very interested in meeting to discuss this further if it is agreeable to you. I enclose my address and telephone number and hope to hear from you.
I hope you and your family are well.
Yours faithfully,
Ray Hardy.

Astonishment joined the joy still bobbing around inside me. I vaguely remembered Mr Blatto saying something about a friend of his, but hadn't taken it seriously for a minute. I didn't know if I should meet this man, but then what harm could it do? If it turned out we were related he might even be able to help with some medical history. We could meet somewhere public to be on the safe side. As long as Luke agreed, I decided to arrange it.

I kept busy over the following weeks and wrote letter after letter, along with preparations for our first Christmas with Yuri. I contacted all the people we knew; my parents and Jade, Frances, Daphne Green, all our friends in Darwin, my university tutor, and even my aunt, uncle and Kim in Brisbane. I also replied to Ray's letter. My mother phoned me just before Christmas but somehow sounded different. I thought perhaps she was ill or something. She said how very, very sorry she was to hear the news about Yuri, but what I found remarkable was her insistence that it wouldn't matter as long as he was truly loved. That was really all children needed, she said.

She didn't mention my father and evaded the subject when I asked after him. It seemed Jade was continually pestering her to move to Australia so we could all be together. I spoke with my sister for a few minutes and she sounded very grown up. She told me whatever happened she would be flying over to see me as soon as she was eighteen and independent. The sound of her voice instantly warmed me and I said our chat was my best ever Christmas gift. Oddly, she didn't speak about Father either.

Luke arrived home on 23rd December for the holidays. He'd bought me a beautiful lemon tree in a gold pot. We put it on the back step and decorated it with a few bits of tinsel and some small glass balls. Luke gave Yuri a bit of tinsel to hold and it seemed he was trying to look at it. It was hot out on the back patio that evening. We drank cool beer and tried to feel festive. We drank to our first Christmas in Melbourne and to Yuri's first Christmas on earth. As the light dimmed I felt truly at peace for the first time in weeks. Nestled together as we'd done so many times on the veranda at Monkey Puzzle Street Luke rested his head on my shoulder and we both wished this moment could last forever.

Yuri woke early on Christmas morning and immediately appeared agitated. Still groggy with sleep we wished each other a Happy Christmas.

'Happy Christmas grumpy.' Luke smiled at his son and kissed his brow. 'I hope he's not sickening for something love.' he said.

I switched on the radio hoping for some festive carols. Instead I heard:

"We interrupt this programme with a newsflash! Cyclone Tracy hit the city of Darwin in the early hours of this morning. At least 60% of homes have been destroyed and further damage is still to be assessed. There have been some 40 reported deaths and we expect this figure to rise. Many more have been injured, and the casualty toll is expected to be high. We will bring you more news as it comes in, on this most tragic Christmas day."

'Oh, my God!' Luke shouted the words and leaped from the bed. I saw his face turn ashen and his words rose above the Australian anthem.

'Auntie Bea!' he yelled, 'and my mates!' He sat down heavily beside me and I clung to him. Yuri was whimpering but we remained frozen together. We held each other in empty shock.

'The hotel,' I sobbed, 'what if it got hit?'

'Not only that love,' he said in cracked tones, 'what if we'd stayed up there?'

Chapter 22

Safe in St Kilda, my thoughts went out Darwin. It had been completely flattened, brought to its knees by the brute forces of nature. The phone and power lines were down, and would be out for some time. The outpost town that fought off the Japanese so bravely was no match for a Cyclone as cruel as Tracy. Gudjewg must have been very angry indeed about something. I hoped it had nothing to do with the house on Monkey Puzzle Street. Never too far away from my thoughts, Maisie hovered as if she wanted to confide in me. Her dreams; her story was now imprinted on my memory. It was like something Luke had said about us being joined together, perhaps because we'd been here before. Some links lasted longer than others he said, and might never be explained.

A jolt brought the tram to a grinding halt, interrupting my contemplations. The conductor leapt off the carriage and reattached the long connector rail to the high cable where it had parted company. Some of the passengers muttered about this sharp corner. It seemed the rogue turn made stopping a regular event. I didn't venture into the city much and wasn't bothered about a small delay. From my seat I could see the sweeping parklands just beyond the approaching buildings and the huge Shrine of Remembrance, reaching up to heaven like an ancient temple. I could've happily gazed out on it all day.

The tram shuddered and lunged forward, cracking into life as the power connected. It quickly gained speed, the swaying motion oddly relaxing. I closed my eyes and found my thoughts back in Darwin. We knew Daphne Green had spent the wet in Adelaide as usual but Tracy had left 66 dead, and countless casualties. Impatient to know if our friends were safe a recent note had at last assured us Bea was unhurt. Quite by chance and at the last minute possible she'd decided to visit Bendigo for Christmas. She'd sent us a late card, the note expressing her own relief at the close escape, coupled with desperation over the disaster. She had no idea what would be left of her or Luke's old home when she returned later in January. I hoped she'd get a chance to visit us before she left Victoria.

The tram snaked into the city. I was on my way to meet Ray at a downtown café. After receiving his letter I'd plucked up the courage to call him on the phone. He didn't talk about our possible link but arranged a meeting to discuss it. Yuri was perfectly safe with Luke but now anticipation pinched at my stomach. I wasn't used to being away from him and the usual anxieties threatened to overwhelm me. I took a deep breath and felt slightly better. Perhaps it was meeting this man that really worried me. Maybe he'd found information that proved the blindness came from my family. It might be me, and not Maisie who had harmed him.

I alighted at Spencer Street, turned off into Collins Street and searched for Josie's Coffee House. After a few minutes I noticed it on the opposite side of the street. A well dressed man was sitting at one of the pavement tables. He was looking around him as if expecting someone. He noticed me and smiled, making him appear younger than his probable age.

'Are you Ray?' I said.

He stood up and held out his hand. 'You must be Rachel; I'm very pleased to meet you.' I apologised for my lateness.

'No worries,' he said, 'I'm just grateful you could come.' He ordered cappuccinos to drink. 'The coffee's very good here.' he said with a wink. While we waited he rummaged inside a case and brought out the map he had of his family tree. 'This is *our* family tree.' He was insistent I belonged on it somewhere. I could see the dates went back to mid 1700.

'I'm probably going to be a hopeless source of information,' I said, 'I don't know anything beyond my immediate relatives.'

'Leave it to me,' he said kindly, 'but you may be able to help more than you think.' The coffee arrived in thick, wide cups. It was steaming hot and had chocolate froth. A little almond biscuit sat in each saucer. Ray lifted his cup. 'You won't get coffee like this anywhere else in Melbourne,' he said, 'now, let me show you where I think you fit in to the tree.'

As I listened I realised how enjoyable this was. I felt drawn to Ray and was glad to have met him. Strangely, there was something instantly familiar and safe about him, something only defined by a genuine blood tie. I hoped we were related, that there would be a reason to remain friends. He showed me the forefather he thought had arrived with the First Fleet. Henry Hardy was a convict on HMS Supply, but after being in Australia for seven years had returned to England a married man. He'd wedded Lizzie, a female convict, after they'd both worked out their sentences. It all sounded a bit shocking, but Ray obviously found it fascinating.

'That might well have been the end of the Australian connection,' he said, 'but this bloke had a cousin, Mathew. Mathew's grandson Samuel came out to Victoria at the time of the gold rush, in about 1855. He stayed over here and I'm directly descended from him.'

'Wow,' I said, 'it's quite exciting isn't it?'

'I really enjoy the research. See here Sam had nine children!' He pointed to the paper. Written on the tree in blue ink under Samuel and Constance were the names of four sons and five daughters.

'Samuel read about the gold find near Melbourne and left England immediately. There's a story that says his mother had some inherited wealth and that she had to sell some of her jewellery to pay for his passage.' He stopped for breath and looked wistful for a moment. 'I rather like that story.' he said.

'So do I, but did he make his fortune?'

'He became very rich indeed, and never went back home. Now your family line is probably from the Hardy's who remained in England. I think you could be descended from Henry and Lizzie, or perhaps from a more distant line.' I slumped back in my seat, wanting to know more.

'How do we find out?' I said.

'Well, maybe you could write home? Your parents or grandparents might have some information.' My face fell as I recalled the tenuous link with my father.

'I suppose I could try.' I offered.

'Bonza, that's the spirit!' he said, and rubbed his hands together. 'Now, do you fancy a cake to celebrate being related?'

Dream Time

Before we parted we exchanged a little about our own histories, and made a date to meet again. Ray told me he was 43, unmarried and an only child. He confessed that was the main reason he'd been compelled to look into his family lineage. He was rich, had inherited Samuel's good fortune and hard work in the gold fields. Ray ran a dolphin rescue reserve out at sea where injured animals were nursed back to health and then set free into the open ocean. He assured me the reserve had nothing to do with training or tricks for human amusement because that was something he truly hated. I told him about Yuri but he thought it unlikely he would find much in the way of medical history. Even so, he promised to investigate for any blindness in the family line.

Bitten by Ray's gold rush story I asked Luke if we might visit Ballarat. It promised to be a nice break for all of us. Ray came to supper one weekend and Luke took to him at once. The two men shared the same sport and by the end of the evening Ray had offered to take Luke sea fishing. Yuri got lots of cuddles from our visitor who seemed to enjoy playing the child himself. He told us how disabled youngsters who swam with dolphins sometimes received health benefits. He asked us to perhaps consider taking Yuri when he was older. We agreed Yuri was a real water baby but he was just too tiny to swim in deep water.

Time was on my side, but there were days when I had too much of it. Then guilt hung on me like a heavy cloak while I busied myself round the house. Yuri's condition was no one's fault, but I lashed myself raw with punishment. Angry and confused, my introspection always brought me to the same conclusion, my blame. In the end, surely I was the cause of my own misery.

Every Sunday I heard the church bells peal as I listened in the back garden. I held Yuri and saw his head move from side to side enchanted with their song. In the same church I gave up my prayers for him. In the atmosphere of incense and echoed voices I sat before Our Lady's altar with Yuri on my lap. I hadn't the need to go to a service, simply needed the familiar feel of her gaze. I prayed for him only, as he was my true hero, my only salvation from myself. Days like this I'd forgotten about our friends. Murray and Belle were distant memories and I'd even push Luke to the corner of my mind. But somehow Maisie endured, even though her visits had ceased. I couldn't forget how she'd given me back the ghosts of my past, or how she'd led me into Luke's arms. If two planets collided they'd probably spark off a bright new star. And like an explosion Maisie had torn me apart, only to allow me to grow whole again.

As the weeks passed we heard from more of our friends. Frances phoned and said she would try to find out all she could. Once more she went over our experience at Tennant Creek and said Yuri was able to feel cruelty as a shock wave through his body. We weren't to be fooled regarding his abilities just because he was a baby, she said. In Flintlock's house he'd felt these crimes radiating from the wall. But the scarred man interested her most of all. She'd seen a similar man herself, and it could have been this picture that set off Yuri's cries. If only she could see it for herself, then it might be possible to get a further message.

Dave rang to tell us his phone was back on. 'How's it going mate, oh, thank God you're okay.' I heard the relief in Luke's voice. After the call he gave me the news.

'Well Marty and Vince are okay, and the pub escaped any damage. No real news from Darwin, but Dave thinks the hotel may've taken a hit.'

Dream Time

'Oh no,' I said, 'I've had a bad feeling about it all along. Let's hope Frances can get some information from the police up there.'

By late March the weather cooled and brought light rain from the heavens. Luke chose a weekend to visit Ballarat and as we loaded up the faithful truck I got a surge of excitement. The last time we'd driven any distance was our journey here from down the Track. This by comparison was just a trip but it fuelled my need for adventure. We had no deadlines to meet and the world was waiting to be explored. Yuri sensed we were up to something and gave me a gummy smile. I sat him next to me on the cab seat and buckled him in. His teeth were coming through and he dribbled over his plastic toy.

'Just like our big trip Rach,' Luke called to me as if reading my thoughts.

'But not quite so far, we hope!' I replied. Luke was happy. He whistled a tune as he checked the battery and tyres. It had been a long time since I'd seen him so relaxed.

'All 'A' okay.' He climbed into the cab and started up the engine. The old girl roared like a lioness eager to join a fresh hunt.

We drove out of St Kilda, and out onto the open road. New relief meant I could relax a bit, but other news saddened me. Frances had found out The Drover Hotel suffered terrible damage in the cyclone and Mr Blatto had been killed. Mrs Clarke wasn't at work that night but Mr Blatto had stayed late after dinner service and helped clear up into the early hours of the morning. Perhaps he'd been unaware of just how much danger he was in, or like a ship's captain had stayed stoically at his post, eventually going down with his vessel. Several guests died with him, and many more were injured.

Mrs Clarke had been in bed when the roof of her house ripped off, like a sardine tin being peeled open. Her leg had broken when it was pinned down by falling furniture, but she was now in hospital recovering well. Bea had returned to Darwin sooner than planned to find her house, along with Murray's more or less flattened. She'd turned round and gone straight back to stay with her cousin until building work could begin. I made a mental note to inform Ray of Mr Blatto's death, as I knew they'd been in contact through the work at the dolphin reserve. But as with Murray, I couldn't believe he was really gone.

In the fields were miles and miles of finished sunflowers, hanging their heads in despair having lost their fiery crowns. I forced my head away and recalled my previous thoughts. Thankfully the couple that swapped houses with us had been with friends over the Christmas holiday. On the outskirts of Darwin they took refuge in a storm shelter at this house. I had yet to hear about Biff, Ringo, and Doctor Treadwell.

Yuri was asleep and I closed my own eyes for a moment. To my surprise I found an image of Maisie. She walked slowly and deliberately round a small bushfire and offered up herbs and fruits. It seemed to be a healing ceremony for those who had died or suffered. I'm returning to the land today, I told her silently before I opened my eyes. As for the house on Monkey Puzzle Street, I could only hope it was still standing, silently waiting among the mango trees for Daphne's return.

Life at Queens Park Crescent settled down and Yuri continued to thrive. Weeks and months went by with a now familiar daily routine. Bea kept regular contact and Ray insisted on paying for therapy to help Yuri with his development. He'd been a little late in reaching the babyhood milestones, but otherwise he coped well with his lack of sight. At family counselling he proved to be a surprisingly boisterous child. Here he played with other blind children and loved every minute of it. His hair had grown dark and curly, inducing people to comment on his good looks. Naturally we agreed he was a beautiful child. Nature had been cruel to give him such adorable eyes and strangers were astonished to discover these had no ability to see. But fiercely proud of him we took him with us everywhere and encouraged him to try as many new things as possible.

It seemed like Luke and I were growing apart. The radio played in the evening but we no longer danced as we'd done in Darwin. Our love hadn't disappeared but was dimmed by the cloud of responsibility we shared. The closeness I'd never thought possible was threatened by sadness. And over time our child's condition inevitably eroded our relationship. A sheer weight lay heavily on Luke's shoulders, while my unreasonable guilt did nothing to lighten the situation. But in one thing we both found real joy, our son Yuri. While coping with each day's challenges unlikely letters of encouragement flowed from England. We spoke on the phone most weeks and now and then I spoke briefly to my father. Mother asked after Luke and I told her he was fine and saw my opal ring cloud over. She joked how she would have to kick Father out if he didn't pack up the drink. This was a bit rich coming from her, and I didn't think Jade took it seriously for a moment. We laughed it off together as real sisters would, hoped they would sort it out and stay together. In their relationship my father had taken dominance but perhaps the tables had now turned.

* * *

'Be careful Yuri!' I called, and he turned to grin at me. It was August, and Yuri's birthday. Now two years old he explored the better-known world of his back yard. In most respects he was allowed the same freedom to interact as any other toddler and his life was really not so different from his sighted playmates. With confidence he lunged towards his presents, all other senses eager to suck in every detail. He ran around and emitted little shrieks of delight at everything he felt. They were usually simple things such as a small leaf, a stone or a tiny puddle of rainwater. Today Luke kept a few steps behind, trying not to be overprotective but careful his son didn't trip over the new puppy. Yuri held up everything he found and Luke made a big thing of checking it out. Every so often the tumbling Sasha nudged Yuri with her wet nose. This brought forth peals of joyful giggles. Yuri was fascinated by her soft fur and by teatime the two of them were firm friends.

Daphne Green's birthday card arrived along with her news. Her letter of several pages told how she was making the most of her time in Adelaide. After Cyclone Tracy she'd phoned and told us how her house in Darwin had survived. But although undamaged, it now felt very different to her. Something within it had changed, leaving an eeriness and gloom that was almost unbearable. She didn't think she could go on living there after witnessing the aftermath of this horrific event. She prepared to rent out the house permanently. At that time Biff was in hospital with a broken arm and it seemed Ringo had run away. Biffs' house had lost part of its roof and the garage door had been flung off, lifted away by the storm as if it were no more than a pocket handkerchief. She lodged with him for a while when he came out of hospital, took care of him until his house was fixed. Ringo turned up two weeks later emaciated and flea bitten, but with enough strength to wag his tail at the sight of his master. That night he was given a decent dinner of lamb shank and in the weeks that followed, made a full recovery.

Daphne wrote that now everything was changed and as she grew older that didn't sit comfortably. She'd visited the library and the Town Hall in Adelaide and looked up as much as she could about her name, Green. Her findings revealed an intriguing drama that slowly unfolded over her time there. In the lounge of her rented apartment she'd spread out the names and dates over the floor. The most difficult thing she had to bear was no one to share her discoveries with and she hoped we didn't mind her writing with so much information.

After weeks of gruelling research she kept coming back to one name in particular; that of *Thomas Green*. His birth certificate was dated 20th January 1788, just days before the First fleet landed at Port Jackson. His mother's name was *Lily Green* a convict, while his father had been cited as *Frank Jarvis* an Officer of H.M.S. Supply. This certificate she insisted, was her link with Luke. Thomas had been given the surname of Green, presumably by Lily, and it was from him that Daphne was descended. Luke she thought was a direct descendent of Frank, and she was now trying to find out more about him and his children's lives.

Later she had found a marriage certificate for Thomas and Rosemary Smith in 1813. Thomas was described as a farmer and Rosemary as a spinster. They were 20 and 19 years old respectively at the time of their marriage. She was beginning to feel old, she'd written, and wanted the names on the paper to speak out. She searched through old journals distributed at that time to farming communities and one day found, quite by chance, the name of Thomas Green. The headline said: *March 3rd 1822, Thomas Green witness to massacre of natives.* Daphne wrote how mixed tears of sadness and joy had fallen when she found this article. She'd finally discovered her link to indigenous peoples. The journal explained how Thomas had also been a friend to the natives, reporting the crime even though he might have got killed for doing so.

She explained how she'd taken the midday bus back to her apartment and stuck the family tree on the wall. It was raining outside but she felt radiant. Taking a green felt-tip pen, she outlined Thomas's name so it really stood out. She could even see it from the kitchen several feet away. Misty eyed, she made a jug of strong coffee. The name shone out at her from the lounge, and all the strength and courage of her ancestor began to fill her with inspiration for the future. She promised to keep in contact, and to come and stay with us one day.

My hands were immersed in soap bubbles and I nodded wordlessly for Luke to fetch a dish-towel from the drawer. After Yuri's birthday party there were extra dishes to clean. Bea had come to stay and was reading him a bedtime story. Tonight he was having the first sleep in his new cot-bed, a present from Ray. Luke flicked the dish-towel over his shoulder and perched on a stool. He hummed to himself as he dried the cutlery.

I looked out the window onto the backyard and adjusted my eyes to the light. But I saw no colourful toys or trimmed shrubs, only swaying mango trees and the stone edge of a fishpond. The cup I was holding dropped back into the bowl with a foamy splash.

'Penny for them.' he said, jolting me back to reality. 'That's what Mum used to say.'

'For a moment I was back at Monkey Puzzle Street.' I laughed. 'I saw the back yard.'

He put down the towel and replaced the dry cutlery in its drawer. 'We've come a long way since then, don't you think?' I nodded and continued washing while he dried the wet dishes.

'Will you ever tell Yuri?' I blurted the words as unexpected thoughts stabbed in my head.

'Tell him what, love?' he asked.

'The dreadful thing first sons in your family used to hear.' Even before I'd said it I knew the ritual was over, but I needed to hear him say so.

'I want that knowledge to stop with us.' he said.

'I'm glad.' I didn't look up but could tell I'd been irksome.

'I can tell you want to discuss it.' he said, 'For a long time I thought the blindness was all part of the curse, the final bit of punishment for the Trophy murder. But now I'm not so sure. I do think now we've been given this child things will somehow change for the better.' I sighed with relief.

'I feel that way too, but I need to know, do you blame me in any way for his blindness?' I raised my head and saw the shock on his face.

'No, of course not. For God's sake, have you been carrying that around all this time?'

'Sometimes, I still feel guilty,' I said, 'even after all the counselling.' The times I'd thought about a miracle cure were over.

'It's okay,' he said, 'sometimes I feel really angry. I didn't want you to see it, so I buried myself in my work. I'm sorry love, I should've been here more, given you more support.'

'I just need to know you still love me.' His kiss held all I needed to convince me.

'Can you forgive me?' he said.

'There's nothing to forgive. As long as we're together I know we'll be okay.' A long time later we drew apart and Luke cupped my face in his hands.

'We must teach our little boy to be aware of the past, but not to feel responsible for it.' he said. 'He loves people; all we need to do is encourage him to always think like that.'

'He sees the world in such a special way.' I agreed, and Luke squeezed me close again. I could feel his power radiating towards me and wondered why I'd ever doubted him. His eyes looked deep into mine, and all at once I was becalmed in a sea of blue. Luke was right; we'd come a long way.

And since leaving Darwin something indefinable had seeped into my blood, had crawled under my skin, and had captured my imagination.

It was Australia.

Chapter 23

Just as in some eastern cultures, so in the western world some say as one soul leaves this Earth, another arrives. From the beginning of mankind, tears have rolled from men and women; tears of sorrow and fear. But those beings who wrought cruelty and vengeance on the creation that surrounds them are not to be feared, for more than most, they need the light that can be brought forth only through love. All cultures possess beings who are enlightened, but once in a while an especially gifted soul prepares to arrive on earth with the one intention of sending out light and peace into the world.

When the world was created the Ancestor Spirits changed into trees, stars, rocks, water holes, and caves. These became the sacred places of Aboriginal culture. In the same way ancient Britain's worshipped the sun and the moon. They were greatly revered, as were the planets, stars, and all of nature. As in indigenous cultures today animals killed for food were honoured. They were respected for their sacrifice and surrender in allowing mankind to expand. Places of worship and thanksgiving were often placed at a particular spot we now recognise as the crossing or convergence of power, or ley lines. Present day churches and cathedrals still occupy these sites and the energy from them still links us to our ancestors; to our past and present, to the people and to the land.

This huge continent had waited patiently for centuries to be found. I hoped one day to share in some of her secrets. I found I was asking Luke to take us outback more and more often, for it was only here I felt connected to the world. This was God's own church; his living breathing creation, unlike the plaster effigies I'd worshiped. The old truck was used to carrying provisions and seemed to enjoy the challenge of each fresh journey. Sometimes we stopped to boil up the billycan and rested if we found some shade. Out in the bush I found myself feeling closer to Maisie again but now it was I who brought her to mind.

Our house squeaked and ticked happily, and now felt like a comfy old chair around us. Meanwhile, time flowed away like running water. Any designs I might have once harboured for a family in suburbia had at least in part reached fruition. But my not so distant aspiration to teach history had evaporated like the desert rain. Still, I wanted to believe the world could open up for us. Our pilgrimage with Yuri was only beginning and already he made us live to the full. For his sake as much as our own it was vital to stay strong, and every day I gave thanks for this wonderful child. Luke discussed his new business idea with Ray. He wanted to design special gardens for disabled children and called them *Sensory Gardens* because they were planted with perfume and texture in mind. He took his plan to the Parks and Gardens Department and they granted him a commission to work as a private designer. That meant any work done on the projects had to be in his time off, but the salary was of a better rate.

Soon he had completed his second garden in the central quadrangle of the Ophthalmic Hospital.

Six years had passed since Murray's death and Yuri was really growing up. He was somehow able to connect to all things and often seemed to understand them far better than we did. Sasha guarded him continually and helped him to find things like shoes and his favourite toy. They played together in the back yard for hours, Yuri throwing a ball to her when she barked to indicate her direction. After retrieving the ball she dropped it solidly on his feet.

When Luke got home from work we often drove to the beach and went swimming. Yuri had always loved water and swam like a fish. In the water sight didn't seem to be an issue in spite of the huge waves. He splashed around and swam underwater for hours as long as he knew Luke was near. Listening for his voice the two of them swam side by side to the shore, but once on dry land he needed Sasha to be his guide again. Luke became unpopular when he had to call an end to the outing. Yuri would then bellow and cry tragically, causing onlookers to glare in our direction.

I was amazed at how he adapted to his blindness. He could even sense the time of day from the sun's angle on his face. Sometimes more in tune with Sasha than his parents, dog and boy spent hours together. But for this I was very grateful. They needed no awkward words or rules between them and until he started school they hardly left each other's side. Now Uncle Ray was a regular visitor and Yuri ran headlong into him as soon as he heard his voice at the door. He became animated when he recognised familiar sounds such as the truck pulling onto the drive. At the group we attended the parents commented on his affectionate, warm nature.

The doctors seemed pleased with his progress and passed comments on how as parents we'd adjusted to his needs. But in my heart I longed for the miracle of sight. I wanted him to see the things I put in his hands, not just listen to my limited descriptions. Frances had said he was gifted and he proved this over time. If I gave him a piece of cloth to hold he placed his other hand over it and told me the colour. I tried to catch him out one day with a multicoloured scarf but after a few seconds he laughed and said, 'This has lots of colours.' I was in no doubt he possessed an unusual intuition.

He'd grown into a handsome boy, tall for his age and with dark olive skin. His sightless eyes were still deep brown; in this Luke said he took after me. Now his hair was almost black, with even tighter curls. These danced and swayed in the breeze, knotted up and caused misery when brushed. Other times he cried and wailed for no real reason, and Luke played his favourite music in an attempt to placate him. Ray urged us to take him swimming with the dolphins, thought he was old enough and saw his obvious unbridled love for the sea. But I remained nervous for his safety. I wanted to wait until he was a little bigger and a stronger swimmer. Luke agreed, saying we would all know when the time for that occasion was right.

The time I'd spent fretting over Luke saw my relationship with my mother improve. The years had delivered a stronger bond and a certain depth of trust. Now we exchanged letters every month and her package always enclosed a note or card from Jade. Her news one day confided she and my father were divorcing. She'd waited until all the details had been sorted out to tell me. They'd separated some time back when she'd given up the booze. The split was acrimonious, not least because of the financial settlement she was due. The hardware stores he'd inherited from his father and the business income made a tidy sum before the house and contents were even considered.

I rang her and said how sorry I was. Mother said she would wait out a few more months. The five years without him had gone quickly and once over she could file for divorce without any challenges. I asked her what had caused their initial separation, and nearly fell off the chair. They'd argued over me, she said. Uncharacteristically she'd fought my corner, told him she should never have allowed his punishments to go unchallenged, admitted if she'd not drunk so much maybe she could've stopped him. Her confession was enough for me to trust her again. I felt the grubby torment peel away, much like scraping soil from the soles of my shoes.

There were other reasons for their break up. Father had become violent, especially after she gave up the drink. As time went on she worried he might take his anger out on Jade and eventually got all the locks changed while he was at work. She bundled up his belongings, shoved them into suitcases and put them by the front gate. This would have required great courage on her part, not least because of the nosy neighbours. They saw the entire drama unfold from behind their twitching curtains.

I was sorry Jade had been through this alone, without a sister to comfort her. But it seemed she was adjusting to life without Father and was doing well at school. I was very happy to hear it, and much relieved my own treatment had at last been considered. I agreed to send a recent photo and reminded Mother she and Jade had promised to visit one day. Ray had been compiling more information for his family tree. Here mother had helped out considerably, managing over time to copy birth and marriage certificates, even enlisting help from a few amenable relatives of Father. She insisted this had helped her get through the break up.

Yuri brought the post from the hall and placed it carefully on the kitchen table. At the top of the pile was a letter from Bea. She'd made the decision to sell her re-built house and wanted to rent a flat near us. She wrote how much she missed us, and how she didn't want to lose touch. I wrote back that day and urged her to come and live with us in Queens Park Crescent, we had plenty of room and she was after all, family. Her news gave Luke an extra spring in his step and he began cracking little jokes and whistling softly between his teeth. Stupidly I'd put to one side his need of a mother. Bea had been as much to him after Ruth passed away. They were so casual together it was easy to lose sight of the devotion they shared. She'd lost her home, Luke and Murray all within a few months. Dear Bea received my letter and came directly into our open arms. I had a feeling her arrival was the start of even better times to come.

A call came late one evening from an excited Jade, who told me the divorce had finally begun. As soon as it was settled both she and my mother planned to book a flight to visit us, but she could hardly wait another minute. Mother had to wait for something called a *Decree Nici*. She said this was the most boring part of all for her. She saw Father twice a week after school when he usually took her out for a meal. Her favourite food was Italian, especially pizza. Father was living simply in a flat over one of his hardware stores, the one in Purley. He kept telling her she should wear proper clothes as she'd started to buy punk fashion. I'd seen such things on the TV. They appeared to consist of fabrics or plastic held together with safety pins. She told Father he was a drag; that he should be thankful she'd not lied about her age to get all sorts of face piercing. I could tell she was headstrong but perhaps in some ways that wasn't a bad thing. The world was changed and people's lives were changing with it. As for Father, it seemed he'd lost everything apart from his share in the business. That, I found was really rather sad.

As if time had rewound, Bea dusted the furniture she knew so well. Yuri followed her everywhere, unable to see her bright housecoat but elated by her presence.

'Shall I dust the Grandad stone?' she said, asking his permission.

'No, I'll do it.' He grabbed it and wiped it on his shirt. Then he held it up to his ear.

'I'll swear he's chatting to Murray,' Bea said, 'it's uncanny, that's what it is.'

Luke laughed. 'Not as uncanny as his disappearing trick.' he said.

'Oh yes, that sounds like magic.' Bea had a twinkle in her eye.

'Always happens at bedtime,' I continued, 'strange, that.' We sniggered but Yuri didn't notice. He was engrossed with Murray's stone.

'What did Grandad say today?' Luke picked him up and sat him on his knee.

'He likes the healing gardens Dad.'

'Does he indeed, he knows about them does he?'

'Yes, he knows about the new one, at the school.'

'But I haven't even told Mama about that one son,' he said, somewhat bemused. Yuri shrugged and bounced down from his knee. He skipped out to the garden with Sasha. Bea's gaze followed him, and her face was a picture.

'Now that's what I mean by uncanny.' she said.

That evening I phoned Frances and we discussed Yuri's progress. She echoed Ray's enthusiasm to take him out to the dolphins and thought we should do it as soon as possible. Thrilled we'd got Bea and Ray's support she had a really good feeling about our future. Life had already proved to me Yuri's resilience. He was never downcast for long and enjoyed every breath of his existence while love flowed from his heart and strengthened us all.

Darwin had slid away from me along with the shadowed memory of Maisie. All that prevailed were my darkened memories of Monkey Puzzle Street. Even they now followed me at a distance. But together they had penetrated my armour, had entered my soul and had entangled me in their eternal song. The vast, limitless oceans of the world link all the continents and islands together. Through this mass swim our guardians, the whales and dolphins. They govern the planet and have existed since the dawn of time. They are loved and revered by those who understand their power.

They swim, play, raise and feed their young. They travel huge distances, singing as they swim. The oceans know of their song because it is the Song of Life. It travels to every shore and all the sea creatures learn of it. The vibration is one of harmony and love. Humans can sometimes hear it but usually make too much noise. But if you listen to a sea shell there is an echo, a memory of the most ancient Ballard of all.

I could hear Ganadja, the Queen of the dolphin's song. Her voice filled my head and made my ears ring. I was afloat in the abyss and she was getting closer. She leaped through the water, swam faster and faster towards me. I could see her power, the sheer majesty as she flew from the waves and crashed on the water like a speedboat. Her song was louder than the rip of the waves, fiercer than the sun. I was frightened. She was nearly upon me when a soft voice brought me back into the kitchen.

'Rachel honey, did you hear me?' It was Bea, calling from Yuri's room.

I got up from the chair and felt my legs shake. I noticed the wattle in the back yard and how the sun made it shine golden like so many fluorescent pompoms.

'Sorry Auntie,' I called, and yawned. 'I must have dropped off for a second.' I soon joined her in Yuri's room.

'Hey, you'll never guess what this little guy just said!' I smiled blearily.

'No, I can't guess! What did you say, little man?'

He held his ears and grinned, his sign of excitement. 'Mama, the dolphins are coming, the Queen is bringing the dolphins!' He skipped round his toys in a little dance.

'Wow,' I said, 'that's right sweetheart, she told me the same thing, just a minute ago.'

'Where? Where did she tell you?' he said banging his fists impatiently.

'She told me in the kitchen.'

Bea was looking pleased, if slightly confused. Yuri ran from the room whooping with joy and found Sasha. I guessed he was telling her the news. Bea and I started to laugh. 'I'm not going to ask what all that was about,' she said, 'but it sounded like a sign to me.'

'I think it's time for that swim, don't you?' Her face nodded approval, but she looked serious.

'You know, I should have mentioned this before, but what with Yuri's eyesight problems and all, well, it just didn't seem that important.'

'What is it Auntie?' I said.

'Well, it's that warrior Murray saw just before he died. I thought he might've mentioned it to you or Luke, anyway.'

'What about it?'

'He only mentioned it once, he saw the same thing the night Luke was born.' My mouth dropped open. 'So he never told you?' I shook my head. 'Or Luke?'

'No, I'm not sure he knows about it.'

'Have you ever thought you and Luke have been chosen for something?'

I looked into her bright eyes. 'It's strange Auntie, I often think we were meant to have Yuri, but I'm not sure why.'

The speedboat *Little Eva* crashed through the waves and searched for a dolphin pod. Yuri sat calm and still beside the quivering Sasha. She had her own doggy life jacket especially for the occasion and was about to burst with excitement. Luke was with Ray at the front of the boat gazing out to the horizon. Bea sat the other side of Yuri, her teeth chattering in the wind. My stomach was numb with fear and I swallowed back the sour, salt air. Yuri immediately sensed my angst and patted my hand like a parent.

'Don't worry Mama, turn off your mind and think with your heart.' he said.

'I'll try to, little man.'

Sasha started to bark and the noise ripped through my ears. Luke settled her at the helm where she stayed for the rest of the journey emitting small squeaks of anticipation. Ray stayed up front with the skipper and checked the wet suits. Bea wasn't planning to swim; she'd brought her camera to take some snaps. Ray told us we mightn't see any dolphins that day, or even the day after. I didn't relish the idea of a second trip and hoped he was wrong. Sometimes it was as if the Queen herself had orchestrated the entire event.

'We're off to meet the dolphins,' Yuri squealed happily, as if reading my thoughts. He'd felt Luke come home dampened most nights, either from a cloudburst or from walking past garden sprinklers. Yuri thought this was very amusing and made exhaustive jokes about it. The boat lurched on a wave and I cradled him in my arms as we sped out to the open sea. Something magical was in the air, and my courage ignited.

An hour passed before the skipper pointed towards the horizon. It looked like dolphins bobbing through the water. Ray checked with binoculars and confirmed it was a pod. I struggled into the wetsuit and Luke helped me with the life jacket. Yuri insisted on having his mask and snorkel as well. It was all Luke could do to stop him leaping off the boat.

'They're coming mama, they're coming!' he cried.

'I know sweetheart, wait a minute now.'

Sasha licked my hands as I fitted her life jacket. Little Eva's engines had stopped and she listed and bobbed on the swell. I began to feel nauseous. It was possible to really see the dolphins now but it was some time before we drifted close enough to weigh anchor. Eventually we were ready and the sea turned as calm as a millpond. Below us the dolphins glided to and fro, foamy water flowing over their silk-like skin. Ray plopped into the water and Luke followed soon after. He asked me to lift Yuri over the side of the boat. Like a clockwork doll I picked up my child and kissed his cheek. I passed him to Luke. In his arms they swam a little way out from the hull. Bea dropped Sasha into Ray's arms then helped me onto the landing board with words of encouragement. The water was cold, even with the suit.

'Are you okay Yuri?' I called.

'He's fine love, I've got him,' Luke said.

I took Sasha's lead and struggled over to Ray. Slowly the dolphins swam up to us and one by one checked us out. But somehow they seemed to know it was Yuri who needed them.

Ray gave instructions to stay as still as possible and even Sasha behaved herself. I held her near the landing board in case of doggy panic. The dolphins became more adventurous, gradually swimming round our little group and giving the occasional nudge with a snout. Sasha sniffed them and woofed softly as she floated in the water.

'What happens now?' Bea hissed from the landing board.

The shore was invisible miles away, and all around us stretched the immensity of the ocean and the vast, deep blue sky.

Chapter 24

The sea remained calm and I detected only the faintest breeze. The life jackets kept us afloat, but I had to move my legs to keep warm. The skipper watched us from Little Eva along with Bea, who'd started to take photographs. I floated in a watery dream, bobbed like a jettisoned cork in another dimension. We spoke little, hoping the silence encouraged the dolphins. I kept my eyes firmly on Yuri but as they closed in on us I became mesmerised by their grace. Pure joy seemed to flow out of them and into my body. It moved through all of us and threaded us together. I glanced at Luke and saw he was already smiling over in my direction.

The sleek bodies circled once more and created a fountain of love within my heart. I wanted to drift there forever, to only hear the slapping of the waves and feel the tenderness I couldn't now leave. Their noises finally opened my eyes. Without hesitation Yuri made a similar click back.

'They're singing!' he called.

Before I managed to reply a large dolphin swam towards him and in a flash flicked him out of the water with her snout. He squealed and flopped into the middle of a group, and was carried away.

I screamed, 'Yuri!' He clung to a fin, his head drowning beneath the waves. I panicked and shouted in vain.

'Oh my God! Please do something Ray, Luke!' I dropped Sasha's lead and dived into the cold water. Through the bubbly murk all I saw were fins, tails and laughing faces. My little boy was gone. Tears blinded me now as I rose choking to the surface of the waves. Luke swam over to me.

'I think he's okay,' he said.

'Hold on Rachel,' Ray called, 'wait, just a second.'

'But they're drowning him!' I sobbed. I could see his hair just above the water and plunged towards him again, but Luke grabbed my life jacket and held me to him.

'He can't drown: look, he's wearing his snorkel. Can't you see what they're doing?'

I looked. Yuri was floating now, alone in the water while several dolphins had swum close up to him. They surrounded him, appeared engaged by his head. His mask and snorkel had come off, and I held my breath as I watched. Very gently, a cream dolphin reached up and touched both his eyes with its snout. Those closest swam round him for a moment before leaping over the waves to join the rest of the waiting pod.

The cream dolphin moved alongside him and Yuri held onto its fin. Suddenly he was in his father's arms again. This larger, almost golden creature dived and disappeared underwater.

'That was something else.' Ray said, 'And that big female, I'm sure I've seen her before.'

Sasha, who'd been extremely patient all this time now swam up to Yuri and licked his sullen features. We waited, but he didn't respond. The foamy waves cradled his body like a blanket and he remained limp in Luke's arms. The pod looked up before finally swimming away. I could've sworn they were laughing.

'You said he was okay.' I said, stroking my son's pale cheek.

'I think he may have just passed out.' Ray said in an attempt to placate me. I didn't like to agree but he did seem to be sleeping peacefully.

'Let's get him back on the boat,' Luke said, 'Rach, you go first and I'll pass him up to you.' Bea helped me change him while the skipper started up the boat and headed for home.

'What in thunder happened out there?' she asked. I told her it looked like he'd got knocked out during the action. 'Strike me,' she said, 'but if it's any help I've got most of it on camera.' We struggled out of our wetsuits in silence and Sasha shook seawater all over us.

'He'll be alright, won't he?' Luke asked me, possible problems hitting home.

'I hope so love, but as soon as we get home we must call the doctor.' My voice choked with emotion.

'We can do better than that.' Ray interjected, 'I'll get the skipper to radio ahead to the hospital.'

Engines roaring, Little Eva surged through the swelling waves towards the shore. The pod rejoined us and swam alongside for a while, a gesture I found strangely touching. The large cream one raced to the front of the pod. She looked up at me holding Yuri, a royal glint in her eye. She held my eyes in a timeless gaze, one that enclosed the secrets of maternal power. I hoped she brought reassurance, not my final punishment. Ray called back to us from the stern and had to shout to be heard.

'I've never seen anything like that in 20 years of field trips!' he yelled. 'They usually just do a bit of gentle prodding. I tell you it's a sorry revelation to me.' He looked over at Yuri, still sleeping apparently unharmed in my arms. 'A sorry revelation, Rachel,' he said, 'and I feel responsible.' The sea whipped up over the bow as we flew through the swelling tide. His sad expression looked beyond Yuri to where the dolphin pod was now swimming, far, far away.

Yuri slept solidly for twelve hours. When the doctor couldn't rouse him he concluded a possible concussion and wanted to keep him under observation. If he woke or was sick, we were to let the nurses know straight away. Otherwise it was best to let him sleep it off, and hope he had sustained no permanent damage.

My feelings of dread had returned along with my shame. I'd been irresponsible and foolish to allow such a risky excursion. I wanted time to be turned back a day so I could have my little boy back. I needed him to wake so I could see he was unharmed. I appealed to Luke for some words of comfort but he said all we could do was to wait. Perhaps he also felt I was to blame; it was hard to tell. He wrung out a cool flannel for Yuri's head and we sat with him in anxious silence.

Bea had fallen asleep but I knew she'd be awake in an instant if needed. I clasped my hands together and prayed at Yuri's bedside, as I'd prayed at Murray's hospital bed and in all the churches I'd visited. I heard the holy bells ring that night in the distance. I prayed their song would reach Yuri's ears to make him open his eyes. Everything must turn out right I thought, after all we've been through. But the harder I prayed the more the silence around me drowned my sense of reason.

It was 4.30 am. Ray had left some time ago, taking Sasha home with him. He'd said something about checking

Dream Time

through his dolphin files and photographs. He wanted to look at some footage taken years back at an unusual dolphin encounter. He'd watch the reel and also look at similar events in articles and books he kept. I couldn't see what possible help it would be, but guessed he just needed to be busy. He assured us he would report back the following morning and made us promise to ring him if there was any change.

Bea was awake and held his little hand while I stroked his hot face. Luke had gone to ask the nurses for some tea. I found him some time later asleep in the day room, slumped across two chairs. It seemed silly to wake him. I took a fresh brew back to Bea.

'No change,' she said, shaking her head as Yuri continued in slumber. 'Why don't you join Luke and close your eyes for a while?'

Reluctantly I joined Luke and settled down on one of the chairs. I tried hard to empty my mind. I didn't want any visions or reassurances from Maisie, surely she'd done enough. I prayed over and again for my child to wake. Please wake up, I implored, so that everything can go back to how it was. Terrible dreams writhed through my mind as I tried to sleep. As if in a dream within a dream, a small child came to me and tugged at my nightclothes. It was Yuri, but different to the child I knew. Luke, Ray and Bea were also there, happy and crying and hugging Yuri. I could see how he would live to become a really great man.

Someone was shaking me, but I was afloat in the sea. I tried to find Yuri and dived deeper and deeper until there was no air left in my lungs. I'd lost him and there was no time to resurface. My life was fading, my dreams dashed to oblivion. Suddenly I opened my eyes and Luke was in front of me. He gesticulated wildly and pulled at me to get up.

'Quick Rach, come and see Yuri!'

'Has he woken up?' I said, trying to reach consciousness.
'Better than that love, he can see!'

I ran on powerless legs. In slow motion I reached his bed, heart beating out of my chest. He was sitting up looking at a picture book.

'Oh my God, when did this happen?' I appealed to Luke.

'Just minutes ago. I think things are fuzzy but he really can see, and he's hungry.'

I kissed Yuri's head while tears exploded silently down my cheeks. In turn Luke embraced me and we exchanged our deep relief.

'Thank God he's alright.' My words were almost inaudible.

Yuri looked up, appeared to see me and said, 'Mama, pretty Mama.' He pointed to a page in the book. 'Auntie said it's a dog, is it like Sasha?'

'What colour is it?' Luke asked. Yuri put his hand over the picture before he looked at it again.

'Yellow?' he said, and I tried to speak but couldn't. Had this really happened, or was I still asleep, lost in another dream?

'Oh clever boy, that's right.' Bea said. Yuri was allowed some water but was asleep again before long. The nurse said he could have some food once the doctor had seen him. Bea went to phone Ray. Pretty soon we were all together again, waiting for a visit from Dr Elkhart.

Outside the world continued as normal as if nothing could stop the sequence of events that made up a day. Children walked to school chatting happily as they passed below in the street. Postmen delivered the mail and commuters travelled to work in the morning sunshine. Ray brought in some very welcome croissants which we ate in the day room. Meanwhile Dr Elkhart gave Yuri a detailed examination. He'd been seen only three months previously when the usual no change was declared. The doctor seemed to take an age with him. Eventually he joined us in the day room.

'Well g'day everyone.' he said, making a disturbance as he bustled into a chair. 'Sounds like the little fellow gave you quite a fright, but he seems to have recovered remarkably well. He'll need to be checked out properly at the Ophthalmic Hospital you understand.' Here he paused for breath and Bea passed him some coffee.

'Yes,' I said, 'that's fine, but what do you think happened?' The words rasped against my dry throat.

'Well, I think I've got some very good news,' he continued, 'because my initial examination shows his eyes have regained near normal sight. I have to admit I'm dumbfounded as to how this has happened, and can only hope it will last.'

'I knew it!' Luke ejected, punching the air in victory. He banged the table triumphantly with his fist. The outburst produced a smile from the doctor.

'Try not to get your hopes up too soon.' he said, 'I've never seen an occurrence of this type so can't say if it's a temporary or complete remission. As for the reason behind it, it's possible the bang to the head was a contributing factor. We'll keep him in for a few more hours and if he remains stable he can go home. But I must stress to keep him quiet, as even normal life will seem chaotic to him.'

Later that day we brought Yuri home. Keeping him calm wasn't an easy task as he wanted to see what everything in the house looked like. He asked to see colours, the garden and of course Sasha. All the details he'd been unable to take in before were becoming clearer. But most of all he wanted to look at all of us. He kept turning from one person to another then held firmly onto his ears. A fair amount of screaming went on if we moved too quickly. We could see how difficult it was and tried to slow down. He'd never seen life in motion and needed to acclimatise to how everything looked and moved.

By the evening we were all exhausted and ended up in a group nap on the sofa. Yuri was put to bed and we said our goodnights as I tucked him in. He dropped off to sleep immediately, clutching his toy crocodile. Bea had collected up the mail but I was so tired I hardly acknowledged her say there was a letter from England.

That evening I became more buoyant as Ray showed us some footage from his archives. The cine film flickered over the lounge wall. It showed a pale dolphin approach a child to nudge her in the ribs. The film was some ten years old and the girl had leukaemia. Ray had dug out newspaper reports following the swim that claimed she'd been cured. I had to look twice but he said the animal had a dent in her dorsal fin.

Another sighting was recorded in a book called *Dolphin Magic Tales*. It described a dolphin with a dented fin and a youth of 15. The boy had a breathing disease and needed medication every day. His parents took him swimming to try and strengthen his lungs but the condition was getting worse. Out at sea the pale dolphin gently slapped his chest using her tail and in the weeks that followed he progressed to a full recovery. Ray seemed convinced both cases showed the same dolphin we had seen. I was satisfied that when she showed up something miraculous took place.

A week later we received Yuri's test results from Dr Elkhart. His sight was for the most part restored and his eyes showed no residual damage. The ophthalmic team were completely baffled. They wanted him to have further tests as he grew older and three monthly reviews with Dr Elkhart. None of them believed this new sight would last.

Yuri slowly adjusted to his new life. He loved going out more than anything but was frightened of cars and trams. Dr Elkhart said it was just a question of time before he became acclimatised to our pace of life. He started school well and made lots of friends. In the evenings I gave him extra tuition while Bea prepared the supper. She was truly as good as any parent to us. Weeks passed before one day I remembered Mother's letter. After reading it I'd tried phoning but got the unobtainable signal for days. Life took over and I forgot about it, until now. I rummaged in the sideboard drawer, found the envelope and took out the letter. I gasped as I re-read it, hurried into the kitchen and checked the calendar. Bea was folding laundry on the table. I let out a loud groan.

'What's up love?' she said.

'Mother and Jade are arriving in three days; I've just remembered her letter!' I passed it to her.

'Jeeze, you're right, and it says they're coming for good.'

'What? Are you sure, Auntie?'

'See for yourself,' she said, 'what're you going to do? There isn't enough room here for both of them. Why don't you turf me out, I can stay at Shirley's in Bendigo.'

'No Auntie, that's not going to happen, this is your home now.' I said as firmly as I could. Her face appeared moved and she reached into her pocket.

'Well, if you're sure Rach.'

'I'm more than sure, and I know we can ask a favour from Ray.'

'Oh, you've just reminded me,' she said, 'I got the photos back from the developers.' She rummaged in her shopping bag and pulled out the pictures.

'Now, just look at this.' She passed me a snapshot of the gold tinted dolphin.

Her body was arched up out of the water and I could clearly see a dent in the dorsal fin. 'Now, if that's not the same as the one in Ray's film I'll eat my hat!' she laughed.

Chapter 25

The doors to Melbourne airport swished open and we stepped onto the hard, shiny floor. Yuri emitted shrieks of echoed delight and made Luke walk him in and out until the novelty wore off. Bea and Ray were at Queens Park Crescent, anxiously awaiting our return. Ray was looking forward to our visitors staying for as long as they wanted. He'd offered his hospitality before I'd even asked and said how much room there was at his place. In any case he now spent much of his time with us. Mother and Jade could have the run of the place he said, as long as they tidied up behind them.

With Yuri between us, we took his hands in ours and made our way to the arrivals lounge. It struck me how many people had made their way to Australia over the last 150 years. This of course included my own family, Luke's and Ray's. Uncle Sid and Aunt May had come over in the sixties as *Ten Pound Poms*, I'd flown over in the autumn of 1973 and now Mother and Jade were about to arrive at any moment. My stomach had churned all morning in nervous anticipation. Now it tightened in a vice-like grip as a loudspeaker announcement told of the landing of flight BA963 from London Heathrow.

Since I could remember we'd been like a broken pot that couldn't be mended, the pieces fragmented, lost far and wide. Now our separate paths led us to being joined again. A broken pot can hold nothing until it's somehow fixed. Perhaps this was the start of our healing. The segments might join up and with luck even stick together. People started to spill into the arrivals lounge, tired, pale looking people pushing piled up cases on airport trolleys. I tightened my hold on Luke's hand and he hoisted Yuri up onto his shoulders.

I saw Jade first. She'd obviously dyed her hair as it was darker than her pictures and she wore thick eye shadow. What must've been Mother beside her looked quite different, even from her recent photos. She'd gained weight and wore clothes of her age range. She looked more like a real mum than I'd ever seen her. Jade noticed our frantic waves and they hurried to us. We hugged and kissed each other if tentatively and said what a long time it had been.

'You look so grown up.' I told my smiling sister.

'I never dreamt you'd end up with these young men!' mother said, and we laughed. We led them out, through the crowds and into the car-park. Yuri skipped along happily holding hands with Jade. Mother nodded in Yuri's direction once he was in the car.

'He doesn't seem, I mean he looks fine doesn't he?' It hit me she didn't know.

'I meant to say before but in all the excitement,' I began.

'We've got some amazing news,' Luke said, 'we think Yuri is cured!' And then we just couldn't stop talking as there was so much to say, and so many questions to answer.

They settled in comfortably at Ray's but soon rented a little house closer to us. Mother surprised me saying they were intent on staying, insisting they had no reason to return to Croydon. For the first time in my memory Mother applied for a job. She was taken on by one of the city banks as a counter assistant. She brushed up on her keyboard skills and impressed her employer with an above average speed. She was thrilled to find how enjoyable the job was and the bank told her they'd be willing to pay for advanced courses. Ray and Bea offered to sponsor them for citizenship. Luke had started to sponsor me after Yuri's birth but we'd not heard from the authorities since we left Darwin. It seemed this might be a good time to chase it up.

Despite her punk appearance Jade had achieved well at school and was of above average intelligence. Like most teenagers she got the sulks and spent more time than anyone else on the sofa, but she was great with Yuri. Above all she shared his fondness for games. They played together for hours and I never heard a cross word. Jade taught him to play soccer and he took her swimming and taught her how to dive. Sometimes Sasha leaped into the waves making sure they were safe then galloped over the sand to shake cold water over my body. Jade enrolled at the local high school and was told after a term she would easily pass to university. Surprisingly her eccentric appearance didn't faze her teachers; she made lots of new friends and said she felt quite at home. But secretly I thought she missed Father, after his calls she became sad, withdrawn and moody.

It was my sister who told me about Yuri's name, that it meant *Peace*. She'd learned about names and their meanings at school. She said it had Russian roots but was probably an Aboriginal name long before that. I showed surprise but knew in my heart that Maisie had suggested it long ago. The conversation took place over dinner and Luke received the news with as much delight as I did.

'I already knew that Mama.' Yuri said, and I thought he was trying to join in with our discussion.

Yuri had become quite a celebrity at the hospital and soon all the staff knew his name. Dr Elkhart was very pleased with him and told him he was a star patient. I found myself exhausted teaching him so much but dear Jade never tired of showing him new things. She had the energy of youth. Yuri hardly stopped, loved to run around and explored all he could every day. His thirst for knowledge was helping at school and before long I held a higher hope for his academic future.

The phone was ringing. Bea was in the garden pegging out washing, while I was preparing lunch. Sasha bounded past me with her ball. She looked for Yuri, unable to grasp he was at school. I thought it might be Ray on the line and was surprised it was Yuri's teacher. She asked if I could come in to see her that afternoon, if someone else from the family could collect Yuri after lessons. My heart jumped as I thought about his sight.

'Is anything wrong?' I said.

'No, he's fine. I'm sure it's nothing to worry about, it's just I'd like you to see something he painted.' We made a time for 3pm and Bea offered to bring Yuri home. 'Don't go fretting now,' she said, 'you know what kids are like. It's probably one of his crocodile pictures; you know how he makes them gory.' We laughed and agreed it was bound to be something trivial.

'I won't bother Luke about it until he gets home. He's working on a new garden and won't need any distractions.' I said.

I met Mrs Brooks at the school reception and she led me to her classroom. 'Thank you for coming in,' she said, 'As I mentioned earlier, I'm sure it's nothing to worry about, but I wanted you to see for yourself. Can I ask you, if it's not a rude question, have you any black relatives?'

'No, that is not that I'm aware of anyway.'

'It's just that he has got quite a dark skin, hasn't he?'

'Yes,' I conceded, 'but what's that got to do with anything?' She was beginning to annoy me.

'Take a look at what he drew yesterday in class. The subject was family.' She pulled out a picture and laid it before me. Instantly a cruel horror entered my being. I looked again at the drawing then to Mrs Brooks aghast. It was my last dream, as plain as day there on the paper. He'd painted a black woman, heavily pregnant and fleeing from white men on horses. The men had guns and the one in the lead had a long black scar down his face.

'Are you alright?' she said, 'Can I get you a glass of water?'

'I thought it was finished,' I said quietly as she left the room. She returned with the water.

'I'm sorry it shocked you, but that's why I had to call. There's one more, but this one's much nicer.' She placed a painting of dolphins in front of me and I took a deep breath. 'It's easy to see why he did this,' she continued, 'because of his sight.'

'Yes,' I agreed, 'it's lovely. Perhaps he was upset when he did the other one? He seemed fine this morning.'

'He's always happy in class. I wondered if he might be having bad dreams. Maybe you could have a quiet word with him?'

My heart skipped a beat. 'I will,' I said, 'and I'll let you know the outcome.'

'Do you think he might have tapped into your emotions?' Luke said later that evening. Yuri was in bed and Bea was reading him a night time story.

'You mean like a birth memory or something? Is that possible?'

'Well, it's not as if you've ever spoken about it to him,' he continued, 'what other possibility is there?' I thought for a minute.

'I'll ask him in the morning if he's having bad dreams, I just hope he doesn't take after me like that.'

Saturday I took him to the park. Luke was still working on the Sensory Garden and I hoped some time together might induce him to talk about the picture. So far he'd been very secretive about it and insisted he didn't have nightmares, only nice dreams. I knew it was pointless to push him on the subject, in this he was very like Jade. My mother joined us for a while in her lunch hour and we sat together while Yuri gave us both bear hugs. Then he sped off to the swings. Mother looked over at him and I saw real love in her eyes.

'You know Rachel, he really is the most wonderful child,' she said, 'I'm so proud of what you and Luke have achieved with him.' She held my hand and I felt my eyes grow hot and moist.

'Thanks Mum, I can't really claim to have done anything except love him.' I said.

'That's the most important thing he needs,' she returned, 'I know that now. I do wish I could make up for the time you had as a child.' She looked away as if worried her own eyes might brim over. It was my turn to squeeze her hand. She hadn't mentioned Uncle Sid since her arrival.

'Do you remember what Grandma used to say about water under the bridge? Let's try to put it behind us and enjoy the future. We've got a chance to make a new start, to be a closer family than I ever thought possible. What do you think?'

'Do you really think we can be that close, after all that's happened?' she said, without raising her head.

'I think we always have been, but maybe we just didn't realise it.' Yuri ran up to us and wrapped his arms around her waist.

'Come on Nana, come and push me on the swings!' I smiled at her and she laughed out loud.

'Oh okay,' she said in mock resignation, 'but I mustn't be late back to work!'

The radio was turned up and I didn't hear the bell ring. Suddenly Ray appeared at the back door and I almost jumped out of my seat.

'Sorry Rachel,' he said, 'I didn't mean to startle you.'

'Hi Ray, it's okay, I was miles away.'

'Is Bea out? I've been meaning to ring you, I've got some news I thought you should hear.'

'Oh do have a seat, Bea's at the dentist and then she's going to the shops.' I poured fresh coffee. 'Not as good as Josie's!' I joked, remembering our first meeting. 'Actually I've got something to tell you about Yuri.'

'You go first.' I told him the tale. Ray shook his head in disbelief.

'That's quite incredible, what does Luke think?'

'He thinks perhaps Yuri tuned into it somehow, but really, it's a mystery. And I had the nightmare years ago, just before he was born.' The kitchen fell quiet for a while and we drank our coffee.

'I'm not sure I should give you this piece of news now,' he said, 'it's about your lineage. Do you remember how I thought your line had remained in England?'

'Yes, while your ancestor came over for the Gold rush.'

'That's right. Well, I've found out quite a bit more with Sandra, I mean your mother's help. She's really enjoying it and we seem to get on so well together.'

'I'm so glad, Ray. I'm discovering new things about her all the time. I found out she had an awful depression after my birth; she said that's what started her drinking. Now she's here, I told Luke it's like being with a different person, she's so happy.'

'Not least, because she's reunited with you.'

'I know, and she's made such a difference to my life. Jade as well seems determined to stay here, and Yuri adores them both.' I said.

'I'm just concerned about him and what the teacher said.' He drew out a paper from his case.

'Is this what you've found?' I said, and sat beside him while he spread the paper on the table.

'Now Rachel, you see the name Gregory Hardy? He sailed here with the First Fleet as a cook but later worked for the Governor of New South Wales. He returned to England when his naval duty was finished and married Louise, a milliner. However, he had a relationship with a native woman while working for the Governor.' A strong band tightened round my stomach as Ray moved his hand to expose a name. It was joined to Gregory's with red ink.

'This is the offspring he had with the native woman. I'm guessing she died, because he took the child back to his home town, Plymouth.'

I traced the name with my finger. 'Fredrick. It says he was known as Freddie.'

'That's it, and while Louise went on to have these other children, you're descended from Freddie's line. You and Yuri have native blood.'

'This is incredible!' Flabbergasted, I stared at the paper unable to digest it.

'The question is,' he said slowly, 'does this have anything to do with Yuri's art work?'

I tucked Yuri up in bed, kissed his brow and told him how much I loved him.

'I love you too Mama,' he said, 'but why do people think wrongly so much?' I snuggled his favourite toys beside him.

'In what way do you mean wrongly?' I asked.

'Because they use their minds too much, they should be using their hearts.' He picked up Colin his toy crocodile and kissed its snout.

'How would that change things?' Sat on the edge of the bed I leant over him. I wondered where this was leading. He gave me an absent look, not unlike his old sightless expression and I held my breath.

'If people opened their hearts and thought with them, they could change the whole world.' He smiled and kissed my cheek.

'Wow, Yuri who told you that?'

'It's a secret.' he said impishly. 'One day Mama, I want to be Prime Minister and I'll make people stop all the wars.' I bent down and kissed his forehead. He must've had a history lesson at school, I thought.

'Goodnight darling, and don't worry about all that now.' He turned on his side and snuggled up to Colin. 'Sweet dreams.' I called from the doorway. Luke came up the stairs, just in from work.

'Sorry I'm late Rach, gee you look all in. Is the little man in bed? I'll just say goodnight.'

'Don't be too long,' I said, 'I've got some very strange news for you.'

In the kitchen I finished preparing Luke's supper and made a pot of tea. Beyond the garden a Kookaburra let out its shrill laugh, while Parakeets and Galahs squawked in reply as they roosted and settled for the night. Off shore on a small island tiny penguins marched along the beach in search of nesting sites. The twelve apostles stood as guardians over the coastal strip, waiting and watching over this sacred land. At their feet the rocks opened craggy arms to welcome the mighty oceans swell, while foaming pools lifted and sank as if they breathed for her.

Ganadja the Queen of the dolphins was out there in the deepest waters. I could hear her song as she swam with her King, *Dinginjabana*. I sent her one mother's grateful thanks and smiled now at my apprehension on the day of Yuri's swim. They were off to distant seas and would continue to travel far and wide with their young, thriving pod. They could understand the message of the rhythm sticks and the ancient songs of the dreamtime. The indigenous ones knew how the same songs linked the land mass to the oceans. These were the very same lines the pod followed all over the planets waters, spreading love and harmony.

I put Ruth's cosy on the teapot. The others soon joined me and I relayed Ray's news. As astonished as I, Bea thought it had to explain things, including why Luke and I had been destined to meet. He in turn was convinced I'd seen a part of an ancestors' life in all three dreams. That alone surely had to be the answer, I agreed.

I prayed every day Yuri would see normally for the rest of his life. But I was already certain his vision was not as others'. What he now saw seemed to be of significance, and in turn that made him different. I longed for him to fit in and be normal, but could see how dissimilar from us he was becoming and how one day perhaps because of it he might be raised to a higher destiny.

Chapter 26

Australia was my home and Queens Park Crescent was the hearth within it. In the autumn of 1980 I became a citizen along with Mum and Jade. All of us attended the ceremony in Melbourne City Hall, Bea and Ray as moved as we were. When we stood up to sing the National Anthem Luke gripped my hand and kissed it. I sang the words from my heart, the printed leaflet blurred with tears of joy. I sang out to the oceans, the blood of the continent coursing through me as I did so.

Nearly two hundred years had passed since the First Fleet. I'd read in one of my books how it had then been viewed as raw and barren, described as *Terra Nullius*, meaning uninhabited. Strangely this term still prevailed in law. I was aware how I most likely held more rights as a citizen than the natives of the land, and I vowed to help those who had lost so much.

'About time,' said Bea. I'd started the long overdue clear out of Murray's old paperwork.

'I know,' I said, 'I don't know why I've taken so long to get round to it.'

'Maybe you were waiting for Luke to give you the nod?'

'Then I'd wait forever.' I joked.

Murray always said there were only two types of folk, hard ones and soft ones. He liked to think of us as the soft variety but it only takes one rotten apple to taint a whole basket. I spent the entire day sifting through the paperwork and left most of it in a pile for Luke to look over before throwing anything out. Moving one pile of papers revealed a large tin. It was rusty round the edges and heavy to lift. I had to fetch a knife from the kitchen to prize it open. Inside I found dozens of photographs, some of them pretty ancient. At the bottom of the tin I found a faded envelope with tattered corners. I turned it over and immediately my stomach lurched.

FAMILY TROPHY was written in thick, black ink.

Bea had taken her car to fetch Yuri from school. I looked at the envelope for a long time before I opened it. My hands shook as I lifted the page of names and dates.

Right at the bottom I saw Murray and Luke, but at the very top was the name Frank Jarvis. Just as Daphne had told us he'd arrived on HMS Sirius and had married Jane Blythe. She'd borne three sons, Tobias, Jacob and Nathaniel. The birth date next to Tobias was 1790 and confirmed the link Daphne had found in her research. There was however, no mention of Lily or Thomas Green. I put down the paper and looked through the photographs. Some were black and white ones of Ruth and Murray as children. Several of Luke I hadn't seen before made me smile. Then a really old sepia print fell out of the pile. Scrawled on the back were the faded words *Tobias aged 60*. I turned the photograph over. The face of a haggard man greeted me.

But the first thing I noticed was the scar running down his left cheek.

*   *   *

The morning was bright and I could hear birdsong in the garden. Mum fussed round me while Bea and Jade amused Yuri. I didn't want to be late on my wedding day. Luke had already left the house and I still hadn't got dressed properly.

'Hold still, I've got to finish your hair.' Mum said.

'I can't, I'm too excited.'

'Well, I'm going ahead with Yuri before he explodes,' said Bea, 'I'll see you there darl.'

The day turned out warm and daffodils were blooming everywhere in St Kilda. Ray gave me away and Jade was my beautiful Maid of Honour. On that special day we became one heart and soul and rejoiced in that union with our loved ones. At the Registry Office Mum and Bea cried tears of joy into their lace-trimmed hankies and chatted away like lifelong friends. My dress was pink with tiny snowy flowers, while Luke and Yuri wore white roses on their jackets.

We received cards from all our friends in Darwin. A painting arrived from Frances of our favourite place in the world, Uluru. Mrs Clarke wrote and told us the new restaurant at The Drover Hotel had been named *ZIGGI'S*. Dr Treadwell sent a note saying how very happy he was to hear of Yuri's progress, although just as baffled about it as the experts. He'd been made head doctor at the new Swanbourne Centre and was very proud of the new building. Dave and Marty were with us and acted as joint Best Man. They brought the news that Vince and Scratcher were well and gave us a huge bottle of champagne. Even Father had sent a telegram and a generous cheque. Daphne Green turned up on route to Adelaide and said she must speak with us before the evening ended.

The reception was at Ray's house and later spilled out into the garden. We ate and drank, laughed and danced well into the night. Sasha happily patrolled the guests wearing a pink bow and made sure Yuri was never lonely. We had music all evening and as we danced the sweet scent of jasmine lingered on the night air. Bea took Yuri home to bed at 9pm, although he insisted he could have stayed up much longer. Daphne found us resting on a garden bench and sat beside Luke.

'You know, this man has been the closest to my own son.' she said. Luke responded by giving her a hug making her eyes light up. 'I want to say I've got complete confidence in both of you and that's why I'm leaving you my house in Darwin.'

'No,' I said, then, 'have you really done that?'

'Why Greenie, surely you've got real relatives to leave it to?' Luke said.

'Think of it as a late wedding present,' she said, 'after all, I may go on for years. I'd better warn you the inheritance comes with a proviso.'

'Go on,' Luke replied.

'I want an artist studio built in the garden and for the house to be made into a centre for children and families of all races. But I particularly wish for Aboriginal art and storytelling for groups and schools. You can begin work as soon as you like, I have some savings to fund it.'

'You mean like a cultural centre, where people can learn about Indigenous crafts?'

'Yes Rachel, well that's what I had in mind. A place they can all come to create their own work, where all art will be made welcome. I've been thinking about it for a long time because since the cyclone I just don't feel comfortable there. This will make you laugh,' and she hesitated, 'it's as if my own ancestors have been talking to me, pressing me to put this idea into motion.' She had an imploring look on her face.

'I can understand that.' I responded.

'You know, this could be just what we've been waiting for.' Luke added.

'Oh, would you really be happy to do it?' We nodded our heads with enthusiasm.

'Luke's right,' I continued, 'we want to do something. It's like giving something back and this idea is the perfect solution.'

'But the distance, the work involved,' she began.

'I'm sure we can work something out Greenie. I've got mates up there that could use a project to work on!'

'And there's Frances, she'd be able to help, I'm sure.' I added. Luke glanced over at Dave and Marty, and Daphne beamed from ear to ear.

A taxi came for us shortly after 11pm. As it drove off I threw my bridal posy into the guests and Mum caught it which made us all laugh, especially her. Ray had paid for a room at The Hotel Collins as a wedding present but it wasn't until we checked in we found he'd booked the honeymoon suite. Bowled over by his generosity and with Daphne's amazing news we flopped onto the bed and dissolved into giggles.

'What a blast!' Luke said. 'What do you make of it, wife?'

'I think I'm enjoying life more than I ever thought possible.' I said. As husband and wife another era had begun.

Dream Time

The family I'd left eight years back was changed beyond recognition and I loved them with all the freshness of a warm spring day. Over the years I'd struggled to cast off the shackles of persecution to embrace my freedom. Now I knew I'd never take it for granted. The once fractured pot was sticking together with Yuri as the glue. One of his bedtime stories was about a vulnerable caterpillar that turned into a pupa. It hatched out as a beautiful butterfly. My own restraints I'd cast aside and thrown to the four winds. My wings were eager in anticipation of the next part of our amazing journey.

Yuri was in bed but I could hear he wasn't asleep. As usual he was chatting to Colin, the toy crocodile. I listened secretly by the door for a while before tucking him up.

'You and Colin are really good mates aren't you?' I said.

'Yes, but I wasn't talking to Colin.' he stated. He put the toy under the covers and pretended it was swimming.

'Oh, so who were you chatting to so seriously?'

'The same person as always; she's my other Mama.'

'You must mean Auntie?'

'No not Auntie, or Nana, my *other* mummy.' He was starting to get annoyed.

'Oh, I see. Do I know her?' I wondered if she might be one of the other mothers from school.

'Maybe, but anyway, she knows you.'

'Did she tell you that?' I'd become slightly alarmed.

'She tells me lots of things, when I'm asleep mostly. She looks after all of us.' He turned over and hugged Colin to his face.

'Sweetheart,' I said thoughtlessly, 'if you dream about her she can't be real. She must be your Guardian Angel.' I patted the bedclothes.

'Oh yes, she is real.' And he sat bolt upright. 'What's a Guardian Angel anyway?'

'Well, lie back down first. A good friend once told me a Guardian Angel is someone who looks after you all the time, even when your parents aren't around. So does she have a name, your Guardian Angel?'

'Of course she does, but she told me she was my mummy.' He sulked and I tickled under his chin.

'Tell me her name then.'

'It's Moree.' he said eventually. 'It means water, because she likes to swim with the dolphins. But she's got another name too.'

'That's a very pretty name, Yuri.' I was intrigued by his story. 'And what's her other name? Why has she got two names anyway?' He sighed heavily.

'Because some people call her Moree and some people,' he stopped talking for a moment, as if listening.

'Yes, some people call her, what?'

'Maisie.'

I was dreaming a different but just as vivid dream. This one was about Yuri, not a young boy but Yuri the man. He'd got honours at university and became a politician. I saw him married with children, a boy and a girl. Middle aged, he stood on a podium giving a speech. He was relaxed and comfortable in his dark olive skin. He spoke about his eyes, about his blindness as a child.

He said he'd been blind but had been given new eyes to see. There were those who had working eyes and ears but even so didn't see or listen with them. Just as we all have hearts, only a few were able to use them for what they were intended. With sight he was able to look at people and see the face of his brother. He wanted to be a new kind of

Dream Time

politician, one that recognised others as family, with no black or white, no rich or poor. He wished no one to be considered high or low, advantaged or disadvantaged and said there was a place for everyone in society no matter where they came from, because everyone should be valued and respected. It's not easy to give love in situations where what we see often fools us, but he asked if the crowd was ready to join him. An Aboriginal Chief was welcomed onto the stage. They embraced, the audience cheered and clapped, and the image faded away.

I was sure Yuri was destined to use his insight to build peace for the rest of his life. His journey might help connect those in his own community but I hoped he would eventually travel to unite whole cultures. If it were possible for people over the globe to join together in harmony, then the impossibility of this task had a chance of being achieved.

Year on year; the first settlers brought to the land buildings, animals and crops. They instilled their money system and social strata and buried their own wisdom with it. Perhaps that knowledge was lost forever. But if those hidden gifts were found it might be possible to remember who we really are and why we are here. The power of the universe could be appreciated without the need of science to enlighten us of its marvels. But a glimpse into the eternity of our existence cannot be grasped at will. And our short history on earth shows us a pattern of destruction that surely needs to be broken.

Like so many I'd been led to this land of extremes. My essence one day would lay in this soil, along with my memories and dreams. From the spark of light where miracles occur, Maisie had watched. I'd come to know her almost as well as I knew myself and now accepted if she'd been a part of my past, so was she instrumental in my future.

Yuri was the child I'd had with Luke, but his soul belonged to her.

Our journey had taken us over the continent but I'd travelled much further. The future was beckoning, telling me of hope ahead. At times during morning yoga I still think of Monkey Puzzle Street. Instantly I'm strengthened by the house that survives through my life.

> The ground heat penetrates the soles of my sandals as I make my way out of the gate and down the hill. At the bottom of the road I glance over to the Botanical Gardens, fringed and dotted with palms and gum trees, silent and still in the morning haze. A giant butterfly flitters past as if suspended on invisible threads. I look skyward expecting to see hands guiding its flight but see only the huge cobalt canopy. Close by Frangipani trees intoxicate with saffron flowers and emerald wax leaves.
>
> The heat is stoking up. In the shaded entrance to the Gardens I pause to wipe the moisture from my forehead. I notice a group of roughly clothed Aborigines; they too seeking relief from the rising humidity. Cooling their naked feet in the dust they glare and point gnarled fingers. They utter words I cannot understand.
>
> The build up is suddenly begun. Gone now is the breathtaking contrast of green against a vast blue sky. Threatening storm clouds move in and bring teasing winds. I return to the house with the leaden weight of heat on my back. Perspiration runs down my face into my eyes. I unlock the metal gate at the bottom of

the drive. The house, standing high on its stilts seems empty now, the heavily shuttered windows guarding deserted rooms.

The climb up the drive brings me to a pile of stones in the garden. These foundations have long grassed over and I hesitate because I hear music nearby. I imagine his face and can also detect the soft hum of cicadas, the melody to his chanting spells. He is here, all round me in the trees and on the winds that sometimes bring a spot of blessed rain. The warrior.

In the shaded living room I feel the cool wood under my feet and hear the squeak of the ceiling fan. A thunderclap rumbles, it echoes somewhere in the distance. A gentle breeze stirs past the veranda and the overhanging mango boughs dance a shimmy. Before me the typewriter holds a waving sheet of paper. The word PEACE is written there, alone in black ink. I'm on the veranda and in the corner see a shadowed figure, his body almost entirely eclipsed by a long shield. It is him. The thunder's nearer now and Barra is coming with the wet. A booming thud enters my body as the landscape sways violently in the wind. I recoil thinking the roof has caved in, then see before me the first precious drops of rain.

Epilogue

Far away in north Australia the last rays of sunlight washed over the veranda. As the light receded, tree frogs hopped happily into the shade, blinking blearily at each other. A soft breeze lifted dried leaves, teased them into the air before allowing them to rest once more on the ground. The tiny whimpers of young possums drifted from the loft. Laden mango trees welcomed the first bats as they gathered for their evening feed.

The house had survived the wrath of Barra, even the anger of Tracy. Enduring seven years since, it was ready to take on a new life.

Dave and Marty unlocked the gate and drove up the drive. In front of the garage they unloaded bricks, cement, tools and planks of wood. They found a radio in the house and listened to it while they worked. Happy to help Luke, they began to build in the garden. It was to be a studio with plenty of light inside. From time to time they heard a dog bark in the next garden, probably at some animal. Occasionally they saw its owner who was moving out to somewhere smaller.

Dave found the cyclone shelter and called to Marty. Inside was a box, carefully prepared with tins of food. They were rusted up and all the other contents had been rifled by insects. The two men laughed and put the box back on the rickety camp bed. Marty noticed something at the back of the shelter. He stepped over the possum trap to get at it and brought it out into the light.

'It's a shield, Mart.' Dave said.

'I can see that mate,' Marty replied, 'nice picture of a fish.' he added.

'That's no fish, it's a dolphin.'

'Right mate, so it is. I'd better put it back; we can sort this lot out another day.'

'Jeeze, but this is a weird place isn't it?' Dave shivered as he said it.

'Nah, you're imagining things.' Marty replied, and insisted they go back to work. There was plenty to get through.

* * *

In January 1788 Killara began his journey homeward. His tribe lived weeks away and he wished to get there faster. What he'd seen at Port Jackson confused him and suddenly he felt more alone than ever. He would visit Uluru, a detour he was happy to make. At the heart of the continent this most spiritual of sites had its own life force, its own wisdom. At only 18 years old he knew this. The son of a Wise Man he was mature beyond his years and already possessed a strong talent with medicines. He took up his few implements and headed west towards the Blue Mountains. After only a week he had passed the Murray River and was on the way to Lake Eyre.

Dream Time

Miles away in the east the strange vessels lay quietly at anchor. A few days passed while the ships rested like huge water birds. The leader of the expedition was confident the soil would grow strong crops and was pleased he'd moved further along the coast before deciding on this location. The Fleet carried a small supply of livestock from England, precious beasts for breeding. They made suitable grazing a priority. Over the next few days the ships stayed at anchor while many men came ashore in rowboats. Over the following months they set up camps, herded livestock and infiltrated the land like a plague of locusts.

Killara reached Uluru. He asked the Spirit Ancestors for strength and protection for his people. So far he'd managed to catch birds with his net but he'd also gathered roots and berries. He would use a digging stick to coax ants from their nest, the twig doubling as an eating implement. If he passed a river he was able to spear fish or eels. Finding Lake Eyre he'd skirted round it and followed the Finke River until it was time to head west. The Lake had been dried up but this enabled him to collect some precious salt from the bed which he carried in a little reed bag. Later, when he reached Tennant Creek, he'd be able to trade the salt for other goods.

Tribes from all over had travelled such rivers since the dawn of man. These waterways were the roads that connected through the land in the same way that blood vessels run through our flesh. The continent was a living breathing soul, joined to its people with invisible threads of love and Killara sang as he walked. He linked with ancient songs and found himself travelling through time and space with no measure of minutes or hours. Here the land was his brother, sister, father and mother. This was rooted deep within him, as it had always been and would continue to be so forever.

The going had been hard but it was about to get harder. Biting flies and hot, dusty soil assailed his body as he was hit by a sand storm. The desert flew up and bit him all over, far worse than the fiercest flies. To avoid being buried alive he had to think fast. He saw a boab tree and hid inside its hollow trunk until the worst was over. He thought perhaps the spirits were displeased because of the pale men. When he emerged from the tree the landscape had been swept into a new world.

In the desert the expert tracker could usually find small lizards and snakes. The type of tracks could indicate age, type and gender. Killara hardly ever went hungry. Out of six hundred clans throughout the continent, his people were known for their strength and tenacity. The men stood over six feet in height. His home was nearer now and some moons later where he would bring his new wife, Talia.

Later when he reached Uluru, he watched in awe the mighty radiance from this vast formation. The sun was hammering down but he remained seated on the sizzling earth. Here he chanted prayers and sung songs. He remembered a story his father had told him long ago. It made him think again of the pale ones he had seen in those fat, indulgent craft. The story told of men who had ears but could not listen, men who had eyes but could not see. They used words without thinking, and they had hearts but were unable to love.

He'd collected some fruits from the boab tree and placed them in the reed bag with the salt. Near the great rock he found a group of eucalyptus trees and snapped off small blood-wood apples. They probably contained moth grubs; these would provide protein and fat for the long journey ahead. Later he was sure to see termite mounds and could use his stick to catch some. But for now he was content to

Dream Time

sit and watch Uluru and to feast on all the beauty of his surroundings.

In meditation he saw it was time for him to step into his new role of husband and medicine man: this was his earthly role. But more than this he realized he wasn't caged by his body, that he was destined to play a larger part than the mere physical. He knew he was part of the trees, of the sky and earth, the rain and stars. He was connected to everything in the Universe, just as it was connected to him. Now he knew he was so much more than flesh and blood. He also felt in that moment, the connection of the pale ones and how they had forgotten this fact. They lived as if in a trance. In them he thought he detected the shadow of a vision; a sadness borne of what lay before him, perhaps the fear of treachery not yet witnessed.

Killara finished his thanksgiving and bowed before Uluru. Once more he gathered his things together and began his final journey northwards. He was going home.

* * *

Now over a century later, he prepared to leave this realm. Alone on the veranda he stood as a tall warrior, his body adorned with ceremonial paint. His thick hair was knotted with feathers and his eyes shone brightly in the evening light. But his figure wavered with the iridescence only a spirit can possess.

Killara watched with amusement some clumsy geckos. They dived and fought over insects while he remained motionless. Only his lips moved to reveal even teeth and a gentle smile. In one hand he held his spear and in the other he steadied a great shield, painted with a dolphin. Over the decades he'd often come here and even visited the artist while he worked. Mulga had so liked the shield he copied the picture several times. Sometime later Killara had enjoyed playing tricks on the gardener and the girl. He needed to test their resilience and at that time his anger outweighed the peace he'd known since the cyclone. But all that was a long time ago. Now he had no need to annoy the men who worked in the garden. He was tired and wanted to be at peace.

Strangely though, he felt quite reluctant to leave. He moved his eyes from side to side to take in as much information as possible and sucked in all the energy of the house and its surroundings. He recalled how the strange men had arrived in their crafts all that time ago and laughed softly to himself. But his smile changed to a sneer at the so-called progress they had achieved, how they only believed in possessions, wars and money. They had no time for those who stood in their way, or anyone who inconvenienced their blinded obsessions. Nor did they comprehend the real meaning of love; they confused it and polluted it with greed and envy. Time was running out and huge chasms remained between the Tribes of Earth. The entire planet was waiting for *them* before it could unite all living creatures in peace.

He remembered how he had married Talia, and the daughter she'd given him. They called her Moree, meaning water. But while Moree herself was with child she'd been captured by the pale men. They took her far away and stole her name. Like him, she was strong and brave. She ran away but they hunted her, cut her down and murdered her in cold blood. Luke the gardener knew it and was sorry for his forefather's cruelty. Rachel also felt this wrong and she saw his daughter in her dreams. The pale men had called her Maisie, even after her death. Out of their bodies and into his realm the spirits of Moree and her son flew. Here they waited for a long time. He couldn't forget how they'd robbed him of his girl child, or how her and his grandson's spirits fled in terror out into the desert air.

His people had long held the secrets of the earth and all her wonders. They knew how everything that exists is connected by its own dance of life. Many years ago at Uluru he'd heard a special song of magic that lifted up his flesh, allowing him to ride through time as a dolphin rides a wave. He saw far, far into the heavens, flying past planets, stars and nebula.

It was here, many years later, where he found his grandson. As if waiting for his grandfather he sat patiently on a young star. Killara asked the Rainbow Serpent if she was strong enough to throw that star back to earth. And one day it fell from his realm onto the veranda at this very spot. He had no need to search for his daughter, because she'd found him long ago. Vowing to return, she came to him while he slept and whispered her terrible story. As he recalled that night a silver tear dropped from his eye onto the wood floor.

But this was the beginning of a new era because his grandchild lived like starlight within the boy Yuri. Even now he advanced the child's learning because he was the prodigy of a Wise Man. He would live to walk with white chiefs in the modern world but his song would endure to be that of the eternal Dream.

He blinked his dark eyes and looked out at the unfolding sky. Soon Barra would return again with the big rains. The wet, able to wash clean all it touched, and strong enough to liberate even his trauma and pain. It healed through the night and purged by day as it had done since the very first dawn.

Exhausted, Killara was nonetheless content for his work was finally completed. Robed in pearlescent light he stretched to his full height, shining with all the colours of the rainbow. For a moment silence hung over the house on Monkey Puzzle Street as all life paused. Then in an instant he was gone and night fell like a heavy curtain.

And because he was very old, like many times before, he forgot his shield.

Printed in Great Britain
by Amazon